# YOU CAN'T STAY HERE

# YOU CAN'T STAY HERE

### JASMINA ODOR

*thistledown press*

Thistledown Press Ltd.
410 2nd Avenue North
Saskatoon, Saskatchewan, S7K 2C3
www.thistledownpress.com

Library and Archives Canada Cataloguing in Publication
Odor, Jasmina, author
You can't stay here / Jasmina Odor.
Short stories.
Issued in print and electronic formats.
ISBN 978-1-77187-144-0 (softcover).—ISBN 978-1-77187-145-7
(HTML).—ISBN 978-1-77187-146-4 (PDF)
I. Title. II. Title: You cannot stay here.
PS8629.D67Y69 2017 C813'.6 C2017-905316-7
C2017-905317-5

Cover and book design by Jackie Forrie
Printed and bound in Canada

Canada Council    Conseil des Arts
for the Arts      du Canada

SASKATCHEWAN
ARTS BOARD

Canada

Thistledown Press gratefully acknowledges the financial assistance of the Canada Council for the Arts, the Saskatchewan Arts Board, and the Government of Canada for its publishing program.

# ACKNOWLEDGEMENTS

The following stories first appeared in magazines and anthologies: "You Can't Stay Here" and "Skin Like Almonds" in *The Fiddlehead*, "A Board of Perfect Pine" in *The Malahat Review*, "Barcelona" and "The Time of the Apricots" in *The New Quarterly*, "Postcard from the Adriatic" in *Prism International*, "His" in *Eighteen Bridges*, "Barcelona" also in *Journey Prize Stories 24*, "You Can't Stay Here", "In Vancouver, with David", and "Peanuts" in *Coming Attractions 04*, and "Everyone Has Come" online at CBC Books. I'm grateful to the editors, especially Mark Jarman.

"Postcard from the Adriatic" and "Skin Like Almonds" owe much to my obsession with Mavis Gallant. The line "a look exchanged, desire as brief as a dream" that appears in "Board of Perfect Pine" is from *Paris Notebooks* by Mavis Gallant, © 1968, 1971, 1972, 1973, 1974, 1976, 1977, 1978, 1981, 1982, 1983, 1984, 1985, 1986 by Mavis Gallant, reprinted by permission of Georges Borchardt, Inc., on behalf of the author.

Many dear friends and fellow writers contributed to these stories' making: Thea Bowering, Scott Messenger, Jill Connell, Naomi Lewis, Barbara Romanik, Joel Katelnikoff, Greg Bechtel, Steve Noyes, Colin MacGregor, Astrid Blodgett, Julie Robinson, Tatiana Peet, Slavica Falatar. Thanks to Audrey Whitson for suggesting Thistledown, and to Will Fraser for the photos. Thanks also to my community at Concordia University of Edmonton. Much gratitude to my mom and dad, my sister Greta and her family, for their kindness and support (and to Adrian, for promising me future book collaborations). Special thanks to dear friends Rebecca Fredrickson, Lisa Martin, and Dijana Obradović. To Dan Mirau, for reading, love, encouragement, and for sharing his life with me.

I'm grateful to the Alberta Foundation for the Arts for financial support, to the Banff Centre for the Arts for providing space and mentorship, and especially to mentors André Alexis and Gloria Sawai. Thank you to Alissa York, for her generosity in reading.

I'm permanently and hopelessly indebted to Greg Hollingshead, my first writing teacher, for his early and ongoing support, and for giving me the language in which to think and talk about writing. His sane voice remains my internal standard-bearer. To Ben Lof, for sharing the vision and the effort from the start, being my first and most reliable reader, for giving me the good titles, and for all his support and love.

I'm grateful also to Al Forrie and Jackie Forrie at Thistledown Press, and all the Thistledown people for their work on behalf of the book. Finally, thank you to Seán Virgo, an extraordinary editor, for his dogged pursuit of weaknesses and generous vision of strengths, whose sharp eye, intelligence, and kindred spirit lifted the work to a level I couldn't have reached without him. The remaining weaknesses are my own.

I owe these imagined worlds to places that I've travelled to or called home, but the people and events in the stories are fictitious.

*This book is for my parents, Ankica and Vili*

# CONTENTS

# Board of Perfect Pine

WE WENT TO BARCELONA THOUGH we'd almost spent our budget in London, where we stayed in a creaky room and feared getting mugged when we crossed the parking lot from the subway stop to the hostel. We needed Barcelona. It was there, in the beautiful eleventh-floor room on Gran Via that we could not afford, that I said, "It's fine, my period just finished, I think it will be fine."

By the end of August it was clear that I was pregnant. I remember the afternoon we sat on this same couch in this one-bedroom apartment not talking to each other. Josh started beers one after another but forgot about each one halfway through the bottle. I watched him hold the lip of the latest bottle between his fingers and swing it back and forth.

"I would like to leave you," I said. "No, I would like to go back in time to when you didn't exist for me. Then I would neither have you nor have to leave you."

He released his fingers then and the bottle fell onto the coffee table, the beer spilling in a foamy explosion over the table and onto the rug.

Still, with or without him, I kind of wanted the baby. I was thirty, after all, almost thirty-one now. He was thirty-three. It's funny how we suddenly become what we are without noticing it. But I didn't want to tell him that I wanted it. Let Josh want it, I thought. Let Josh convince me.

"Maybe it's just the thing we need," he said. "And then you wouldn't have to worry about leaving me." The foam sunk into the rug under the coffee table, and we both looked around our apartment at the same time.

That was four months ago. Now, on the couch, he surprises me when he says, "Nin, your elbow."

I realize my elbow has been pressing into his shoulder.

"Sorry." I bend my head to kiss the soft part between his shoulder and neck, and we shift our slightly sweaty bodies on the sticky leather.

"Is it you here or is it the husk?" He holds my eyes.

In Barcelona one afternoon we rode the two-tiered Bus Touristic for two hours, hot and hungry, and when I asked Josh if we should get off on Gran Via, he said, "I don't know, this is just my husk here, my real self is eating tapas and drinking beer on a shaded patio." Since that day, we are always on about the husk. "Is it you or the husk," I'll say, when he leans his head back and closes his eyes in the middle of an Almodovar film we're watching, Penelope Cruz's character dragging the body of her murdered husband down the stairs — "me, he'll say, it is I," he'll say, opening his eyes.

Outside, all I see is that the snow, of course, is still falling, uniformly, as if inside a glass box. Two people, their heads hooded and their faces scarf-wrapped, walk slowly through the silent scene.

The blizzard hasn't let up by nightfall, but still we drive out to Josh's parents' suburb for the party his mom Trudy is hosting after the Christmas concert at their church. She didn't sing in the concert the year before, when her next-door neighbour and long-time friend, Cindy, was dying. She is emotional about the whole thing, the concert going on without Cindy for the first time, about Cindy's husband Bob, who has been drinking too much, who is seeing a woman who used to be Cindy's friend. Josh's brother Matt and his girlfriend Nicole are in the back seat, tipsy, like me. We'd planned to make it to the church, but instead we kept drinking at our place. We finished the wine Matt and Nicole brought, and then, because there was nothing else left in the house and no one was going to go to a liquor store, we drank warm champagne and then some gin that Josh's sister had brought us back from Tanzania and we'd been saving.

Now the snow is driving sideways and the roads are thick with it. On window ledges, awnings, and mailboxes, the snow has made clumsy, sparkling shapes, skewing all recognizable things, hiding the edges. Pink, milky air. Few people anywhere, only some drivers who had not listened to the weather warnings either. All human and mechanical movement is cautious, the ordinary rules of motion through space not applying. Climbing Bellamy Hill we watch the cars ahead of us sliding back, their rear ends dancing. I hold a dish with spinach dip covered with plastic wrap in my lap. Josh curses and brakes when it looks as though the car in front of us really will continue slithering down. But then it is moving up again, and we too are moving up, slowly and uncertainly.

"Let's forget the party and go drink somewhere," Matt says.

"Yeah, just turn this car around," I say, "just pull a U-turn." Josh looks at me like he's taking me up on it and makes a quick motion with the steering wheel. We are sliding for a moment, and then he rights us, with some effort. Groans and laughter. I wonder just how tipsy he is.

Ten minutes later we get stuck at a light and the three of us push while Nicole takes the wheel. It takes us nearly an hour and a half to get to Josh's parents'.

By the time we walk into the house we are jubilant in our achievement. We jostle each other in taking off our coats, let them fall to the floor, throw our toques across the hall. The smack of Josh's leather gloves on the hallway stand. His mother with her arms outstretched and a glass of red in her hand.

"Oh, it is just terrible out there, just terrible, isn't it," she says. She hugs me tightly.

"Oh it's the worst."

"We nearly died at least twice," Josh says.

"You owe us for this, is what he means," I say.

Josh hugs his mom, holds her by the waist, kisses her cheek, makes her disappear in his long arms.

"I'm so glad you're all here," she says, a little glassy-eyed now, "even if you didn't make it to the church." Josh's dad, Karl, joins in from the sitting room, says, "Well it's lovely weather, don't you think?"

"Get a drink, get warm guys," Trudy waves with her wrist.

"Help me with this dip, will you," I say to Karl. Nicole hops along with him ahead of the rest of us. Josh's mom takes me by the elbow and walks me into the kitchen. Josh and Matt follow, still shoulder checking each other.

The kitchen is full of people, women in red and black satin shirts, men with thick wrist watches, wine glasses in everyone's hands.

"Let me introduce you, I don't think you know everyone, let me introduce my wonderful daughter-in-law," Trudy says, looking back and hoping Josh has heard her.

She taps a woman in front of us, a short woman with bushy dark-blonde hair.

"Marta, this is my daughter-in-law, my son Josh's wife, you know Josh, he's good friends with Eric."

"Hello," I say, after I look pointedly at Trudy, who is really not my mother-in-law. Marta smiles widely, takes my hand. She has big breasts inside an open-neck blouse and a nice waist and a sun-spotted chest.

"Marta is Bob's friend." Trudy turns to me here. "Eric's dad Bob, you know Eric's dad."

"You guys drove out in the blizzard, what good children!"

"We sure did."

"You need a glass of wine," Trudy says. I see that Matt and Nicole already have drinks at the other counter.

"What are you into tonight?" someone says behind us and I swivel on my heel to turn toward the voice. A man in a pink shirt quite open at the neck, ruddy face, smooth hairless head.

"There's Bob! Perfect, you remember Nina?"

"Good to see you, Nina," Bob says. Bob Hrypchuk. Josh always says their last name whenever he mentions Bob or Eric. Bob's holding a bottle of wine in each hand. Thick wrists, rolled-up sleeves, attractive sturdy hands. But it is his throat that catches me—pale and tender between two sharp clavicles.

"Now, there is Karl's homemade shiraz, and then there's the good stuff I'm drinking." Happy eye-roll from Trudy, a little teasing punch on his arm.

"Hello, hi, Bob. Well, I have to stay loyal. Give me the shiraz." Laughter from everyone. They're already sauced.

"You poor soul!" Bob has a great deep laugh. He pours briskly but precisely into a glass that Trudy has handed me.

"Good," Trudy says, "now I'm going to borrow you, Bob — can I borrow him, Marta? — and make you bring those bottles right over to that crowd in the living room," and then she turns to me. "I'll be back, okay, Nina." They move past me, past Marta. As they do I feel the smallest whoosh of air between my chest and the sleeve of Bob's pink linen shirt.

I prop my foot up against the cupboard and lean on the counter, the edge pressing into my lower back. The glass of wine is loose and light in my hand. The charm on the stem of the glass is a yellow bunch of grapes. Marta talks to some men about a cruise; she keeps her body angled as if to include me in the conversation. I wish Josh were here: I see him across from the kitchen table, his blue-and-black striped sweater. He's only about six people away from me, but already I feel I couldn't reach him if I tried. Trudy comes around with a plate of someone's homemade spring rolls. Other people come and say hello. I say things. I pour more wine, regularly.

I move through the crowd, into the smell of musky, sweet perfume, the carefully arranged women. But though their hair is streaked and stiff and their fingernails painted, their laughter is loud and unbuttoned, their arms playful. I fill my plate with broccoli and carrots, crackers and part of a cheese ball. I talk to one of the women about the cheese ball, encrusted with real bacon and rosemary. I look for Josh again. There he is, the husk of him at least, with Matt, pouring whiskey into tall shot glasses with palm trees on them. On the other side of me the flat, brisk sound of a wine bottle pushed across the table.

I decide to go to the bathroom. As I walk I look down and see patterned men's socks, women's bare feet and stockinged ones. The water dish for the dogs, who are temporarily shut up in the basement.

Inside the bathroom, I lean on the door. I close my eyes. Slight buzz inside my head. I think of Bob's wife, Cindy, try to remember her face. Mostly I remember the hair, a dark bob, pre-cancer. I also remember her as she was when we visited her once, thin, pale, queen of the living room, in the hospital bed that had been set up for her. I think of Josh pouring whiskey into those tall narrow glasses, slowly, carefully watching the progress of the liquid. I think of the last time I saw Bob, early in the summer, before Josh and I went to Europe, the only time I had seen him since Cindy's death. It was here, at a barbecue. I'd come into the kitchen to find him slicing tomatoes at the counter. You don't expect a man, at a barbecue, to be inside slicing vegetables. He wore a white button-down shirt then. "Do you need a hand," I'd asked. His tomato slices were big and uneven. "I'm bad at this," he said, seeing me look at them. "It's the knives," I said. I was uncomfortable. But then I found another knife in the drawer and took a tomato from Bob and started cutting. Josh and I had been searching for flights to Europe that morning, and I told Bob about the trip. After a while I asked him how he was doing. "I'm staying afloat," he said. Then he told me about him and Cindy in Europe, the year before they got married. Driving from Barcelona, up through the south of France, then Italy, then down to Yugoslavia — there, on the narrow, winding, two-lane highway along the Adriatic, they in a rented Fiat van. Cindy held the passenger handle tightly, eyed the precipice, asked him to take the turns slowly, but he teased her with them, revved up and swung into them, wanted her to loosen up.

I hear voices outside and open my eyes. I run the water for a moment just to produce a normal bathroom sound and then leave. In the hallway I run into Trudy and Karl saying goodbye to people leaving and taking the coats of a couple just arriving. I nod and slither by and head for the kitchen. But Josh doesn't seem to be in the kitchen anymore. I hover near the dishwasher where no one is standing and then put some random abandoned plates into it. I put the salsa bowl in, though it's not quite empty. I put in three little forks. I make one section of the counter very clean.

"It's too early for that," Trudy says, coming in from the hallway. "You just leave that, now," she says, taking my hands into her own. "I'm going to bring out the cake soon."

"Okay," I say, as she moves past me, but then I stay where I am. There is a crowd under the arch between the kitchen and living room, and I see Marta again, an absent-minded hand in her hair. Bob Hrypchuk's clean, loud laugh, and another man's dryer, more cackly one. A woman walks by to the kitchen table, helps herself to spinach dip on a little paper plate. Then she is talking to Bob. His throat looks flushed. I put another stray wine glass into the dishwasher, letting the wine spill onto the other dishes. When I look back Bob meets my eye. He moves toward me.

"Nina," he says, as if I were an old friend he hasn't seen for a long time, "how's the party treating you?"

"Bob. What can I tell you? I'm staying afloat," I say.

He laughs, so I do too. "You are, are you?"

"The currents are strong though. Excuse me. I don't know what I'm saying. I'm a little bit drunk. How are you?"

"But this is only the beginning," he says. When he smiles, his cheeks stretch and long lines spread from his eyes, and I feel suddenly like he is all there, all of him on the surface of his friendly face.

"Heck, you're right," I say, and top up my glass from the bottle of red at my elbow.

"I haven't seen you two in a while. How are you, how's Josh?"

"We travelled this summer, and the fall was busy, so we didn't come out here much."

"You went to Europe, right?"

"Yep. London, then Spain. Barcelona."

"I remember you telling me about it. I've been to Barcelona. So did you like it?"

"I don't even know. I don't know sometimes why anyone travels, you know."

But then there's Karl, putting his hand on Bob's shoulder, squeezing it.

"It's good to have you here, Bob; it's good to have you both here." I don't know whether "both" means Bob and me or Bob and Marta. Bob nods, and looks away, and I can't tell if he's touched or irritated.

"Nina was just telling me about Europe," he says when he looks back. *It's a struggle, this talking, isn't it,* I want to say to him.

"Oh great. You've been to Europe, right?"

"Cindy and me. 1976."

"Right."

Trudy walks by with a cake that looks like a giant brownie.

"Trudy will need me in there, won't she?" Karl says, giving Bob's shoulder another squeeze.

"I'm going to follow that cake into the living room," Marta says, passing by, and following Karl.

"There's a cake," I say to Bob. "But is there more homemade shiraz?"

He finds a bottle on the other counter and pours into my glass, glug glug glug.

"There's a cake," Bob says.

"I don't care for cake," I say. Then Bob pulls a loose hair from the sleeve of my shirt. I look toward the sitting room, where most people are now. I don't see Josh's sweater anywhere. Bob's touch was a flicker of motion anyway. I think maybe it has not really happened.

"Excuse me," I say. I feel woolly, like all the clatter and shimmer of the party is padding the space inside my head.

I sense myself about to sway and I grip the counter more tightly. "I think I can't stay here," I say.

"We don't have to stay here," Bob says.

He pours me a glass of water from the fridge. He drinks one himself. His eyes are bloodshot, but otherwise he is a model of glowing late-middle-age health.

I drink the water. "There is a bathroom upstairs," I say.

"Okay," he says.

I walk, not toward the living room, but the other way, where the stairs are. Bob walks behind me, soft steps in socked feet. He follows me into the bathroom next to Karl and Trudy's bedroom and I close the door behind us.

"Here," Bob says, running cold water in the sink. He passes me a cold little towel. He half sits on the counter next to the sink, and I sit on the other side of it, not far from him. I hold the towel between my palms. Fine cold towel. The bathroom is looking a little shabby. The guest one has been renovated, but this one has not. The tub faucet is from the '70s, the rugs are pilly. Bob Hrypchuk's wife died of kidney cancer. She died in their living room, on the hospital bed they had set up for her where the loveseat had been. Marta was a family friend.

"Are you doing all right?" he says. "Is that better?"

I'm holding the towel to my forehead. My face is cool. Sometimes, when you're drinking a lot, there's a moment when you think you're going to be sick or you're going to pass out or you can't go on anymore, and then you come back from it. That's a good moment. You can keep drinking then. It's as though you've been strengthened. I look at Bob. Bob has strengthened me. I put the towel down.

"So do you want to hear what happened in Barcelona?"

"Sure," he says. "I'll take a story. Just hold on a second." Then he turns over the toothbrush cup, rinses it, reaches inside his pant pocket and brings out a flask.

"We just need a little more, I think." He pours a generous amount into the toothbrush glass. Bob understands. Steady doses. This place is not ideal, I think, but I would be anywhere with Bob Hrypchuk right now. He drinks, then passes me the cup. Scotch warmth. I feel perfect. I hope never to leave this bathroom.

"So. We were to land in Barcelona at eight in the evening and we hadn't booked a place to stay, so at two that afternoon at the London airport I'm phoning numbers I'd got on the Internet to get us a place to sleep. So I find a guy with a vacancy, and he says he'll send someone to wait for us at his place. The cab drops us off at this high-rise, downtown, and sure enough there's a guy there, looking impatient. "This guy looks sketchy," Josh says, as he's lifting my suitcase out of the cab's trunk. And I'm thinking, who are these people? Where did that number even come from? Anyway, the guy — a bit older than us, white T-shirt, black jeans, ugly black runners — he unlocks this metal door, and we go into a lobby, quiet as a graveyard, lit with only one bulb, all marble and stone. Josh and I are trying to look at each other, but we can barely make out our faces. We ride the tiny elevator to the eleventh floor, no one saying a thing, and up there it's the same silence, a view down a spiral staircase. But the point is — I'm thinking, we're about to get robbed and raped, and instead we end up in the most beautiful place I'll probably ever stay. When we enter — the man uses three different keys on three different locks — we hear soft classical music. We're in a marble-floored foyer lined with dark-wood cabinets, on top of which are these huge glass sculptures of birds, like birds of paradise, blue and yellow and red, like nothing I've ever seen, and the sun is shining on them. In the doors of each cabinet are carved patterns, also of large birds. The man stands in front of us and spreads out his hands, as if to say, this is it. There are two closed doors to our left and another, more striking one directly ahead of us, a double door with shaded, patterned panes, the patterns like those on the cabinets, and it is closed. These are for guests, our guy says, and this here — pointing to the double door — is Ferran's apartment. He's not around very much."

Bob puts his hand on my knee. It's a warm, heavy hand, and content, as if it doesn't need to move in one direction or the other. I smile right into his grey pebble eyes.

"On the third day we meet Ferran. He's in his fifties, polo shirt, nice jeans, smooth tanned skin. He tells us where the beaches are beautiful — not in Barcelona. He's been skiing in Banff. We pretend we have too. The next morning from his apartment, through the double door, a woman comes out, young, twenty-three, twenty-five maybe, a petite, Slavic-looking girl, with thin, blonde hair, glasses, dressed in yoga wear. For the rest of the week she's there every day though there's no more Ferran. She seems to have the run of the place. One afternoon I find her on a ladder, in her little shorts, cleaning out the top cupboard. "*Hola,*" she says, smiling, when I come into the kitchen. "Check out Ferran," Josh says every time we run into her. Well, one night I wake up, just like that, and Josh isn't in bed. He must've gone to the bathroom, I think. But he's not coming back and I'm not falling back asleep and so I go and check. He's not there. I patter down the long hall. I call him quietly. I walk to the end of the hall. Well, in the kitchen, there is Josh, in nothing but his gaunch, holding this girl, Ferran's girl, holding her to him like he's going to save her from drowning. They don't even notice me standing there. She's in her usual gear, her little pants and spandex shirt, except that she's taken off her glasses. When they finally separate I see her eyes, small, myopic eyes, like the eyes of a baby animal waking up."

Bob is looking at me the whole time. He doesn't move his hand, but it's a living hand, nothing dead about its weight. I take a swig of the scotch from the flask, since the glass is empty.

"So what does he say?"

"What does he say? What does he say? He says, 'It's okay' — to her, not to me. That's what he says."

"Go on," Bob says, "they won't miss us just yet."

"No. Listen to what happens next. The next day in the early morning, while Josh is still asleep, I get out of bed when I hear the caretaker, the guy who met us on the first day. He always came in the mornings to change the towels, turn on the dishwasher, fill up the coffee. So I hear him and I go into the kitchen and I make myself an espresso and I sit at the little nook by the window. Well eventually he comes into the kitchen to do his things. 'Hola,' I say. 'Hola,' he says, a little surprised by anyone being there. He refills the coffee capsules — there is some fancy coffee system there, and he says something, half English half Spanish, which I under-stand to mean the guests drink a lot of coffee. I down the espresso. He offers me another. He takes a fresh cup, presses the button. He passes the little cup to me, moving in just slightly closer than he needs to. Our fingers touch. He looks at me and I don't look away. And there it is, all I wanted. A look exchanged, desire as brief as a dream. I'm quoting that part."

Bob shakes his head. His eyes are looking a little small and dreamy too, eyes looking at me from the border between here and elsewhere.

"Nina," he says, and squeezes my knee. He closes his eyes as if he just can't keep them open any longer.

I put my hand on his. In a moment he opens his eyes again, and he's back. He's here, strong. We can go on together.

"What happened with Josh and Ferran's girl?"

"Listen. Josh had come into the kitchen and found her sitting on the stool at the breakfast nook. Just sitting there. Something was wrong, he could tell. She was folding and refolding a napkin in her hands. She didn't say *hola* this time. He poured himself a glass of water from the fridge — what he had come for — and drank it slowly. Then he offered her a glass. Just on a whim, he said, he offered her a glass, because he didn't want to leave without a word, her looking the way she did. No, she shook her head. He saw her eyes welling up, though she kept her eyes down and tried not to cry. So of course he put his hand on her and of course that's a sure way to make a person trying not to cry, cry. So she cried. She cried and cried, he said. She took off her glasses, slipped off the stool, slipped into Josh's now open arms and she cried. She cried in quiet whimpers, then in quick choking spurts, snot and saliva and tears all mixing together, then in huge, full-body dry heaves, she cried, he said, until all her body was empty and clean and light like a piece of pine, a board of perfect pine, smooth and clean and too perfect to use for building anything. That's what he said — until all her body was like a sheaf of light. He held her all the while she cried, held her to him without shifting a muscle. When I walked in was when the crying had stopped, the dry toe-to-head convulsions had stopped, when they were both still. When she made the transformation into perfect light, I suppose."

Bob is quiet. The flask has been going back and forth between us. He looks at me with some pain in his face, as if he just got heartburn, or some other human, bodily pang.

Eventually he says, "It sounds right. Sounds like just the kind of thing that might happen. Girl had a bit too much to drink earlier, probably, the drink brought out the despair, that will happen. Josh also had a bit too much to drink, needed a glass of water around 3:00 AM. It sounds right." But I know that's not what he's thinking about.

"Oh it's a true story," I say. "And that's it. Well, I also got pregnant."

"In Barcelona?"

"Yes, the day after the kitchen and the crying business. We didn't find out until we got home of course. In any case, I miscarried one morning in October, at home, just like that. Since then all I can think about is either having a kid with Josh, or leaving Josh and never having a kid. I think about it driving home, stuck in rush hour on the bridge. You know how the light can be on the bridge, when the sun is going down? Coming through the ironwork it blinds you every other second — bridge, cars, then blinding all-erasing light.

I imagine the apartment Josh and I would buy, the breakfast table we would sit at with our child, exhausted but fully present in the world, bound to each other and the child. The child one day with his complexion and my eyes, another day all him, all in shades of brown. Then I think about not living with Josh. Moving back in with my parents. Or moving to Spain, alone, renting a room somewhere — phoning my mom and holding the receiver away from my ear while she tells me I've ruined my life. I would always have to speak to her with the receiver away from my ear."

"There's no way of knowing about the children stuff. Cindy and I weren't sure we would have children. In fact the deal when we got married was no children. Then she hit late thirties. In the end you do or you don't. And the other stuff — I don't know if there's any way of knowing about it either."

Bob's shirt is open one button below the standard. His shirt sleeves are rolled up. Bob was married to Cindy for almost thirty years, but he has made love to many women, I suddenly know it. I move toward him on the counter, so that half my bum is in the sink.

"You know what," I say. I look at his face, his sharp jawline, the solid chin, the clavicle.

"You know what, it's not just that. It's the sex that's difficult. It needs opening. I can't open. I won't. Something in me won't give over."

"Oh, sweetheart." He puts his hand in my hair, finds my neck, gets his fingers all tangled up in there. "I know. I know."

What I think is, I will fold myself into the light of Bob. I will be sucked into the vortex of light that is in the part of his chest other men keep buttoned up.

"You know what?" I'm perfect. I'm outside of time. No, not quite. I'm not quite perfect. I need a little more. Do I? Sometimes you have to pause and rethink whether you need more.

"In the end there are only two reasons to have sex: love and curiosity."

He laughs. "You're silly." His hand is below my neck, on the back, travelling down. "That's silly. There are so many!"

"Bob! Okay, but just exclude the perversions." I put my arm around his waist near the belt, feel the girth right above it. I pull my one knee up, let the other leg dangle.

"Exclude them? Are you nuts?" He keeps his hand on my hip bone.

"Fine. Fine." I look down on my dangling leg, the leg dangling close to the ground, the leg that could be not my leg. What a relief that is, that any part of you could be not a part of you.

"Anyway . . . love, that's vague," I say, still looking down.

"You said it."

I do it. I fold into him. I pull up my leg that is not my leg and bend the other and take his shirt in my fist and scrunch up into him. What can he do but hold me, pulling me back to lean against the wall.

"Josh was my own true love," I say.

"That's how it goes," he says.

The knock comes as if from some other place.

"Nina, are you in there?"

My own voice comes up, automatically, like a rote reaction, though the existence of Trudy and her hallway, her house, is not of concern to me at all. "I'm here, Trudy, yes, I'm fine."

"I've got her, Josh, she's here," I hear her call down. "Are you sure you're all right? Do you want Josh to come in?"

"No, Trudy, I'll be out in a minute."

"Okay, then." Then I hear Karl say to her, "What's going on? She all right?" Then Josh is there. "Nin," he says, "you've been in there a long time, let me in."

But still I think it can't really be over.

I put my hand inside Bob's shirt, find his shoulder, his neck.

"This is trouble," he says.

It's too late. Already the beyond-the-door exists. And outside the door there is a pause and then Karl's voice. "What is going on in there?"

Bob pulls my head from his chest gently and looks at me. He looks at me and looks at me. Then he moves off the counter, unfurling me with him. He opens the door. It hadn't been locked.

The two of us look directly at Trudy and Josh, and Karl behind them.

"Oh, what on earth?" Trudy says, "You're both in here?" She sounds almost like she will laugh.

Josh looks from Bob to me, and back again. Karl looks at us and then quickly away, and fixes his eyes just to the right of Bob.

"Marta's gone home, Bob," Karl says, looking at the frame of the door. "I better take you down." Karl's face is a pale, limp rag. I regret it because I like him, and I like Trudy too. But then I think it's all right. It's just how it is. Let them see. This is just how things are now.

Josh is pale. He's looking at me.

I should say something, but instead I turn to Bob. He is flushed in the face but calm. "She wasn't feeling well," he says, looking back at me, and it seems as if he is about to extend his hand to Josh. He doesn't, thankfully.

"What the fuck, Bob?" Josh says. Trudy quickly puts a hand on him. Her mouth is tight.

"I'm not going home with you," Josh says to me.

"Oh, don't be hasty now, Josh," Trudy says.

"Come to the kitchen," Karl says to Bob.

For a moment no one moves and then Bob turns to me. "I'm going to go downstairs, okay? Okay, Nina? You'll be okay." And he does walk away, with Karl, down the stairs, Bob, Bob Hrypchuk, bald head and warm chest, disappearing.

"I'm going to go downstairs too," Trudy says. "Okay, you two? I'm going to leave you up here. Okay?"

"It's all right," I say to Josh, once she leaves.

"What were you doing with Bob Hrypchuk in the bathroom?" When he stresses the word bathroom, it comes out in a squeak, as if his voice hadn't broken yet.

"Talking," I say.

"What's wrong with you? Just what part of you is not wired right?"

We go on like this for a while. I would like him to forgive me. Oh, yes, I'd like that very much. I am full of regret. But I don't tell him that, exactly. Because between the attacks of regret, I think it's for the better. He should see how things are too.

We move into his parents' bedroom. "I'm so embarrassed," he says, curled up on his parents' flower-printed duvet. "You know what, actually? I don't care. What do I care?"

"No one's really noticed but your parents."

"Oh, just my parents. Right. Great."

We don't say much more. We lie there. Josh smells warm. I don't know why that word comes to me. He turns over onto his back and with one hand rubs from his temples over his eyes, back and forth. When he does it the skin around them wrinkles and releases, wrinkles and smooths. It's just an organ, the skin, after all. Josh is with me in Barcelona, looking at the lights strung up over someone's rooftop patio. Josh smooths the bedding. He lifts my suitcase from every luggage belt and into every subway car and carries it up and down every set of stairs because it has a hard handle that hurts my hand. It's all coming up, warming my throat.

"Josh," I say, "you're hurting my throat." I move in tentatively, lift his arm up, put my forehead to his armpit and the faint trace of white that I know on all his sweaters.

He shakes his head, hand over his eyes. He must know what I mean. Before long his lip pouts slightly and his chin trembles. It has been there all along, this, and I should see it too, I suppose.

He won't let himself be held, so I lie there, smelling his warmth and hoping he can smell me too. He doesn't cry for long, and then we are silent for some time, until Trudy comes in, not at all tentatively, and stands in the doorway with her hand on her hip.

"Well are you guys spending the night here? I really don't care one way or the other, I'd just like to know so that I can get the bedding out."

Josh lifts up his knees, and leaps off the bed. It's the first he's moved in about half an hour. "Nope, we're leaving."

"Come on, Nin," he says to me. I come. One way or the other, I'm not going to stay here and sleep on Trudy's bed.

"Fine," Trudy says, with her tight mouth. Maybe her mouth has been set in that way since I first saw her in the hallway outside of the bathroom. "I'll tell Matt and Nicole then."

We go downstairs, not passing through the living room to avoid the few people sitting on the couches, slowly finishing their wine. Matt and Nicole, blank-faced, slow-moving, meet us in the hallway. We sling on our scarves, stuff the gloves and toques into our coat pockets and purses, and move through the snow on the driveway single file, in flapping coats and unzipped boots. It has grown colder and the snow has not stopped falling. Our car on the street is snowed in, but the doors are not frozen, and Matt and Nicole get into the back seat, not caring about the snow that falls inside the car. I stay on the sidewalk, because I know we won't get to just drive away from here, I know the car is stuck. Josh has the keys in his jacket pocket and he starts the car and then gets out to brush off the snow, the way he always does, with fast, wide movements, not bothering with corners. Karl and Trudy are watching from the picture window, their arms hugging their bodies as if they are outside and cold, and when Josh tries to pull out, but can't, they emerge through the front door, with gloves and jackets on.

Matt gets out of the back seat, and he and Karl and I start to push. Josh accelerates and the wheels spin. We rock the car, push it forward and let it slide back. Try now, Josh yells, his door open, and we push hard and again the wheels spin. The noise is an incision into the brittle armour of the street, the cold, hardening snow and the cars parked in driveways, immovable. We rock again; my arms hurt and my feet slide and Matt's hands are bare and red on the trunk and Karl is breathing hard. But on the next upswing Josh accelerates and the car goes up and over and glides down the street. It just glides. Our arms are suddenly free, warm blood coursing through them, hearts beating fast. The car is rumbling, dutiful, obliging, forgiving. We climb in and drive away, yellow light of the street lamps, wheels gently crunching the snow. The air in the car slowly loses its tightness and Matt and Nicole start to doze in the back seat. But I imagine tomorrow, how desperately hungover we will be, void of serotonin and hope, how we will try to return to ourselves over cereal and coffee and maybe something more, frozen waffles and sausages and sunny eggs to bring us back to life and smother our shame. Or we won't, we will try to force things to their logical ends. "Forget about the eggs," I will say. "And then — "do we have to do this, couldn't we just have a nice breakfast, get back under the comforter in our T-shirts and underwear and hold each other's dry, vibrating, nervous bodies." But some part of me, curious and yearning and unapologetic, will still be with Bob in the bathroom, and I will wonder, what do other people do, when this happens?

# In Vancouver, with David

I'LL ALWAYS REMEMBER THIS LUNCH I had with David's, my boyfriend David's, Aunt Joyce. I had gone to her apartment, for the first time, to pick up some tickets she had promised the two of us. She worked at a small theatre that put on satires, black comedies, and such; I think she was a sort of secretary there. So I came for the tickets, and she said somebody was just about to bring them by — they were late, in fact, she said — and so she invited me in for lunch. "It'll give us a chance to visit, love," she said, in her pleasant voice that *carried*, like everyone's voice should if they plan to be generally successful in life. She rubbed my shoulder with one hand and motioned me in with the other. She was very heavy, with a familiar kind of pretty, friendly face. I sat down at a little table separated from the kitchen by a counter. I liked that she called me 'love', and in general I liked women, older women, calling me by terms of endearment. Joyce wore big tunics and ornamental earrings with stones that matched the colours of her outfits and her polished fingernails.

As I sat, her dog Milka — Joyce told me that she was a field spaniel — occasionally came to sniff and rub up against me. "Milka got her name from the German chocolate," Joyce said as she set the table and brought out garlic mashed potatoes, a pan of veggie sausages, and one of those store-bought potato salads. Then she called for the dog, who had disappeared a moment ago, saying "Come here girl," over and over; she must have said it eight or nine times, with the same intonation each time. Milka eventually bounced along and climbed onto a chair beside me.

"You don't mind if Milka eats with us," Joyce said — said and not really asked — as she set a soup bowl in front of the dog. I didn't know what to say. The dog put its paws beside the bowl. It raised itself up and leaned in to smell the sausage, tongue hanging out. Joyce motioned Milka to sit back down and began cutting a sausage for her into small pieces. I still didn't know what to do, or where to look. Then I caught the smell of the dog's breath, and with that the obscenity of the situation struck me. And I began to feel shamefully uneasy. My parents, whom David sometimes — inaccurately, I think — called "properly European," came to mind. What ridiculousness, I remember thinking. Then, as if scripted, the man with the tickets came. He leaned in through the door, extended his arm in a wave and called out in a baby voice, "Hi, Milka girl, well look at you." When he left, Joyce sat down and spooned some sausage and potato stuff onto my plate. I ate it, the dog ate hers, Joyce prattled on. Finally I excused myself and left the whole circus.

When I met with David that night — at Murky Waters, a small café on Edmonton's Whyte Avenue, a café with a clientele that considered itself artistic and radical, I thought disdainfully — I broke up with him. I saw him through the glass front, sitting at a table by the wall, bent over a magazine and, in a characteristic gesture, stroking his jaw. I walked up to him, laid the tickets on the table, and said, "Here, you'll have to find someone to go with, 'cause I'm not going with you, I'm not going anywhere with you again." David said, "What the heck are you talking about?" But I just walked right out, with all my anger tight inside me. We got back together, so to speak, the next day. David had a way with me, I should admit. He called me on the phone in the morning, five or six times before I actually answered. The first thing he said to me was "Lidi," in that soft, sort of vulnerable, voice, and I knew that we weren't, of course, over.

That was in May, the episode that David later called my mini-breakdown. We had been dating for a year then; I worked in a bookstore, and David was a bartender. My hours were long and leisurely and occasionally contemplative, and David's charged and tense and exhausting. David also took creative writing courses and wrote poems that used words like *lacunae* and *orbits*, poems I didn't understand. I looked for pieces of prettiness, tongues pressed to petals, stuff like that in his poems, and for any oblique mention of me. But he wasn't pretentious, David. My parents liked him well enough, although he wasn't the Croatian boyfriend they had hoped for, just a Canadian, Anglican boy whose background had nothing in common with mine, with *our* background as my parents would say. "He'll never understand that," they'd say.

In June of that same year a cousin of mine who lived in Vancouver, who was older than I and married with children, invited me for a visit and said I should bring David.

"I love the West Coast, Vancouver is great," David said. "We should go." West Coast, East Coast, out west, up north, these are the ways Canadians orientate themselves around their country, I thought, such a shockingly large country and all there is to it is left, right, up, down. So we went to Vancouver, drove the twelve or so hours in David's blue Pontiac Sunbird. We were well past Kamloops when the sun started to set, so we were driving into the sunset.

"Write that, David," I said, "write that we are driving into the sunset, that your hand is inside my clothes, that we are the only survivors of an apocalypse." David often smiled with just one side of his mouth. "I would," he said, "but I don't have a free hand. You write it."

My cousin Zrinka and her husband Marco lived in a white and yellow two-story house in the Grandview area, next to a corner store. Their daughters were six and eight years old. One was named Lidija, like me, except they spelled it Lydia, the English way, and the other Antonia; nice universal names, my cousin said. Zrinka spoke to them in Croatian, Marco in Italian, and the girls answered in English. David and I slept on the futon in the guest room. Zrinka had lived in Vancouver for twelve years, twice as long as I'd been in Edmonton. Marco had lived there since he was five years old, and I wondered sometimes, listening to him repeat simple instructions in Italian to one of the girls, how much of the language he had lost. It was my first time meeting him; he was pale, with dark hair that must have only recently begun to recede, and seemed to wear flip-flops and Adidas shorts everywhere. At breakfast, the morning after we arrived — it was Saturday — Marco asked me what

I was planning to do, now that I was "finished school and everything."

"Your degree's in English, right?" he asked. People always ask what you're planning to do, this ridiculous question, and everyone, I've always thought, lies, says they're looking into things, mentions a school or a company they've only heard about in conversation, say they're taking a year off to travel. But whoever considers that there may be a natural disaster, or something of the sort, that decides for them. Falling in love, I thought, is a natural disaster, and I secretly considered myself clever for thinking so.

"Zrinka said you were thinking of going down home for a while," he continued. Their kitchen was small and neat and entirely white.

"What's with you and the questions? They're here on vacation," Zrinka said, and took away his plate with half a slice of bacon still on it, and so breakfast was over.

David and I meant to go to the University of British Columbia campus during the day, but it was already dusk when we got there, because we had an argument about his socks. "Dress pants and loafers and white socks?" I noticed them just as he was opening the screen door to let us out of the house.

"Aw fuck," he said, and rolled his eyes. "I'm gonna wear pink socks with sandals one day, just to piss you off." While I looked for socks in our as yet unpacked suitcase, he went to the kitchen to open a beer. When I returned, he got me a cranberry cooler, and socks in hand we sat in the living room and watched a talk show. Some two hours later we finally got in the car and drove to the campus. We walked and walked, with no clear goal, through mostly quiet grounds, neat and lushly green, past a wide mansion of greystone and another one of glass and steel. In truth, I could hardly believe how green and open and beautiful it all was. We walked until we got down to this pavilion with stone arches, bushes and flower gardens, a fountain in the centre, and a view of the ocean. At the edge of it was a stone fence from which you looked down on a road, and beyond that was the ocean stretching out. It was a dense blue that night. Zrinka had been right when she told me, a long time ago when she had first invited me to visit, that the ocean wasn't really like the Adriatic, where we had both spent many summers, and a few of them together, at her parents' summer house. But that was when I was still a kid, when I watched Zrinka enviously as she went out every night (bare-shouldered, skin smelling of coconut suntan lotion), when neither of us could have imagined we would meet here, of all places, one day. David and I leaned our torsos on the low wall and hung our arms over the edge. "Hot skin against cool stone," David recited in a mock-poetic voice. The stone was actually warm and suddenly it all seemed strange, this perfectly manicured and fake little pavilion behind us and the ocean distant and inconceivable.

"Let's go," I said, turning away from the view. David looked at me, looked back, and stayed as he was.

"I'll meet you in the car," he said.

We were all meant to go out for drinks that night, but at the last minute Zrinka said she would stay home with the kids, and so it was the three of us, David, Marco, and I who got into Marco's old Volkswagen and headed downtown.

We scored a seat on a patio of a café whose name I don't remember, on Robson Street, or off Robson Street, either way. We smoked cigarettes, drank gin and tonics. The patio was raised three steps from the sidewalk and surrounded by a low railing, next to which we sat and watched the crowds that poured by on the street, the night warm and lovely in a way I couldn't remember it ever being in Edmonton. At some point Marco started talking to someone at the table next to ours. I didn't pay attention because I didn't want to become part of the conversation. David seemed to be in the same mood as me and just sat looking out at the people on the street. We were joined by our forefingers, our arms over the railing. Marco spoiled the mood when he began introductions with the man at the next table, who wore a suit jacket, was in his thirties, and was apparently drinking alone. On his table sat a cell phone, a cigarette case, and something like an electronic day-planner, or Palmpilot maybe. He promptly offered his Marlboros around. I still tried to look uninterested, smiling faintly and staring off vacantly. The crowds were engrossing, never-ending variations.

Street people passed often, but few stopped beside us; we were part of the background to them, I suppose. A round of drinks arrived, courtesy of the man David and I were trying to ignore. I toasted with everyone and turned away. Then a homeless-looking guy walking slowly along the sidewalk made eye contact with me; he had a greying beard, and a canvas bag with the word Vancouver splashed on it in several colours, slung on his shoulder. He walked over and, without touching the railing said, "Can you spare, ma'am, I haven't eaten, ma'am, a dollar or a quarter." As I was reaching for my purse Marco's yuppie friend said, "Hey, why don't you come over here, I've got more money for you." He pulled out a five-dollar bill.

"Five bucks if you'll suck my cock," he said, dangling the bill, elbowing Marco to laugh with him. The man with the canvas bag frowned, muttered something vaguely angry but indistinct, and walked away.

Back at Zrinka's house, David and I lay on the futon with the lights turned off and the window open, still in our clothes. My back was turned to him and he held me because I was crying, sobbing and crying, for I don't know how long before he calmed me down. He turned me around to face him and then held me like that, my face in his chest, so that it seemed I cried into him and he absorbed it all. I wasn't sure why I was crying, because of that stupid man, or maybe the ocean, or David himself. Certainly I didn't like to be crying for no clear reason. At the café I had tried to throw a drink at that guy, but I'd done it so awkwardly that most of the scotch, which he had ordered us a moment earlier, landed on the floor, only some on the guy's knee, and a fair bit on Marco. Ridiculous, it all felt; even leaving — shaking as I was for some reason — could not be done right because the place was so crowded. David's hand found me just as I started down the sidewalk. Then Marco caught up with us, looking embarrassed, I don't know for whom, and we drove home in silence. Now David was holding me so tight that I had to laugh a little and say, "I can't breathe, David," and he said, "You don't have to breathe air, you can just breathe me." And then he started reciting lines, nonsense lines, "Beneath the surface of the ocean we'll be joined; your hair will be a nest for my lips — do you hear, or have you suffocated?"

"I've suffocated," I said, mostly into his chest. He continued, until, with a word still half in his mouth, he fell asleep. I knew the precise moment because I felt his limbs go heavy and, within seconds, his breathing became regular. I wanted to stay awake, to feel him sleep like that, but the next thing I remember is the opening and closing of doors, feet on the stairs, dishes clinking, and outside, the purring sound of cars softly turning corners.

# Bless the Day

I WAS WALKING DOWN A street with those modest wartime-era houses on the one side, and 1970s, three-storey walk-ups on the other. Tall elm trees lined the street and threw shade on the sidewalk. The sun was high and fierce, but a soft, undulant wind lifted the heat, and the sky was bright blue, the clouds puffy and harmless things. In fact I was fairly sure I had lived on just this street, with David, when we first moved in together, into the basement of one such humble house, a surprisingly roomy, light basement we had thought ourselves lucky to have. Now David lives in a house of his own, with another woman (they are getting married this summer), and our daughter, Mia. Their house is a heritage home with a mock pond and mock Chinese bridge in the enormous front yard, and a little balcony on the second storey, a child's wicker armchair with a pink cushion in its corner. I've driven by there, so I know. The little armchair is for Mia, of course. Let's keep her in one place a little longer, for the sake of stability, the social worker had said that morning. He looked tired, the social worker, and I don't blame him: he must see tiresome people like us all the time. But I would not think of that anymore today. It was a nice day.

I was smoking a cigarette while walking, trying to recognize our old house. On the front lawn of one walk-up sat a man and a woman. The man nudged her and she called out to me, "D'you have a cigarette?" I had one extra in the front pocket of my blouse, wrapped in a receipt. I took it out and walked toward them, out of the shade of the sidewalk and onto the sunny grass. The woman took the cigarette without getting up and lit it awkwardly, with thick dirty thumbs. They were sitting on a blanket with some Subway sandwich wrappers beside it. Behind them on the grass was a shopping cart, full of empty bottles, flattened carton boxes, a folded blanket, and on top of it two mugs that said Magic 99! Next to the man was an open tub of oily cream, and also a plastic bag with an empty-looking bottle of Canadian Club and some other messy thing — noodles and beef growing rank, red sauce spilling. The woman passed him the cigarette. His left cheekbone was noticeably lower on his face than his right. A lump.

"Thanks for the smoke," the woman said. I wished I had another. Instead I had pretzels in my purse that I had bought in a bakery after leaving court. I'd bought them because I saw other people buying pastry and buns, eating them on the bench in front of the bakery, with their little children, their loved ones, biting into steaming sausage rolls, happy, in the sun.

"I'm very tired," I said. They did not say anything. I looked down at the ground, and then sat down next to the woman, a foot away from her, on green grass.

"Tired, eh," she said.

There was something very wrong with her nose. It was flattened and I could not be sure, but it seemed as if there was only one nostril. I took out the paper bag with the pretzels. There was also a cheese bun in there that I had forgotten buying, and a poppy seed muffin. I put my nose inside my purse to see if it smelled like greasy baked goods; it did. I asked the woman what she would like; she chose the muffin. The man also chose the muffin. I watched the woman break it into rough halves and I watched as she ate her half. Then she stretched out, closed her eyes and lifted her face to the sun.

When David and I lived in that basement we were doing grad studies in comparative literature at the university. David's favourite author was Turgenev and for a while we read one copy of the *The Jew and Other Stories* again and again, passing the book back and forth between us. In one story, "The Duellist", one guy says to another, "You can't believe that about me, you know me." And the other responds, "I know you? Who knows you? The heart of another is a dark forest." It became a joke between us. I'll clear my books from the kitchen table when I get home, really, you know me. Know you? The heart of another, etc. Yes, I thought now, that was an easy one. Also, I thought, this must be the street, since I have thought of Turgenev. But it bothered me that I could not be sure. Which house was it? Where was the house?

I lay back, and when I did I felt the grass on the back of my head, and the breeze on my neck and on my stomach between the buttons.

"God, what a day," I said.

"Oh, it's a beauty," the woman said. Her eyes were still closed. She stroked the grass next to her with her hand, lightly. A car rumbled along on the road. I had the banal thought then that you only get one face — and if someone, say, rams that face into the edge of a table, crushes the nose, well, that's it. It's the only nose you've got. I felt around for the paper bag with the pretzels. I tried to picture walking to campus from that basement home — did I ever walk by this building? The man and the woman laughed at something. I could not hear well what they were saying, because of cars going by. I turned my head to their shopping cart. I understood the shopping cart. I said to myself, I have to get it together.

Then a cop car pulled up on the other side of the street, slowly, and two cops, two tall, fit men, got out and walked toward us.

"Hello, there," one cop said.

"You folks don't live in this building, I presume," the other said. This one was shorter than the other, but just as fit looking, with nicely combed black hair. I looked at the man and woman. They were shifting.

"No, we don't live here," the man said. The cops then studied me. My clothes were okay clothes and my purse was new. I had dressed well for the morning's meeting. The shorter cop with the black hair squinted at me.

"This is private property here," he said. "People live here. You know you can't hang out here."

I didn't know why they were bothering to do this. It wasn't such a fancy neighbourhood.

The taller cop said, "You'll have to take your stuff and leave. All right?"

"Ok," the woman said. She turned to me. "I guess we're getting the boot here, eh?"

"I haven't seen you folks here before," the shorter cop said. "Where did you come from?"

"From nowhere," the man said, "that all right with you?" The two cops looked at each other.

"You've been seen about by a few people today. We've had a few calls about you. Are you carrying any illegal substances, by chance?"

"Nope." The man again.

"But you had smoked some earlier. Is that right?"

The man rubbed his jaw and squinted at some distant point.

"You see," the shorter cop continued, "families live here. They don't want their kids seeing people smoking drugs or getting drunk."

"We ain't drunk," the man said.

"There's a public park around the corner and no one will stop you from sitting there if you don't bother anyone," the taller cop said.

"We were just enjoying the day," I said. It was a weak thing to say.

"May I see a piece of identification from you, ma'am?" I saw now what bothered me about the shorter cop with the finely combed hair. He was smug. The question was politely phrased but the tone was an order, smug.

The woman got up. She was not steady on her feet. She nudged at the man with her foot for him to get up too. The cop looked over my driver's licence.

"It's a nice day, but I still have to do my job, don't I?" he said, without looking up. "I don't tell the chief, it's a nice day, so today I'll go have a picnic on the grass instead of patrolling."

The woman rolled up the blanket, put it on the cart, picked up the smelly plastic bag too, and the man wheeled the cart off the grass and down the sidewalk. She followed him, then turned to me and said, "Thanks for the smoke, lady." It gave me a chance to look at her again; I wanted to remember her.

Both cops watched the man and woman walk away. I looked up at the windows and balconies of the little walk-up. Behind them, the curtains hung undisturbed.

"They'll turn the corner and plop themselves on another lawn," one said.

"They're like squirrels," said the other. "They always hop somewhere else before you can catch them." I picked up what was left on the lawn, the sandwich wrappers and the paper bag with the baked goods.

"You need a ride somewhere?" the taller one said.

I said, "I wish I did."

"Pardon?" The taller cop had a patient look on his face.

I turned to the shorter cop. "We were only sitting down for a rest."

"Take a rest on your balcony, next time," he said.

He said, "I don't get high and sit on other people's lawns with my junk spread out just because the sun is shining." He only then handed back my licence.

I probably should have taken a ride with them. Instead I walked along thinking of an image from a relief camp I had seen recently: a mattress on the floor, slippers placed neatly next to it, clothes folded in short stacks on three wooden boards made into a bench. Two photographs tacked to an otherwise bare wall. Then I thought of the shopping cart again, and of Mia, reading on a sunny balcony — quietly missing me, perhaps. I turned around and saw the police cruiser a gleaming white in the distance. The heart of another and another and another. I decided it didn't matter if this was the street I'd lived on with David. That house and that basement, even if they still stood intact in the same place, were not really there anymore, anyway.

# You Can't Stay Here

IVONA WORKS AS A CLEANING woman; she vacuums a restaurant, after 2:00 AM when everyone has gone home. The restaurant is called Comfort Food Den, and it is on the ground floor of a three-storey pink-stucco structure, below a set of law offices. Though all of the staff have left by the time she arrives, she sees traces of them in many places: notes posted by the front till, *Groups reserving for eight or more must be told about fifteen percent gratuity* written in a bubbly cursive, or in the bar section an ashtray with two butts in it tucked away beside the sink — last indulgences of the night while closing, perhaps. She doesn't clean the kitchen, but she wanders in there occasionally, on nights that feel long and expansive; sometimes she slides open the clear-glass door of the dessert cooler to cut herself a slice of pie that she then eats with her fingers. And she has taken to eating pie — apple, or lemon meringue — while standing in front of the staff table in the corner and reading notices posted above it. Messages on white letter paper in purple marker — *All staff: The days-off book is getting ridiculous. I'm trying to run a business here!* Signed *Will*. Every few weeks a new message pops up and sometimes a whole bunch, giving the impression of a crisis; their tones are threatening, exasperated, sarcastic. *All staff: Our closing time is 10:00 PM. Which means we serve customers until 10:00 PM. If anyone has issues with this please see me personally. Will.* One of her favourites is *Staff: eating gummy worms while on shift (or off!) constitutes stealing.*

She has been cleaning the restaurant for about six months when she sees the notice (on the board that stands on the front lawn) seeking, immediately, an evening hostess. The idea of being present in the same space, but when everything happens, tempts her. The only barrier is her uncertainty about her English skills, her ability to pronounce menu items clearly, without mixing up round and flat *o's*, to deliver the daily special without the awkwardness of misunderstanding. But she feels facing such a challenge is a necessary step, and imagines her accent will at least bring an unusual note to this comfy, middle-class family operation.

She knows enough to apply after 2:00 PM, when the restaurant is nearly empty. The girl at the front is young and pleasant and uninterested. She takes Ivona's resume, typed up the night before on a neighbour's computer, and hands her an application form, a crooked photocopy asking for employment history and personal interests in crowded block lettering. Ivona is working through it in a booth near the door, when a man wearing a tie emerges from the kitchen. As he sits down opposite her and shakes her hand — "I'm Will" — his smile seems calm and real. He looks young to her, barely in his thirties. He is neither middle-aged, nor pompous, as she's imagined. He is of average height, slim and pleasant looking and chatty. He mentions his teenage daughter, who apparently has the same curly hair Ivona does. He tells her he is actually forty-three, after she comments that he looks too young to have a teenage daughter.

"It's been a kind of a crazy house here," he says, "so don't mind me if I seem a bit cranky." He asks where her accent is from. She tells him it's Croatian, and he replies that his parents are from Belgium.

"I'll be calling you by tomorrow, I think," he says. "Everything looks good. I'm pretty sure everything will be good."

༒ ༒ ༒

When Ivona and Sven got engaged seven years ago, his parents disliked her, for intangible reasons, but nonetheless sharply. After Ivona visited the house for the first time, Sven's mother said, "She is a little, well, a little *važna*," and she did a strut from the stove to the table, with her nose held high and her hips jerking from side to side. Sven repeated this to Ivona once, when he was a little drunk, several years later. They tolerated her well enough perhaps, in that way parents can have with their children, affectionate but underneath a little spiteful, a touch hateful. "I don't understand what they want out of me," Ivona would say to Sven. He in turn soothed her, said they were just overly possessive of their only son, and besides, she wasn't marrying *them*. She agreed, generally; she never doubted that he was worth it.

In honour of their engagement, his parents held a supper at their house, where some twenty guests ate in shifts of eight, as many as the dining room table could accommodate. Ivona wore a dress she'd had made a few weeks earlier, a present to herself; she was feeling lavish and loved and eager in those days. While the second round of guests was eating, she walked around the table, adding dishes, taking away plates, nudging children to eat. Sven's father sat at the head, having grown impatient and not wanting to wait for the last round. He was bald, sarcastic, and funny. As Ivona was taking the full bone-plate beside him, to replace it with a new one, he said casually, looking at her sideways, "I see you're looking stylish. What are those, flowers, on your dress? Roses are in bloom for you guys, I guess." People looked over to smile. She put a clean plate on the table. "But maybe it should be a little longer, your dress" — he looked down — "to cover your calves. You have calves," he continued, "like a Frenchman who spent his life stepping on grapes in a barrel." It was moments like these that still stood starkly in Ivona's mind, part of the landscape of her marriage.

కకకక

Will starts flirting with Ivona after a few weeks of hiring her as night-time hostess. She notices he flirts with all the weekend girls (she works a few weekends), most of whom are in school or filling time after finishing school. He pulls lightly on their ponytails and leans in to smell their necks. He gets a little frantic when asked for days off, but usually gives in. "You are such a lady, you know, Ivona," he says to her almost every day now. "How is your husband," he asks, "is he treating you right? Because if he isn't, you shouldn't take that." She's heard it before and found it curious, this turn of phrase connecting love to being "treated right" — it makes her think of pets, or livestock, something helpless.

Dogs should be treated right — not kept inside too much, fed regularly, petted a lot. Will's wife Kim comes to the restaurant only occasionally. Her hair is dyed a solid, yellow blonde, and curled into large, girlish locks. When she is around, she spends most of the day assessing staff habits, the clutter on the counter, the cleanliness of the glasses, and Will stays mostly in his office at the back of the bar.

One day, as Ivona is giving Will her daily cash out, he motions her into the office. He asks how her day was. While looking at him she has a brief thought that he has been crying, there is moistness in the corners of his eyes.

"I had a dream about you," he says, after some small talk. "Oh, this is embarrassing," he says, "I shouldn't say this, it's really bad, but you were naked in it."

❧ ❧ ❧

In the fall of 1990, Ivona and Sven simply locked up the small flat that had been the home of their married existence, and emigrated to Canada. Times were uncertain, Ivona was five months pregnant, and the opportunity was not to be had again. Sven's uncle sponsored their emigration, and after two years, Sven attempted to bring his parents over. Ivona didn't object, but most of her focus in those days was on her son, his unusual behaviour, and the doctor's tentative suggestion that he might have a condition called autism.

It's taken until this fall for Ivona and Sven to work out a visiting visa for his parents and, with the help of Ivona's hostess tips, gather the money for plane tickets. The two arrive looking distraught and lost, Sven's mother constantly on the verge of tears. They sleep in the bedroom, and Ivona and Sven and Mario on a garage-sale mattress in the living room. The parents haven't brought much — only one photo album, some clothes, and one particularly dear, and aged, ceramic tea set.

"We thought we would be back in a few months," Sven's mother says repeatedly. She also says, a day after arriving, "I thought you would have done better for yourselves."

What she mostly means is the lack of furniture. Ivona tells her it's minimalism they're going for.

"But where are people supposed to sit when they come over?" She wants, as signs of their success, heavy armchairs with carved wooden armrests, Oriental rugs, perhaps a wall unit filled with crystal.

"If I sit on the floor, my friends sit on the floor," Ivona replies.

"What will become of you two here?" the mother wails.

"This is it. What you see, is what we've become."

At first, both grandparents fuss over how handsome Mario is, but after a little while they talk more and more about why he doesn't even answer to his name, why he continually wriggles out of grandma's lap. Insinuations of guilt hover above their words. Mario is indeed a beautiful child, with smooth, shiny brown hair and flushed cheeks, and perhaps for this reason, people expect him to be exceptionally responsive and affectionate and bright.

When the parents go to spend a weekend with Sven's uncle, Sven and Ivona fight the whole time over a missed appointment with the pediatrician, and for the first time ever, Sven sleeps alone on the mattress in the living room. On Monday morning, the day Sven's parents are to return,

Ivona wakes in her marriage bed, a double bed with no bed frame, with her son's sleeping body next to her, his head at her hip. Her first thought is of her mother-in-law, the small-shouldered, black-haired figure, nestling into a corner of the living-room mattress, propped up by pillows, like a small animal, burrowing. Bringing crumbs of pastry up to her lips on fingers wet with saliva. And the father-in-law, calling over to Mario, "Come to Grandpa, little man," then throwing up his hands when Mario ignores him. Murmuring words to himself. Then she hears the front door unlocking.

They are in the hallway, the father struggling to get his coat off, the mother holding up a plastic bag and saying to Sven, "We had the best veal at your uncle's."

Ivona emerges from the bedroom. "You know what, I'm sorry, keep your coats on, you can't stay here."

Sven turns from his parents to her, his face first stunned then colouring red. When she just stares back, he throws his arms out, disbelieving.

"Have you gone crazy? Don't listen to her." He tries to move them inside, but his parents stand immobile, with long, blank faces.

"No, no, you can't stay here, there is no room, go to your brother's house, he's rich, we're not rich." Neither of them speaks, Sven clutches his head, and Ivona continues, "I'm not fucking around. If they stay" — she turns to her husband — "I will go."

Now Sven's mother's eyes moisten and her chin trembles, and she drops the bag of veal leftovers she's been holding, while his father stands very still, as if he were standing on one piece of blessed solid ground amidst an earthquake.

"I will go," Ivona says, "and I'll take my son, you goddamn assholes."

❧ ❧ ❧

At the end of a Friday closing shift, Ivona is the last one in the restaurant, except for Will, who has stayed in his office for the last three hours instead of leaving at dinnertime, as he usually does. She wonders if he's been waiting for her to finish up, and she can't avoid going to his office to hand over her cash. The door is open a crack, and as she enters she sees that he is sitting still, a calculator and a book open in front of him, but his thoughts, surely, somewhere else.

"Thank you," he says. At first she would like to just leave, but then she asks what he's doing here so late.

"Kim's off somewhere, one of those Avon parties or something. So much freakin' paperwork to catch up on." He rubs his eyes. "Maybe we should have a drink, you and me, now that the place is empty. I've got keys to the bar, you know." He smiles.

After a moment's silence, she says, "Do you want to take a ride, Will? Just a ride, we can talk for a bit."

He looks uncertain and a little excited. "A ride?"

"We'll take my car," she says.

It's cool in her old Subaru, the fall night is getting colder. They drive in silence, and she isn't sure where she's going, or why she's going anywhere at all. She is driving toward her own apartment, she realizes. Here is that Baptist church she passes by almost every day. She has no idea what a Baptist church might be like; she has only once back home heard of

57

someone who went abroad and became a Baptist — strayed into it, rather. She turns into the parking lot of the church.

"Well, this is an odd place to stop."

"I live close by here. I just didn't want to go any further."

"Ivona, Ivona. Is your husband up waiting for you?"

"He usually is."

He unclips his seatbelt; she hasn't bothered putting hers on to begin with. Will shifts slightly to turn toward her, and she does the same. In the light of the streetlamp that enters the car, he looks soft, his mouth pursed, his eyes slightly sad.

"How old were you when you got married? You're twenty-nine now, right?"

"I'm thirty. I was twenty-four. Had my son at twenty-six."

"That's like me, I was even younger. Too freakin' young. Lots of things I haven't done, travel and stuff. I'd like to travel, go to Belgium maybe, that's where my parents are from. All these girls working for me, they take vacations, go to Europe, go to — I don't know — Latin America. They're young, they can do whatever they want." His hands are on his thighs, his plain slacks, and he's looking at the dashboard, not at her. His moustache is perfectly trimmed.

"Maybe I'll do all that stuff when I retire, I want to retire early, definitely. Right now, the way things are going, with the restaurant and everything, I could probably retire in ten years, if I don't lose it before then. My kids'll be grown, I'll ship them off to school somewhere, and then I'll just lie somewhere on a beach drinking those fruity drinks, whatever they are. But you need about a million to retire decently, you know, that's what I figure."

"A million dollars? You need a million dollars to retire?"

"Well, I figure — What are you looking at me like that for? Hmm? Am I boring you, are you laughing at me? You're quite a beautiful lady, you know."

This dreamy look in his eyes, this fake dreamy look, fake husky voice, mockery of seduction. He doesn't even really want me, she thinks.

"I'm not, obviously." She means beautiful. "Will, you should ask her, you should ask Kim, about all this retirement. You'll still be young in ten years."

They sit in silence for a little while, each looking out their own window.

"I feel like kissing you. Is that really bad? I shouldn't be saying these things to you, but I do want to, I do, I'm an honest guy, a simple guy."

The car has been running the whole time and now she shifts it into gear.

"I'm sorry, you're right, we should go home," he says.

She drives back to the restaurant. That's where his car is. If Sven knew this was going on, he would say, "You can quit, if it's a problem. We can do without the money." In front of the restaurant, as he's about to get out of the car, Will says, "I'm sorry. I'm out of line. Forgive me." His eyes have cleared from the haze of dreaminess.

"It's forgotten," she says.

She drives back home, past the same church, its parking lot empty. She and Sven have been fighting for weeks. "Do you know there is a war on? Would you have them go back to that, is that what you want?" She has never seen him so jerky with rage. Mario had several hysterical crying episodes in the days after Ivona sent her in-laws out of her apartment.

She's read somewhere that children with autism often suffer from anxiety. "You are such a hard woman," Sven said to her on the third day, when they were getting worn down. He said he might never forgive her, and in revenge she took back her forgiveness for everything she had ever held against him.

She finds Sven sitting up in the kitchen with Mario, trying to get him to draw. Mario is puncturing the paper with the crayon, and Sven keeps saying, "Easy, son." She sits down beside her husband. He is a dark-haired man, with a wide face, and his skin is milky-pale, inherited by their son. There is a spot of black grease near Sven's temple, and a stray eyelash nestled near the bridge of his nose. Ivona, before she kisses them both, and touches both of their faces, can see all this clearly.

# Postcard from the Adriatic

IN THE SUMMER OF 1992, Ivana and Melita tanned themselves mercilessly: Ivana was naturally olive skinned and dark-haired, and Melita blue-eyed and freckled, but both burned, peeled, and burned again. That summer, the four hotels of the beach complex *Luna* on the Dalmatian coast were filled with refugees. The girls, though also displaced, weren't staying in one of the hotels; they had to walk for over an hour to get to the beach. It was worth it: the beach stretched for kilometres; it was sand and rock and forest and picnic tables and waterless swimming pools and endless possibility. They had both turned thirteen that year and had boyfriends, of a sort, who lived in the hotels; these boyfriends were a recent, start-of-summer development. Ivana and Marko would swim out far and hug and grope in the water, or walk off into obscure, wooded parts of the beach, to squeeze each other tightly on a bed of pine needles. Melita and Johnny had their places too: one a room with a small window, through which the sun shone as if through a tunnel's opening. The possibilities of the beach were grand.

Today was an ordinary weekday in early August, and the girls lay in their usual spot near the defunct blue waterslide.

Melita glistened with oil and sweat and Ivana was fingering the bikini knots that stuck out from her hips. But when Ivana saw her boyfriend Marko approaching, she did not wave at him, as she usually would.

"Village boy," Melita said. She'd spotted him walking towards them through the wavy haze of the hot sun. She wiped at her sweat with a small towel.

"You deaf?" she said.

Ivana frowned and didn't move. When Marko came up, he crouched next to Ivana's legs, and ran a finger upward on her thigh, upsetting the bleached fuzzy hairs there. He had thick, curly dark locks that she loved, but at the moment his curious, probing, benevolent brown eyes irritated her.

"Want to go for a walk?" he said.

"I can't now. Melita was just telling me something important."

He looked silently at her for a few moments, unprepared for refusal. "Going for a walk" was what they did every time they saw each other.

"Well, all right, I'll see you later?" He was a muscular and almost stocky boy, and watching him walk away in a moment's time Ivana felt something close to disgust at his slight bowleggedness.

Melita raised herself up on her elbows and saw that Ivana's chin was trembling.

"Hey," Melita said, and moved Ivana's raised knee back and forth like a swing, "He-ey, hee-eey, heeeeeey."

"Stupid idiot ass," Ivana sniffed out, as he walked away. She explained: last afternoon she and the boy had been in a little grove of olive trees and low shrubs, when he had put his hand inside her shorts and inside her bathing suit. He tried to pull her shorts down; he put his fingers in places. From where she had lain under him she could see, over a low stone wall, people's thighs and torsos and lazy, curious heads, and she was ashamed — before that it had been all tingly, teasing, fluttering, clothed touching. Though he had touched her breasts before that afternoon — had kissed the middle of her chest where the ribcage meets, and said she had the most phenomenal breasts he had seen on the entire beach. (The girls had both already agreed that Ivana's breasts surpassed all standards, so perfectly full and firm were they, and it was Ivana herself who, on a whim of vanity, had offered to take her top off for him.)

Melita looked out at a calm, green and blue sea, her view obscured in part by a large male belly a few feet in front of her, then down at her cousin. All day she had been wanting to tell Ivana about yesterday afternoon with Johnny. She waited a little while. Then, trying not to sound overly happy, "Well, it's funny, you know, um, you know Johnny?"

"Yeah, I know, you probably love him, yeah, I know."

Melita edged closer on her towel and began to whisper. The girls put their towels down on this less glamorous side of the slide because here entry into the sea was shallow and gradual: they weren't the proudest swimmers. The big-bellied man and his wife turned toward the loud static of their whispering and the lady could be heard saying, "Ah, youth" in an amiable, indulgent tone.

As Ivana listened to Melita's story, her hand went over her mouth; with her other hand she squeezed Melita's forearm.

Melita said, "So what?" She looked flushed and possibly even smug. Johnny was popular on the beach, even though his face was pockmarked and he had a slight limp. He was older than the girls; he'd told them he was nineteen. They'd told him they were sixteen. Why did he have his eye on Melita, skinny and small, definitely less well-breasted. But he did, and it had been clear to Ivana from the day he walked up to them near this very spot, a long time ago now, at the start of summer. She wasn't jealous, anymore; there was something skulking about him, about the way he pretended not to know them if other people or families were near.

Ivana offered to oil Melita's back. The older couple near them was eating apples and arguing a point. "No, no, no," the man was saying emphatically as the woman waved him away. Nothing about them, about the way their body language suggested both intimacy and indifference to each other, helped Ivana understand why Melita had enjoyed herself and she hadn't.

A cloud from some far corner of the sky crept up to the sun and drew a shadow over the girls. They groaned. But the cloud would pass, they knew. They might have thought that it would never not be summer again. They sometimes felt as if they had been here, in the cabin and on the beach, forever, and that nothing before this needed to be remembered.

They were cousins, and at the moment were living with Ivana's mother and grandmother; Melita's mother was in Austria, scrubbing toilets and polishing armoires, and sending German marks to the cabin's address every month. Ivana's father was on the front, and Melita had never known hers. The cabin was the summer house of a distant relative — that much the girls did know — but the reason that they ended up here in particular was one of many things that the adults (whether carelessly or deliberately, it was hard to tell), didn't explain to them.

To walk home they took a shortcut up the hill, way at the wild end of the beach, where nudists made their home on muddy sand, and dark weeds flailed in the water. It was a steep foot path, and they were halfway to the top where the highway was, when they turned to see a naked man with a hand around his penis, waving to them with his underwear in his other hand. They rushed up, stubbing their toes, and once at the top, stood and watched as he waved wildly and laughed. Ivana was so unnerved by this mysterious laughing cartoon that she wanted to tell her mother about him. But Melita made her swear on her own grave never to do that.

Darko's arrival was the most unexpected, exciting thing their household had seen in weeks. The cabin was in a cul-de-sac at the end of a street and any car coming in could not go unnoticed. Mrs. Vela came into the yard to see her cousin unfurl his tall frame out of a loud white Golf. Darko was shirtless and unshaven, and carried a watermelon under his arm. He was at the kitchen table slicing into it when the girls returned from the beach.

"Young ladies!" he nearly bellowed, as they left behind their flip-flops in the hallway.

"You're not being shy, are you?" They stood still, unsure how to greet him. "I've been here all afternoon waiting for you princesses to get home."

After they had hugged him, loosely, Ivana said, "Did Dad come with you?"

"Soon, he'll come soon." Darko started cutting the melon again, and seemed already to be thinking of something else.

Mrs. Vela said, "Melita, dear. Someone with your complexion can't take that much sun." The name followed by endearment, period, was her intro to gentle chastisement or advice: "Ivana, love. Don't create a feast for the ants on the floor." Or, "Melita, honey. The water has to boil before you put the pasta in."

When she had the chance to talk to her friends on the phone, Mrs. Vela found that their voices sometimes reached her as stark and as startling as scent. So it was now seeing her cousin — his presence was like a car engine idling in an otherwise silent night: she could hardly focus on anything else. They were born a month apart, were the first grandchildren of the family, and always together. There was a family legend told ad nauseum about how Mrs. Vela, Marija, four years old, had abandoned Darko and not let him play with the puppy she'd got for her birthday. Darko locked himself up in the pantry of his parents' house and howled for hours. When he finally came out, he said he didn't want the puppy, he just wanted Marija to love him again. They were reconciled within the week, but legend of her fickleness and his devotion lived on. The truth was that jealous four-year-old Darko had tried to twist the puppy's leg — a thing no one but her saw or believed. She could never correct the story later, couldn't muddle it with the truth.

While they ate supper on the terrace at the back of the cabin, Melita was brave enough to ask, "How are things out there?"

"Melita, sweetheart. Don't pester," said Mrs. Vela.

"Beautiful, Melita, you just take an interest, that's what I like to see," Darko said, and simply kept eating his pasta without answering. Mrs. Vela was finding it somehow repulsive how much she and he were beginning to look alike. Both had long faces that looked old before their time — and not because they were weathered, exactly. The two lines under her eyes, where cheekbone met cheek, she'd had even as a child. In some of the childhood photographs that had caught her when she was sad, she looked as worn and oppressed as a prisoner of war.

Ivana observed her mother strumming her fingers on the table and humming, tunelessly. Ivana thought it meant she was cheerful. Her mother's moods were familiar but difficult to predict.

"How long will you stay?" Ivana asked with a glance at her uncle.

"Christ how curious children are. Aren't you?" He peered at Ivana. Ivana looked to her mother for help, and saw that her face was clouding over.

"But they're not children," she said. "By the age of twelve they're already fully formed. I'm not 'raising' them anymore. At best, I can be a mentor, an — "

"Example," he finished for her. "Mirror. Guiding light."

"What mirror?" she said. "Shut up."

Ivana then looked at her grandma, who sat with her hands clasped on her round belly, with eyes closed and a wide smile. Ivana was still looking for clues to help solve her problem, but she found none in her grandma's squat pumpkin of a body. Since she had started taking walks with Marko, Ivana had collected a number of things from him:

earnest and rather clever love notes, matchboxes with special meanings, a flower he had made for her out of the paper that lines cigarette packs, a school photograph of himself. Last night she threw some of them in the garbage and felt a creeping exultation — at freedom from this bond, at her own cruelty? What stopped her from destroying everything was remembering what he'd said after she'd taken off her bikini top for him: that her breasts were scoops of vanilla ice cream and the tanned skin around them a sugar cone.

Uncle Darko, passing Ivana in the hallway on his way out, said to her, "Your mother is in her uncommunicative mode. I'll see you later." He let the door slam behind him. The cabin shook and echoed with the force of it.

Later, the women watched soaps on a small beige television, Grandma with her knitting and Mrs. Vela with her battered copy of *Anna Karenina*. She claimed not to be interested in soap operas, and so it was necessary, while sitting in front of a television screen showing *Santa Barbara*, to have the book near — an alibi.

In a few weeks the girls would be starting grade eight. At the same school, she hoped, but couldn't be certain; the Swiss relative who owned the house was unhappy with the arrangement. What precise relation he was Mrs. Vela could not figure out, being unclear on matters of first and second cousins. She had never spoken to him and news of his displeasure reached her obliquely and with delay. She sometimes wondered if they could have found a better place for themselves; that was what she daydreamed about more than her real home, the apartment she had left behind in a hurry. Since the occupation, it was likely being lived in by someone else. You have to make clear to them that I have no money to pay for living here, she told Darko. It was he, not her husband on the front, or she herself, who was in charge of contact with the relative — another thing the girls were not expected to understand.

*Santa Barbara* was heading for its climax. They watched unblinkingly, devouring chocolate candy for sustenance through the drama. Considering first *Santa Barbara*, then *Anna Karenina*, Mrs. Vela thought — all that for the love of a man, the love of a woman, the most ordinary of passions?

"Better than all that passion is closing the balcony door whenever you want to," she said aloud, and indeed got up to close the door of the terrace. The way she said "passion," mockingly, made Melita feel sorry for her. Her skinny, dark aunt must never have felt the transgression of fingertips on her back, the force of a man's desire. Ivana considered the statement and ended up feeling she had been given a corner piece of a puzzle, the whole picture of which could have been anything — a horse at pasture, a Dutch windmill, a field of violets even.

The show finished and the girls looked sadly let down, their chocolate candy gone and their appetites unquenched. Ivana got up and turned off the television.

She'd not given the boy a picture of herself. There were simply no good ones. The photograph he'd given her was his official grade school portrait: his mother had not had time to pack photo albums, and this was one of the few pictures he had left. (Ivana's mother might not have packed her albums either; but her husband had frightened her by saying, Bring the photos you want to keep, a coat, boots, doctor's records.)

Melita, taking the picture from Ivana's hands, said, "He's cute. Look at that cowlick."

"I wish he had nicer teeth," Ivana said, snatched the picture back, and flicked it into the garbage.

Later, waking up in the night, stifled by heat on the lower bunk of the bed, Ivana let her head dangle from the mattress and felt a breeze from the large window. She heard her grandma's light snoring, and then, distantly, her uncle's voice. The door of the bedroom was open. She got out of bed quietly and, realizing her mother and he were on the terrace, sat inside the frame of the bedroom door.

"There's as many of them as that May first weekend," her uncle was saying. "You remember that one?"

"Of course. Like the plague, we kept saying. We couldn't figure it out, there had been no rain."

"The river," he said.

"Lake," she said. "You are mixing it up. He's told me three times he's coming the next week and each time it turned out not to be the truth. What do you think of that?"

Ivana thought there was a pause, then Darko's voice, "You and him, disappearing without warning. All the time. Everyone knew, but you acted as if you had just come back from filling the water bottles at the well pump. I was jealous of how much time you devoted to him, the way you picked up and folded his shirts."

"I did no such thing. Did I? That was another time. Now I daydream about good books. A big window with a view, to sit at, alone."

"But when I think of how you had begged me to take you along to places where he would be. When I first introduced you, those precious manners, politeness. Then later, imploring that I get the keys to Grandma's house when she went away. A switch up from the back seat."

"Oh, that's not true," she said. She would never have called it begging. But a film, like gauze, seemed to be draped over most of her memories. What she did remember was the chafing of the seats. She was thinking of the way everything was funny then, the mosquitoes were funny, the car breaking down on the way to the lake made for great adventure. As if she had been saying it aloud, she continued, "It must be like that for the girls now."

"I could tell you right now which of the two girls will give you more trouble," he said.

"Why do people talk like that?" she said. "A girl gets to be a certain age and suddenly she becomes collateral. Risky business."

"I'm only saying you should take some of the responsibility. She *is* your responsibility now." Ivana heard a chair scrape and hurried back into bed, promising herself to remember everything in the morning. "She" was Melita, and "he" was Ivana's father.

❧❧❧

An overnight rain made mud out of the rust-coloured earth; the girls kept forgetting to take their sandals off in the house and left red footprints on the white linoleum. Darko collected buckets of pebbles at the nearest beach and spread them around the perimeter of the house, to keep the rain from splattering dirt onto the white stucco. The sun, which had been direct and insistent for days, now hid and re-emerged from behind large clouds.

The rain brought freshness: the leaves of the fig tree, the ripe cherries, the roof of the neighbour's old car, all glistened. The girls were flipping a coin to decide if a trip to the beach was worth it. Their uncle snatched the coin, threw it high into the air, and without showing them whether it was heads or tails, said "Go."

They did. The sea was calm after the rain, and they stayed in the water a long time. There was an advantage to being alone: they could climb on each other's shoulders and dive off, swim underwater between each other's legs, eyes open for direction, without embarrassment at their lack of skills. Even so, they had scanned every group of boys, without admitting, even to each other, that they were doing so, hoping to see Marko and Johnny. Ivana had, after all, rescued most of Marko's mementos from the garbage.

When the guys did come along, everyone's enthusiasm suggested a joyous, unexpected reunion. Soon, the girls were arranged comfortably but carefully on their towels, the guys smoking cigarettes. When it started to rain again, Melita stood up, straightened the clip of her bathing suit, and said, "We should swim, it's supposed to be the best while it rains."

Johnny stubbed out his cigarette, lifted her up and ran with her into the sea till the water was past his knees, and threw her in. In the overcast light her kicking limbs looked shiny and unreal, and part of Ivana wondered if she hated being plunked in like that. But then Ivana and Marko followed, and the four of them swam for a long time, as far as the other leg of the "U" shape that the coastline made, and there they got out. They lay stretched out on rocks, quieted by exhaustion.

Johnny said, "One day we'll swim all the way across to the island. Not from here," he added, expecting the girls to be confused, "but from the part out by the camp."

"When we get there we'll take a boat back," Marko said.

The persistent rain and the sudden coolness had unsettled Ivana. For the first time since the start of summer, she thought about its end.

"What else is there on the island?" Melita asked.

"Oh, everything," said Johnny. "Fig trees and old folk sitting in front of their houses. Don't worry, we'll provide the entertainment."

"I've never been on an island," Ivana said.

The rain had stopped and they were looking up into a slowly darkening sky. Melita and Johnny got up to leave, startling Ivana.

"But we have to go back," she said. "It's almost dark. I don't even know how we'll get to the cabin."

"It won't be dark for another hour at least!"

"We'll borrow some motorbikes and drive you home. You'll be there before you know it," Johnny said. Marko was silently twirling one of his curls around a forefinger.

"Uncle Darko will give us grief," Ivana tried. She felt they had to leave right now.

Johnny laughed. "Let me handle uncle Darko."

"You don't care," Ivana said, addressing her cousin only. "She's not your mother so you don't care."

"I don't worship her, if that's what you mean." Melita flushed and turned away.

Ivana was shamed by her own outburst, and it had not helped: they were already walking off.

"I'm cold," she said. She was also weary, and afraid. "Let's go back to our towels on the other side."

Marko laughed. "They'll be wet anyway."

"Oh, I'm so stupid." Waves could be heard nudging at the rocks beyond their feet, and there were the crickets. Still a few people around too, though so many seemed to have cleared out that Ivana wondered how she hadn't noticed. She pulled herself closer to Marko, testing the feel of it. Then she slowly arranged his hands on her body, as if he were a Ken doll and she a Barbie. He let her.

"Just like those hills over there," he said, running a hand over the curve of her hip, where she'd placed it. It was how she wanted things to be — warm hugging and words she could mull over in her mind. She dipped her head into his neck. She left things up to fate, choosing to trust Marko, Melita, Johnny, all of them; they fell asleep.

❧ ❧ ❧

In an old-fashioned café and ice cream shop on the main city square, Mrs. Vela and her cousin ordered gelato cups that were pictured opulently on the menu but arrived at their table small and melting. Darko asked for a little umbrella for decoration, and the waiter, not caring for the joke, said the state was at war and who had time to care for little umbrellas and other crap. From the café they could see the slippery, polished stones of the square, that common postcard image, the imposing building of the National Theatre, and other canopied cafés, nearly empty. It had been months since air raids were heard here and only some mortar damage suggested there ever were any. She thought he looked anxious. She wouldn't have been shocked to see him unravel in some wholly unremarkable way.

"I'd spend my whole budget for the month if I wanted to take the girls out for a play and ice cream afterward," she said.

"Isn't that a library there?" he said, pointing to a door with a plaque above it on the side of a shorter building next to the theatre. Why don't you get your good books there?"

"I . . . it's only that when I'm there, I can't seem to . . . I pick up a book, but it's not . . . I can't seem to find the right book."

"Everything will be all right." He continued, talking about her husband, "He has that terrible integrity. He carries a picture of Ivana with him everywhere."

She could remember her husband leaving the cabin last winter during a blackout. He had bathed and showered before heading out and when he leaned in to hug her, the outline of his neck and jaw made him seem so vulnerable, it was a task for her not to whimper and beg him to stay.

"I could have left him once, do you know? He'd been away, two months in London. Before he left we fought, and while away he hardly called. It was a beautiful time. I painted the garage. I read three, four books a week. I easily decided what I would keep and what he could have. Such relief. Ivana was seven, eight maybe. But when he got home he seemed so happy to see us. I didn't leave. I could have done everything I've ever wanted. Renovated the entire apartment. I could have been somewhere else right now."

He reached over and took her hand, then leaned over to kiss her mouth. His chair scraped and clanked and people turned to look. She didn't bother wiping her lips. The setting sun shining between walls and canopies and foliage created a pattern on the stone tiles of the square and they both stared at it. He padded the front pocket of his shirt for his wallet, took out a couple of photos, put one back.

"Some of the guys started shaving their heads, but leaving hair at the back, like — like half a Mohawk, see? One guy did it and everyone thought it was a hoot. You think I should do it?" On the small photo were young men, naked to the waist, hugging, their faces smudged with tar, wide smiles. They all looked bald, except for one smudge of hair on a guy turned partly sideways. She felt like whimpering, like that terrible winter night during the blackout.

"It's a nasty picture," she said quietly.

"You don't understand what it's like."

"You never sleep," she said. Their ice cream sat in puddles at the bottom of the glass dishes.

He said, again, "It'll work out," and put a hand on her shoulder. "But try looking at ads, just in case, for someone willing to take in a family. If it were just you and Ivana."

The rain started to fall again, drop by slow drop. Her husband had said, "Pack the photo albums." She tried to make a deal with the same power that made the sunlight tremble on the tiles of the square. As her part of the deal she offered all the small good things she had done in the course of her life and would continue to do. But that was not much; they really were small and she wondered what they added up to.

He put the picture carefully back into his pocket. The waiter passed by their table with a tray of empty glasses.

"That punk wouldn't have talked to me so if I hadn't dressed as a civilian," Darko said. The waiter was at least fifty years old. Darko flicked off a cigarette butt that had fallen out of the ashtray. "I might go across the border. I mean I might volunteer to fight. We're needed."

That was what they were always doing to each other: raising the stakes. She should have played along and said, "Yes, well, why don't you?" She didn't look at him when he pulled her wrist to him and held it.

Then he let go, stood up, and left the table. She had expected a sudden departure. She counted out bills to pay for the ice cream, while the waiter watched, hostile. It was still early evening, not late, and she stood just outside the café, didn't want get on the bus back to the cabin. She crossed the square. The city had a beautiful core. Hilly, with stone staircases and winding alleys, those lovely green shutters and wrought-iron balconies. But the insides of those tall houses, built centuries ago, were stinky with mould; she would never want to live in one.

She let a man buy her a drink. He was just an ordinary man. She sat at one table in a café, a café along the harbour-front she picked randomly, and he at another. They happened to glance at each other at the same time. She was thin and perpetually stricken-looking, but still it was hardly the first time a man had started talking to her out of the blue. She found herself telling him, "I haven't worked in almost a year, that might be the worst thing of all." Sorting cans and underwear at the Red Cross office did not count, not at all. He was older than her, late forties, early fifties maybe, and quite grey. "I'm not a healthy man," he said. "They wouldn't have let me on the front even if I'd wanted to go. Truth is," he said, "I wouldn't have wanted to go." She found she didn't mind his company at all. Before leaving he handed her a number, if she ever needed some kind of help. "I would never want to go to the front either," she'd told him. "I would escape in the dead of night as quietly as a hypocrite if I had to."

By the evening she was back at the cabin, and found Darko there. Grandma said, "I thought the girls would be home by now."

"Are they not?"

"No."

After eight o'clock Grandma walked out to the road outside of the cul-de-sac to wait for them. When it got to be after nine, Darko and Mrs. Vela got into the car, the same white Golf Darko had rolled out of, to look for the girls, see if they might spot them walking back. They knew it was a long walk, and dangerous after dark, for they'd have to walk alongside the highway, and through long stretches without houses or streetlamps.

Darko had the windows rolled all the way down and was smoking; a strong and cool wind gushed through the car. Mrs. Vela could hardly have been heard even had she wanted to say something. She thought of how he had said, "She *is* your responsibility now."

"I've *always* assumed my responsibilities," she shouted at him then in the wind tunnel. He turned to her, but did not hear what she had said. She kept shouting. It's understandable, he thought, that she would shout. She should

have been more careful, but he would certainly not say that
to her now. She thought, I'm thirty-seven years old and I
don't know what I have left to risk in this game: no doubt,
though he is trying to appear indifferent, he is waiting for
me to move.

രൗരൗരൗ

Ivana was on the back of a bicycle; Marko was taking her back
to the cabin. She didn't know what time it was. Fate had let
her down; she didn't know where Melita was either. The boy
was pedalling hard. Cars zoomed by them on the highway
and Ivana held on tightly. The bike didn't have a night light
and the boy had woken up his mother while digging around
the hotel room before he finally found a fluorescent-striped
pencil case that he attached to a handlebar. There was no
telling how useful that was.

The restaurants along the highway were emptied, their
terraces covered, only here and there a warm light glowing in
the distant interior. When they turned off the highway onto
a gravel road, they stopped to rest. The bike ride itself felt
to Ivana as if it lasted an eternity. They had to do the whole
roundabout loop, couldn't take the bike on the shortcut.

"You have to ease up on the ribs," the boy said, breathing
somewhat hard, because the last stretch had been uphill.
Ivana thought she had failed, in some new and unprecedented way. This stretch of gravel would be unlit, she knew,
until they reached the factory properties. The unrelieved
darkness was like nothing she had known at home. The boy
stopped keeping up conversation. The bike was not his, he'd

taken it without permission and would have to return it before morning. He'd have to clean it, too.

She sent him back before they quite reached the cabin. He kissed her near the mouth, his parched lips rough on her cheek, and she said nothing. She had displaced Melita as easily as a favourite pencil.

She was turning to go when she saw a white Golf coming toward them from the direction of the main street.

"Go, hurry up," she said, and the boy started to ride away. In a moment the car pulled up and her mother got out. Staticky dark hair made a halo around her head. She only stared at Ivana.

"You don't know where Melita is," her mother said, with finality, in a tone as if she were answering a riddle. They were standing under a lamp, and in its light they could see grass-hopper corpses strewn all about their feet. Mrs. Vela looked off in the direction the boy had gone. He hadn't got very far.

ॐ ॐ ॐ

Not long after, they were all on the terrace — Ivana, Mrs. Vela and Darko, and Marko. The older Mrs. Vela retired to bed without a word, though it was unlikely she would sleep until Melita was safely home; Ivana saw only a glimpse of her braided grey hair at the door. Marko was drinking a tall glass of cherry juice. He'd just told Mrs. Vela that all his friends were very nice, and that one of them, or one of their mothers, is surely bringing Melita home.

Mrs. Vela, like Darko, was standing. "Which friend?" she said. "What's the name of the friend she's with?"

"Probably — " he looked to Ivana for help, but she was too mortified to even look up.

"You'll get in the car with me and find them for me," Darko said. Mrs. Vela was silent. She thought of all the dark corners of the beach, the hundreds of rooms in all the hotels.

"Where did you leave her exactly? In a room? Outside? And with whom?"

"Johnny," Ivana mumbled, "but I don't know his real name."

"Dear God." Her mother put her head down — and just as Ivana was ready to spill everything, exactly as it happened, they heard a car, and her uncle and mother ran into the yard, their steps as if practiced, her mother clutching a fistful of T-shirt at his back. Jealous of how you picked up his shirts, Ivana remembered. Her throat burned with a sour sweetness. The car stopped, and Melita's foot emerged, then a shoulder, then a head that started low, and slowly — as if there was something to be gained by delay — straightened itself out. Marko kicked Ivana's leg under the table, and rolled his eyes as if to say, Look at all the trouble they've caused. She could not stomach him here; he could not be this chatty, comfortable boy, and that eloquent lover, all at the same time.

The car would have pulled away but her uncle smacked the driver's side window with an open palm. Perhaps nothing was as terrible to Ivana as the sight of Johnny, disoriented and vaguely frightened, ugly, walking across the yard between her mother and uncle. Why did stupid Melita not even think to have him drop her off down the street?

But her mother — she was as dark and unpleasantly shocking as the weeds at the bottom of the sea. She made Melita and Johnny come onto the terrace and sit down at the table too. She pretended the situation was ordinary: she got everyone juice. She asked Marko where he was from, and how he'd ended up at the hotel. He talked for a while, and Johnny stayed silent. Darko sat perched on the corner of the terrace railing, in army boots and army fatigues, periodically staring at Johnny.

Mrs. Vela said, "The lack of public lighting around here is what really appalls me. You can see why we worry when the girls don't make it home before dark."

"You know, I've heard that people have written petitions," Marko said.

"Yes," Johnny added, finding a hoarse, dull voice.

"I hope you don't mind, but I think I better get back. I have to return the bike before it gets too late. But thank you for the juice."

"Of course," Mrs. Vela said. "It was good of you to borrow the bike and take Ivana. I can just imagine," and here a throaty chuckle escaped her, "how she suffocated you on the way. She clings like a crab." And then she rose out of her chair.

"Good night then," she said. "Johnny will take you back, won't he? The bike can fit in the back seat. Otherwise we'll take you in our car." Everyone else rose swiftly, and once they'd wedged the bike in the trunk, not the back seat, the car reversed and turned around — slowly, as if trying to be respectful.

Mrs. Vela was frightened. She knew that her sister was a different sort of mother and Melita had looked so small next to that man and Mrs. Vela had to wonder how much her niece understood and what had already gone on. She would have to deal with that. Her sister lived poorly where she was and there weren't even schools nearby, but she'd fetch Melita if Mrs. Vela said a few right words. They were clearing the table when Ivana said, "I tried to tell her we have to go home." From the way the two of them weren't looking at each other, Mrs. Vela thought this was probably true.

"I wouldn't care if I never saw this place again. There are creeps everywhere and . . . " Ivana stopped, because she saw Melita's face.

"Ivana," her mother said, dropping the endearment, "how could you have tried to send that boy away, without so much as a glass of water? You — both of you girls," and here her mother took in a small slice of the entire universe with the sweep of her hand, "only want your fun. You only want what you want."

And mysteriously, unbelievably, that was all the trouble they got for that night.

Later, Darko said, "I told you which one was trouble, didn't I? Did you notice how old that asshole was?" Melita was, amazingly, already asleep, but Ivana, blood stream racing with sugar and anxiety, was not.

"I wish you hadn't sat there like a gargoyle. Sizing them up. What's the use of that?"

"Your husband might try to tell you to call your sister."

"I don't intend to tell him. In the event I see him anytime soon."

"*He* is the tree blocking your window view. He doesn't understand you. Being loved in the morning, shunned in the afternoon. But I — "

"He was more like the light inside the room preventing me from seeing what's outside. But you — I don't know what it's like, as you said."

A gust of wind shook the shutters, lifted the tablecloth on the terrace. Ivana worried that she was missing what was being said next. Then she heard, "When you're out there it is something like an intimacy, merely because you're in danger, in danger together. Because otherwise some of these people are just assholes."

"And this?" her mother said.

Ivana tried to line everything up and start over again: she had the best breasts, but Melita was the one in danger of getting pregnant. Her uncle understood this, understood her mother's mysterious moods. But still the puzzle did not become whole. What kind of light was her father? She was ashamed that she could, in this moment, recall hardly anything precise about him. Her mother had once begged for him, and now . . . But Melita was safe with her. Her mother wouldn't let anyone separate them. She could be kind, her mother; Marko too was kind. Her breasts were scoops of beautiful vanilla ice cream. What if I love Marko, she thought, but then the thought made her nearly sicker than she already was. In the other bed, old Mrs. Vela wept quietly. Later, no one heard the younger Mrs. Vela say, while dreaming, "Some bastards are living in my house."

# The Lesser Animal

HE LIVED NOW IN A duplex on the north side of Edmonton, and there was no one here to ask him about the ugly things and remind him. But still he thought of the things, as he drank a whisky with ginger ale, a Canadian habit he had taken on, sitting at his kitchen table, which his Kate had set as usual with a tablecloth and a vase and the big glass ashtray. He had a kind of family now, Kate and her eleven-year-old daughter Frida, who was his daughter now, too, wasn't she. He had lived here for ten years and there was no one to remind him; the faces looked different, the houses, the streets, all set up differently, and only among the ex-Yugoslavs did he feel naked, transparent. But what need was there of reminders, anyway. He knew.

Last month the Canadian government found a man who had lived in Ontario for more than a decade, but would now be extradited and tried, and since then Toma has begun to wonder if it was a matter of time before they found him too. It was irrational, his cold brain told him — he was no one, as nameless as the victims. But each time the fear came, he had to ride it out. It created first heat, a rising fever that made him slow down — butter-knife moving slowly over slice of bread — and then stop. He let the knife drop, stood still at the counter. Then came the sinking, a falling through earth's layers, fields and waters, summers and winters, nights and hours. At the bottom was just a pit, a hot, dark, slowly suffocating place.

He had not been like the others, nor nearly as bad as the other side, in wanton shooting, in locking people in attics to torment and debase them. Still, he had been there; he had been high on battle and victory, on testosterone and other hormones. On history. He had been there and had done ugly things, even if he was among the better of them and not in charge.

He felt the heat now, rising past his throat, and he placed his hands palms down on the kitchen table. It's all right, he said to himself. He freed one of his hands and swirled the rest of his drink shakily. No one is coming for him. He is only Tom of North Side Painters, known to his neighbours as a quiet guy, decent enough, with a nice common-law wife and a shy step-daughter, trying to get by like everyone else, trying to pass the time, maybe even to make something of life — not something grand, but something decent. And who among his neighbours did not have a dark spot, somewhere — who had not been ashamed, or despised himself? Who arrived to live here on 154th Avenue, or on any street or avenue, with only a clean path behind him? He was only Tom, a painter, and he did enjoy things, having his rye and ginger, Frida teasing him about his English grammar when he helped her with homework, even slicing vegetables and potatoes as Kate told him they should be sliced.

But still, it was not really the true picture. Still there was the pit. What, on earth, did Kate know of the pit? That told him it was not the true picture. Oh, he hated her, sometimes, when she was the happiest, when she was falling asleep nestled into him, content.

ॐॐॐ

Once a week he had drinks with his niece Ana. She was more of a sister than a niece — during the war she had been in a camp in occupied territory, and after it was freed, the Red Cross had sent her to him, the nearest surviving family. She was fifteen. He was in Germany, trying to get to Canada. He took care of her then, and when he came here, he took her with him. He was so happy — so flatly and at-the-core-happy, so happy in the bottom of himself that it could not show on the surface — to arrive at the Edmonton International Airport, give his forms to the clerks and have their blessing to be a free, different man.

Ana was trying to study accounting, but instead read novels and philosophers and testimonies of Buddhist nuns, and some self-help stuff too, and saw herself in the paranoia of Kafka's fictions. She was vivacious and unhappy and carefully fashionable. She smoked pot sometimes, on her lunch break, when her son Noah was in daycare, to manage her mood. She worked at clothing stores, worked as a bank teller, as a lab assistant. Her salaries were always modest, and Emil, Noah's dad, who had been with her through several degrees, felt bitterly that the degrees had not materialized into income. Emil blamed society, he blamed the schools, but now he blamed her too. His accusations did not make her try to earn more, but only smoke more pot to be steady enough to make it through a day at her underpaid job. Toma worried for her. Every day she checked in with him, and he didn't go to sleep at night until he heard from her.

Toma and Emil had been part of the same brigade, except that Emil was not at that one terrible, victorious battle; he was pulled out of it because he had broken his leg. He'd fallen through what looked like brush into a deep hole, and another soldier had landed on him. It was a bad break, in three different places, but Toma was envious — only now, in retrospect — and would gladly have suffered the pain of that break, the agony it must have been to get carried by three men for more than an hour, then to finally reach a car and be driven to a hospital low on morphine. Awful it was, but small, very small in comparison to the other thing, which Toma cannot think about as often as it comes to him, because it deadens him, and he came here, after all, to come back to life.

He did not think Emil a bad character, back then, only a bit crass, a touch unpredictable, childlike, even. But now he was obstinate. He checked up on Ana even when she was with Toma. And when she went out to friends' houses, he demanded she be home by ten. If she wasn't, he didn't think anything of it to call the house and tell whoever answered the phone, "Tell Ana there is an emergency with her baby." But their son Noah would be happily watching cartoons, tucked in among pillows in the big bed of the master bedroom, coming down from a sugar rush after Emil fed him berries and whipped cream for supper.

"Emil, you donkey, tell me the truth now or if I come home and find that you lied to me, I'll get the police on you and send you out of the house."

"I don't know what it is, but you better come home. If you care about your son you better come home." So she would, and stomp to the bedroom in her shoes, and, seeing Noah asleep among the cushions, the television muted, stomp back to Emil and push him into a wall, in the hallway, away from the bedroom, and hit him again and again over the head.

"Now it's enough — do you — now, all right, enough. Seriously, enough, or you will be sorry. Do you hear, enough!" He wrestled himself away and raised his hand as if to hit her.

"You're degenerate. You've lost your mind. A normal person doesn't do what you do. And that I should have tied myself to you! I wish you had been killed in the war! It would have saved my life."

"You wish your son never was born then, do you? What a mother! If we go to court, no judge in the world will give you custody of my son, do you hear? You think I'm stupid but I remember everything."

And so it went. When she didn't talk to Emil the next morning, he said, at breakfast, "Come now, I know you love your son, come. How could you not love him when I gave him to you?" This while Noah was in his room, playing with Thomas the train — it was how Emil joked around.

"Remove yourself from my sight."

"Who would have given you a better son? Look at him — he's a prince. No one could have made you a better one, not one of those puppies who follows you around."

89

Those puppies were the friends she'd collected over the years, men she went to school with once or worked with at this job or that. They were lab technicians, DJs, yoga instructors, lawyers. About half of them were in love with her, and the others, Toma thought, holding on because they got little attention elsewhere. They bought her things, called her at bad times. Most were young but a few were in retirement and sent her postcards from cruises to a PO box she kept without Emil knowing.

"If you don't shut up, I will scream." Then Noah sprinted into the kitchen, *choo-choo*ing quickly like a rushing train.

"Look at him!" Emil said.

"Come to mama, love, shall we feed you now? Shall mama give you a bottle?"

*Choo-choo.*

So it went.

It seemed to Toma a nasty jealousy Emil had. Toma was not especially jealous, amused mostly when he thought someone flirted with his Kate. But he thought that Emil was not stupid and probably sensed that only by some cosmic accident he had held on to Ana, that really she had wanted to leave him for years, that she was loveable and charming and restless. But there was Noah. If only there was no Noah, thought Toma, sitting in his kitchen looking at the empty vase, not feeling guilty for wishing Noah out of existence — he loved Noah, and it did not hurt Noah for Toma to think things would have been easier were he not to exist.

Ana loved Noah too, but she worried there was something wrong with him. She had her peculiarities and this was one of them, always worrying there was something wrong with Noah.

"But really, do you think it's normal how he bites? I'm asking everyone. Do you think it's normal?"

This on a downtown patio, squeezing her pint with both small hands. She had fears for Noah's health and for his mind and soul. She had refused vaccines, fearing they triggered autism; then, feeling guilty, gave in to the vaccines, fearing everything else. She worried there was insanity in Emil's family, and was sure that at the very least Noah would develop a behaviour problem. He was too energetic, too excitable; he ate too much, more than she did and would not go to bed without an extra bottle or a treat.

"Look at what I've become with these fears," she said to Toma, "I'm old. I've become old next to that man. Oh, how I'd like to fall in love again. I think it would cure me."

"You're barely thirty. You can have anyone."

"What good is only thirty when I'm like this? To fall in love with someone young. To sleep with someone young — God, how many beautiful young men there are."

Toma too wished sometimes to sleep with someone else, he thought about it a great deal even, and yes, as if it could cure him. Not that his Kate was not good enough: no, perhaps she was too good, perhaps that was what people said about them. But she was too much a part of him now, and he wished for someone unlike him and unlike Kate to come along and give him that attention peculiar to love that reinvents one.

Once, when he was having a new picture taken for his driver's licence, the clerk at the empty registry office, a young woman with red lipstick and straight-across dark bangs, startled him by asking where he was from, what he was doing here. The phone had rung, and she put the caller on hold and just kept talking to him — for a quarter of an hour at least, not getting back to the phone at all. And when he went home he was so happy that he called Ana and told her about the lovely woman, how she had ignored the phone, how she'd told him, in parting, "I work every day except tomorrow, if you need to come back."

"Good, I'm glad to hear it," Ana had said, laughing at him. He indulged the lightness of the meeting, of telling Ana. But he knew that he wouldn't go back to the registry office, that the lovely woman would not fall in love with him and take away his heaviness.

Emil had no heaviness, Toma thought.

"I don't know how many I've killed," Emil had said to him. "Really I only know of one for sure. Listen how it happened — "

He had said it to Toma but he could say it to anyone, his buddies at the Italian café, people he'd just met at a church-sponsored picnic for refugees in Berlin, to the neighbour who'd come to ask if Emil's toilet was leaking too; say it with a perfect innocence that left people wondering if he was sane. There was no reading him. You could get along with him fine but you could not see to the bottom of the waters he swam in.

In the war, Emil had seemed more or less like Toma, clear on what they were there for and excited when they shot down a jet or captured a tank. One needed those lighter moments, to admire the spectacle of force as children admire fireworks. Toma had no desire to kill, but he did not feel conflicted about firing at men who were shooting back at him — he was not indifferent about dying, not at all, but neither did he think there would be something unjust about his death. So he'd remained clear headed and wasn't tormented for a long time.

But he did start to dislike things. People he liked died in bad ways. Such things mounted and he became irritable. Emil had not been there when their brigade had retaken that town. They had broken through and had to secure every-thing. People came out of their basements, their houses, some with white strips of cloth they'd ripped off sheets, and a few with rifles held high, surrendering.

The ones with rifles were led a short distance away and shot. Toma and his friends had been at it long enough to know also that everyone had to be doubted. Old women lying under duvets could hide hand bombs, so they heard. It was a nerve-testing job, holding onto a sense of danger after you'd broken through. And yes, he had been angry at some of the people there, because he could see in some of them that they despised him. It had shown in them through their fear. One man, moustached, middle-aged, sinewy, and dark had looked at him with teacherly, patronizing disapproval. And just-suppressed hate. Toma walked over and hit him in the back with the butt of his rifle.

He was excited and he fired shots in the air as others did and he'd snickered at a trembling old man who had urinated in his pants. And later he'd entered a room in which were his good friend Filip, three other guys, and two girls, who were standing near the wall. The girls were maybe sixteen, maybe eighteen, maybe twenty, but they were still girls. They looked like sisters, they wore old tracksuits and had long greasy hair and frightened eyes.

He entered the room and said, "What, monkeys, avoiding your work?"

Filip stretched out an arm and embraced him, "Friend," he'd said, "this is long deserved," but Mihael, whom Toma joked with often but did not like, said, "Fuck you commander wannabe." He pretended to lunge at Toma and laughed.

"There's work to be done, what are you fucking around for?" Toma said.

"Don't worry," Filip said, "don't worry about us. Hey," patting him on the chest, "it's me." Filip was a bit drunk and he was a silly drunk, and the others were drunk too, they laughed as Filip held his arm around Toma and kept patting his chest. Ivan, who was barely nineteen, turned toward the girls. "Fuck this war when this is all we can get. When'd you last have a shower?"

"Not longer ago than you, prick," Mihael said and smacked him across the head, then took one of the girl's chin into his hand, shook it, and hit her across the face.

"Let's get on with real shit," Toma had said, motioning toward the door. He was hot and angry.

"Friend, everything here is tip-top and we'll be with you real soon, and everything here is just tip-top," Filip said.

What were these girls even doing here? He wanted out of his sweaty uniform and into a cold, clear lake. "File," he'd said to Filip, putting a forefinger to his forehead, "you watch, all right? I'll be coming back here." He walked away, leaving the door open. Then he heard someone kick it shut.

He did not see the women again, but he has dreamt of them. They were probably a little bit older than Ana was then, fifteen. As far as he knew they too were alive. He thought often of how he would like to encounter them in a normal world. They might have become friends — he used to have a lot of girlfriends. It was not good to meet people in rooms you were sending them out of, to meet them over guns; not good for this to be the connection between him and another human being, for those girls to think of him as he was then, walking away from the room, a coward. Not good for him to be part of their dream that deadened the morning, part of that other side about which they had to say, "Why must there be this darkness? "

And since then he'd thought often of what he was to other people. It mattered very much that in colliding with others making their way on this earth he be himself again, and decent; even if only to balance things out on that side of things, overall, a little bit. It bothered him when he couldn't do it, when he was a coward or made mistakes. It bothered him about the woman at the registry office, that he would not honour the small moment between them that had revived him. It upset him even more that he watched television with Kate happily curled into him, and imagined someone else falling in love with him. That he let Emil be nasty to Ana.

Though the part of Toma that tried to balance things told him that Emil had to matter too. Did he matter? Toma could not tell. Emil once called Toma at 2:00 AM, his voice trembling, because Ana had gone out and he knew it was with a man. He found a card in her drawer, one of those cards people stick in bouquets. It said, "Thanks for the lovely walk." It was signed "A." Emil said it's Afsheen, this yoga instructor she knew. She wants to fall in love, to be reborn, Toma thought, while listening to Emil beginning to cry, trying not to cry. Toma understood Ana, but still, there was Emil. Emil did not dream of falling in love; he did not have many women friends and he did not keep a secret P.O. box for secret correspondence, for gifts of wanting and reaching. Toma had the impression that there was nothing to Emil that he or Ana could not guess; one could look through all his emails and text messages and listen to his phone conversations and find nothing unpredictable; and yet he would still be what he was — a particular, almost-manageable mystery.

He asked Kate if she would move. If no one would rescue him by falling in love with him, maybe he and Kate and Ana and Noah could move.

"This is a good neighbourhood," she said, tying her pyjama top into a knot at her belly. "I want to build relationships here. I want roots. This will be the house Frida remembers as her house, that's what I want." It was a fine enough house for growing roots, yes. What would Frida remember — how easily that leap of the imagination came to Kate and not so to him. Frida, Frida, surely he loved her after these five or so years. It mattered to love Frida.

"I don't like that he calls here so late, I mean it's a bit, you know, dramatic." Kate's parents had been dramatic, and so had her husband — phone disconnected because the bills were unpaid, asking the neighbours to borrow theirs again and again until they get less polite about it, that sort of person — in a perpetual crisis. She did not want that anymore. She was building a different life and a different self now: she wanted to grow a garden, to read books, and to listen to music from parts of the world her ex-husband did not know existed.

"Ana would leave him if she could afford an apartment."

"I like her. But you should distance yourself from it a little bit, bun, don't you think? I mean just for — him being the way he is."

"She could stay here until she got a place."

"It's not good to take sides."

"It's not good to take sides."

"Oh don't get like that. Don't repeat after me. You know what I mean."

"Let's move to the country. Get a plot of land."

"No."

"Will you be good to me Kate? I'll give you everything you want. Just don't leave me."

"Oh bunny, this again. I won't leave you. Take Frida to dance tomorrow."

"Dance?"

"I'm making her take dance. She must do stuff."

"My Kate."

ॐ ॐ ॐ

"Noah's not right," Ana was telling him, "I said to Emil, 'Look — ' I showed him the plate Noah had finished off — two peppers I had mushed up for him, two big stuffed peppers! 'I eat one in a sitting — is that normal?' 'How can you say that of your son? he'd said." She mimicked his voice. "'How can you look for faults in him with such malignance?

You will bring the illnesses on him yourself, as punishment.' Do you think so, brother? Will I bring it on him?"

Toma looked at Noah, who had mangled most of the sugar packets on the table of the restaurant and was eating sugar from his little palms, wet with saliva.

"Listen," she said, "this here on my shoulder." She pulled her cardigan down at the shoulder, showed him a yellow and purple bruise. "It's from three days ago."

Okay. There was a bruise. Toma tried to absorb the reality of the bruise. How much force would have gone into a bruise like that?

She continued, "He pushed me into the wall. I didn't want to tell you. But that's how it gets now."

"I didn't watch over you from Bosnia to Germany to Canada so that a monkey like him can push you around."

"Don't talk like that."

"I'm s — "

"Shut up. Enough now."

"Listen — I'm going to get you a place. You can let him visit Noah, or not, you decide."

"What's wrong with you? Emil not see Noah? And I can't work full time and pay for daycare." She took Noah's hands roughly into her own and wiped at them vigorously with a paper napkin. He let out a single wail.

"All right. All right. But he's got you thinking too much about money. You think money makes things happen."

"I can't pay for daycare."

"You'll live with us." He would have offered, promised anything, for time was slowing down and he was heating up now. He had let this go on for too long, and now it made him sick.

"You shouldn't have let it go on for so long," he said to her. "Noah."

"If I'd had these brains then. In the beginning, you know, he was always a bit crazy like this, but then it was like we were on this adventure together, he was funny; you remember him at my window when I lived with roommates, yelling, 'I love Ana, I don't care if she wears pyjamas all day.' I liked that then, and I didn't care when my roommates asked, 'What's wrong with him?' We were crazy together. Now, man, it's only him yelling at the window and me hiding inside hoping no one will hear it.

"But this child wants him. You should see how he jumps when Dad's home, how they love each other. Emil would make enemies with anyone over Noah. He's too much that way. Man, how many people we don't talk to anymore because their kid took Noah's toy!"

But Toma was only on the edge of listening to her. He thought, Let me make Ana happy and then let them come for me, finally, and free me of the wait. How he wished to press a gun into the softness under Emil's jaw-line; how he wished to have put his gun into that jerk Mihael's face, to have pinned his arms behind his back and told the others he'd blow the guy's head off if they don't clear out, get away from those girls. He might have threatened to blow up the entire room, with all of them in it. Or he could have wounded someone, at least. What would have happened then? Someone would have shot at him, killed him.

"Toma."

"I'm here," he said. "Don't worry."

⮞⮞⮞

He was in Red Deer for a two-day painting job, lying on the bed in his motel room with the television on. He was reminding himself to get a gift for Frida's birthday: he tried to pay attention to her, to notice if she was in a poor mood, because she was sometimes a melancholy child. Every now and then he got her a gift and it made him feel close to her if she liked it: when she was in grade one he got her a leotard that she fell in love with, and he felt they had a month's worth of mutual understanding on the strength of that leotard. When Ana had come to him in Germany, he'd taken her to a big department store and bought her jeans and a hairbrush. He'd borrowed money to be able to do it, because all she had when she came to him were oversized sweatshirts. But how glad she had looked to see him, and how happy he was to be reminded of himself. That's who he was: the man Ana saw when she looked at him. He was not that other guy, not that other guy at all.

While he lay awake in his motel room, smoking cigarettes in bed, Kate sat in the kitchen, alone, Frida having gone to sleep already. It was a quarter after midnight when she heard a knocking on the door — quick, loud, and she worried it would frighten Frida. Through the peep hole she saw Ana, holding Noah wrapped in a thick blanket, so that he was huge and she was tottering under him, moving their joint weight slowly from foot to foot.

"Toma," she said, controlling her volume but loudly enough to be heard, "it's me, open up, quickly." Kate opened the door.

"What's happened Ana? Tom's not here, he's in Red Deer on a job. What's happened?"

"Oh no. I forgot. I'm sorry, Frida must be asleep. I just — I didn't want to bother my friends."

They were still standing, Kate inside and Ana outside, straining under Noah.

"I left Emil, that's all, I didn't say a word about it to him, just threw Noah's clothes and some toys in the car when he was out. We had a fierce fight before he left, oh, it was something. Never will he see this child again. Oh, Kate." She was shaking. "I will be free now. I can feel it. All it took was courage, do you see?" Kate now moved aside slightly and Ana cautiously stepped over the threshold and Kate gently closed the door behind her.

"Did he hit you?" She saw Ana's jaw was red, as if chafed.

"Hit me, that's the least of my problems. But there he is now. Yes, that's him. Listen."

In a second Kate heard a car, accelerating then making a sudden brake in front of the house, then a door slamming and the sound of feet running.

"Don't let him in here, just don't. Did you lock the — " and as she said it Kate reached behind her and turned the lock.

Emil knocked on the door with a quick loud rap.

"Friend, I know Ana is there. Ana, you goose, listen. Leave these people alone and come home. Toma, don't do this to me." He rattled the doorknob, hard. Kate moved Ana from the door toward the living room. Noah squirmed and cried out from under the blanket.

"Toma's not here, it's just me and I can't let you in," Kate said. "She'll sleep here tonight and you can come in the morning for her, and then she'll talk to you." In the morning she would make Toma come home, in the morning she would send Frida to school. The morning was much easier.

"Forgive me, ma'am, forgive me, I did not know you were awake. I did not want to disturb you."

She thought, that stupid ass, always calling me ma'am.

"I just want my wife and son and then I will leave you in peace. It's late, I know; you just tell my wife to come out."

"She's gone to bed. Leave now or one of the neighbours will call the police, you hear? It won't be my fault."

"You understand, you have a child. I just want my child. Ana," he continued, "even if Toma should kill me for it tomorrow I'll break this window and come in and get Noah."

Kate looked at her. He won't, Ana mouthed and shook her head, he won't.

"Leave now, you understand, leave," Kate said through the door.

He hit the soft side of his fist against the window. He won't, Ana mouthed again, just don't let him in. Noah was crying.

"Ana, it will be your fault," and he hit the window again, harder.

"I'm going to call the police," Kate whispered to Ana. "He's insane. Frida is sleeping upstairs."

Now a rock at the window, loud, startling them.

"You idiot," Ana yelled.

"It will be your fault," he said. Then another rock and they heard the loud crack of glass.

Kate turned to Ana. "He will break the window. Listen, you — I don't know what to do. Are you afraid of him? If you are I'm calling the police. I can't have him here like this."

There was a thud by the door, and Emil's voice now came from down low, as if he were sitting on the ground. "Forgive me, oh please, forgive me. I'm going to sleep at this door like a dog, just please come back." His voice shook.

Ana stood, Kate facing her. "All right," she said quietly. "All right. I'm sorry Kate. I shouldn't have come." She reached for the door with one hand.

"Well don't go," Kate put her hand on Ana's, "don't go if you're afraid — if you think he'll hit you — I'm not telling you to go."

"I'm sorry Kate," and she turned the lock and opened the door, at which Emil reached for her legs.

"My queen," he said, holding her calf, "my queen and my little prince. Look at what you've done to me." Then he raised himself, Kate was watching cautiously through the half-open door, and he took the big sausage that was Noah, who let out intermittent sobs. Ana's body seemed relieved. Emil cooed to Noah, shook his head at Ana, reached out one arm to stroke the back of her head, as if he would pull her in for a kiss.

"Look what you've done to me," he shook his head, smiling. Damn it, Kate thought, looking at the girl, her face droopy under the outdoor light above the door.

"Be quiet and let's go," Ana said. Emil turned to Kate. "Please, accept my apologies too, ma'am, I am sorry. But I

103

was like a lost man, believe me. Toma will kill me but really I will never do such a thing again, and I will fix your window, believe me."

Ana moved finally, saying to Emil, "Go now, go."

"Leave the van, we'll drive together," he said. Ana looked back at Kate, for permission it seemed, and they stood for a moment looking at each other before Ana turned away and got into the car.

Toma drove home from Red Deer after Kate called him around one in the morning.

"I wish you hadn't sent her away," he said to Kate, around eight in the morning, after they'd slept for a few hours. She was washing dishes while he sat smoking cigarettes at the table.

"I told you she left on her own. Damn it, I told you."

"Oh I know you didn't mean to. If you had just called me. If she had just called me. Why didn't you call me, tell me again?"

"It all happened in — in less than ten minutes. As I've already said. I wanted to call you, or the police — I said to her, Do you want me to call the police? I've explained this part to you. And then she was already opening the door. And then they were off."

"Yes. Right. I'm sorry. I just wish I'd been here." She put a plate in a slot next to the others. She pulled the plug and the water began to drain loudly from the sink.

"I wish you would think of Frida a little more. I wish you'd think of Frida half as much as you think of Ana."

Yes, that, he thought or perhaps said very softly, to himself. But nothing would have happened to Frida. Yet Ana had needed him and he was watching a Sylvester Stalone movie in a motel in Red Deer. So it went.

"I'm sorry," he said. "Truly." He had to remind himself that it was not right Kate had to do that alone, that it mattered.

"All of you with your 'sorry, truly sorry,'" she mocked. "What good is that?"

He let the remnant of his cigarette fall into the ashtray without butting it out. He took the ashtray, a large square of thick, dark blue glass, and stood up. Kate was scooping with her hand the bits of food that had collected in the drain, her back turned to him again. She opened the cupboard door under the sink where the garbage was.

"I can't have a window cracked like that in the winter, it'll collapse. What are you doing?"

"I'm weighing the ashtray," he said, moving his hand up and down, with the ashtray balanced on it.

"Settle down," she said, turning to fully face him, "just settle down now." She wiped her hands on the tea towel, as if preparing, not taking her eyes off him.

"Look now. It's all right," she said. Trained from years of crisis intervention, he thought. Ashtrays are a dead art — no one smokes anymore. You only see the grand old ones at garage sales. And they used to make great gifts. His mother kept the best-looking, heaviest ones in the living room for when company was over, and she made sure ones people had brought her from vacations were prominent too, even if they didn't fit the décor or they wobbled.

"Here, I'll wash it," Kate said, reaching out her hand.

"There's no need." He walked with it past the kitchen table and into the hallway, and threw it against the window cracked from the night before. The window collapsed into large shards; cigarette butts and ashes flew onto the floor and over some homework papers Frida had left on the bench near the window. Kate — as if there was a fire — ran up with a pitcher of water and poured it over everything.

"So you too," said Kate, without looking at him, as the water puddled around broken glass and pages covered with Frida's large, uncertain handwriting.

The smash, then the glass, the ashes, and the water, seemed appropriate to Toma. He passed his hand over his eyes and went out the door. Outside, he picked up a piece of glass from under the window and got into his car. He rested the glass — slightly larger than his palm — on the passenger seat. He hadn't owned any weapons since he'd moved here, never thought of getting any; and he didn't like cutting, didn't even like to have in the house those specialty kitchen knives that Kate had ordered. The glass was just the nearest thing.

He drove to Ana and Emil's place, hoping Ana would be at work and Noah in daycare.

He parked the car in the front and walked around to the back of the house, holding the shard gingerly, feeling a bit absurd with it. Nonetheless.

Emil was in the front living room and Toma walked in through the unlocked back door. Hearing the creaking of the screen door, Emil walked to the back.

"On my mother," he said. "I knew you were coming. But what is this? What are you holding there?" He laughed, a laugh of surprise. "Toma! But we made up! I know, I tried to break your window. I'll make up for it. But she came back. Didn't Kate tell you? She came back and everything is going to be fine now."

"You need to understand something," Toma said.

"Come on man. First of all, sit down. We're not strangers, are we?"

"Listen."

"I have a gun here, you know. But should I come out here with a gun and wave it in your face? I wouldn't do that to you."

"I know you don't have a gun here, you idiot, I was with you when you took it apart and threw the pieces away because Ana didn't want you to have it."

"I could have got another."

"Shut up." He pushed Emil toward a chair and motioned him to sit down. "Why is your house so bloody hot? It smells like burnt milk."

"I fried eggs for Ana. You should have seen us this morning. Fried eggs, coffee, our child eating cream of wheat."

"Open the window, I'm dying here." Toma felt the heat was going to choke him if it continued to rise past his armpits and reached his throat.

"I think you must have a fever. It's only twenty-two degrees in here. But if I walk past you to open the window, don't attack me from behind."

Toma laughed, he had to, for here was the man as he knew him best. He coughed then, feeling the back of his neck burning. He stood still until a breeze from the window reached him, a whole half-minute later, during which Emil stood watching him.

ॐ ॐ ॐ

Ana waited for Toma in the park. Edmonton's Fringe festival was on, and this park was one street over from the busiest section of performers and food stalls. She sat on the bench near the sandbox with the slide and swing set. Her hair was arranged carefully in a side bun, with pins holding everything in place and one wavy strand of hair let out on the side. Her blouse was ironed and she had painted her nails the colour of brick. To do these things gave her a semblance of life, Toma knew. Noah, with his hair slicked also to the side, sat in her lap, content for a moment, drinking from a juice box. She was texting, with a man she met recently, an Algerian with curly hair and glasses, who hung about and sometimes wrote in the coffee place near the bank where she currently worked.

When Toma arrived she let Noah play in the sandbox. She'd brought him a plastic shovel and bucket and toy bulldozer. She told Toma about the man, as Noah drove his bulldozer from one end of the sandbox to the other: he emptied and refilled the sand each time he reached their feet.

"You shouldn't have been so harsh, perhaps," she continued, talking now of Emil. "I'm worried about you. He's going to take that job in Lacombe." She looked at him as she said it. He said nothing.

"I guess you meant it for my sake, sending him away. He'll be home only on weekends. Maybe that will be good. But Noah's going to exhaust me. Emil always plays with him. I can't. By the time I wash and feed Noah and prepare his clothes, I'm so tired that I yell at him for asking me to play. How will I handle him all week?"

"I'll take him sometimes."

"I suppose you got lucky with Emil's mood and so he took your advice. Anyway, now he says he's going to take the job and earn enough so we can move back home."

"He's been moving back there for years."

"Is Kate still upset?"

"I'll make it up to her."

"I really like this man," she said brightly. Noah was by her feet and she brushed sand off his cheek. "I wonder how old he is, I haven't asked him. It's so nice to talk to someone normal. To talk about something you've read. He's a writer. If I try to talk to Emil about anything interesting, he says, 'It's because you're always thinking about things like that that you're never good at any job.' So he's right. I'm not good at any job. I got another warning today for poor attitude."

"All your jobs sound like school. What of these men? How many are in love with you?"

He meant it lightly. The day should have been light, what with the sun and the festival and the ice cream eating crowds.

"It's not really what you think. Only once or twice, and I felt guilty, I felt sorry for Emil afterwards. I've always felt sorry for Emil. I feel sorry for him now: I could probably make myself cry this moment just thinking about how foolish he looked trying to give presentations in university, in history class. People have always laughed at him. I did half his work that year and he still just scraped by. But I gave him Noah. That must make up for things."

"By accident."

"I know I said that. But I did want Noah. What I wanted was for this body, since it has suffered, since it has not had much pleasure, to at least bring something good into the world. You know my mother had all those growths in her uterus and couldn't have any more children after me. I thought, what if I can't make a child, ever? What a waste it would be of the one thing I could do."

"I wish you'd told me." But he wasn't sure he wished it. He imagined her alone in a bathroom, contemplating coldly the few possibilities of her body.

She said, "I'm worried. About you. And about Noah."

"There's nothing wrong with Noah. He has a good appetite."

"I was picking him up from the daycare, and I saw him pinch this small boy, younger than him, who had touched his train. He looked around first to see that no one was looking, and then, like this, pinched him on the arm, hard. The little guy wailed and Noah sat down and just kept on playing as one of the nuns ran up. It's Emil's fault, he gives in to him on everything. So that's all that's wrong with him — a mean streak. If only this kid could have saved me. But no, even that was too much to ask."

"He'll be good."

"What's Frida like?"

"I don't really know," he said quietly. "She's sad a lot."

"Would Kate have another?"

"I wonder if she would." Maybe that was the thing — beg Kate to have a child. More roots, he could say to her.

"Well, Frida is lovely. And I can tell she loves you. You have to stay on this side of the abyss, my Toma — that's what my mother used to say to me. Maybe I should have another." She paused. "I have a cyst on my ovary, this big." She held

110

up her hand and made a small circle with her thumb and forefinger. "That's small I guess. But I can't sleep at night from fear. Do you know what I did last night? I stayed up the entire night and I wrote out everything I could remember about Noah's childhood until now, and also everything I thought he would want to know about his mother — about how I loved gym class in school and always wanted to play with the boys. I thought, I will die and he'll have nothing of me. You know I hardly have photographs from before coming to you and I wanted to leave him something."

"Toma," she continued, "you should have another child. For me, I will love it like my own." Noah was at Toma's feet, putting a shovel into his hand, pulling at him insistently.

"You strong little man!" Toma said. But no, he thought, he would not beg Kate for a child; there was nothing left in him for another child. Ana took it all and hardly left anything for Frida.

"Ana," he began, "what would you do if you'd hurt someone badly and couldn't, didn't know how to fix it?"

"You didn't do anything like that, did you?"

కిలు కిలు కిలు

One of the girls who visit Toma in his dreams, with their dirty hair and scared eyes, the older of the two sisters, lives now in Minnesota. She was asked by the therapist assigned to her, at a centre for victims, to write an account of her experience as she remembers it. She wrote: *It was a bright clear day. I and my sister and mother — my father was long dead — spent the morning listening to mortar and gun fire, together with the neighbours, all in one house. I could not tell*

111

from the noises if anyone was getting ahead. But some of the men seemed to read this language of noise and now and then exclaimed if it were good or bad. It was clear what was about to happen when we heard yells and shouts. They marched us, all of us, out of the house, and one guy pulled me away, and then pulled away my sister. My mother — I don't like to think of my mother then. She put up a good long fight for us, but there was no helping it.

The worst part is the mind accepting the reality of what is about to happen to the body. The mind and the body have been the most intimate companions — the hand reached out to stroke a dog's muscular back when the mind was moved to it, the mind looked for a blanket when the body was cold, laid it to rest when it exhausted itself. Yes, they were the closest of friends, and the mind protected the body. Now it has to give it up, into the hands of those who care nothing for it, hate it perhaps. The mind has to accept that the body will be hurt, unpredictably, badly, permanently. No, it's too much for the mind to accept, and it cowers in terror and impossible panic. What could be worse? Only perhaps seeing the body of one you love about to be deliberately damaged. Thus my terror over my sister; my mother's terror. Love then seems like only that, a self outside of the self.

That is the trouble with all of us she wrote, ten years later, living in Minnesota now and trying to explain things.

# *Skin Like Almonds*

THE SUMMER WE WERE TURNING twenty-five, Eva and I
spent three weeks together on the Adriatic coast. The things
that were on our minds were men and money and getting
ever closer to thirty. We saw thirty as a cut-off point before
which we wanted to do everything worth doing. Eva had
come from our hometown, and I had come from London,
Ontario, where I'd emigrated with my family right before
our last year of high school. Not spending that last year of
school together was a loss neither of us could quite recover
from. As for money, it interested us because we had grown
tired of having little of it — even I, who was expected to have
some because I lived abroad, had spent all the money I could
earn on tuition fees, two old cars, and summers visiting
Croatia. Eva had been almost engaged, but the engagement
was put on hold and she now considered herself in a state of
more-free-than-attached; I too was unattached, and we felt
this state of temporary liberty needed some concrete action
or it would be wasted and forgotten.

  We arrived on the overnight train. For the last two
legs of the trip we'd shared a compartment with four
French guys, younger than us, and spillover from the next

cabin — a large group of French people, friends, none older than twenty. Being six in the compartment, the maximum number, meant that at least we didn't have to worry about being joined by someone drunk or pestering — though the French boys *were* a little bit tipsy when they got on. The trains brought out territoriality, and if you got on a train already full, you knew the drawn curtains, the spreading of belongings, the averted eyes, the pretending to be asleep. The boys drank beer and from about eleven until 3:00 AM we drank their beer also and talked in stalled English and ate the cold chicken sandwiches Eva's mother had made. They were nice boys; their friends kept coming to the door of the compartment and talking in loud, excited tones.

At about three, we did turn off the light and tried to sleep, wedged head to foot with each other. When we woke we were near the sea and through the open train windows we could smell the familiar pine and sap and sea salt. The French gang was staying on the train, and in the morning we all said goodbye politely.

Eva knew the way to the house we were going to stay at because she'd rented a room there last summer, without me. The gate was open and when we entered the yard a man walked out of the darkness of a hallway. I guessed from what Eva told me that he was the caretaker who lived here with his family; they had come from Bosnia. He was slim and dark-haired, youthful even with his worn, sunned skin.

"You two are taking the smaller apartment, yes? I remember you" — turning to Eva — "from last season, you were here with a fiancée. And now" — turning to me — "you've brought a friend. Leave your bags, I'll carry them up."

Later Eva said to me, "You see the tone that man has? You do what he says before you realize you've been given an order."

He led us up the stairs and unlocked a door behind which was a fragrant, spacious room with two single beds, a sofa, and a table. While we were peeking into the kitchen, the owner of the house appeared, an elderly woman, a widow, Eva had told me, who wore the kind of housedress that one always saw on women over fifty — sleeveless, with buttons down the front, of a light fabric and small floral design. She shook hands with us, as the man hadn't done; Eva's hand she took in both of hers for a brief moment. Eva was always well liked by landlords, and the elderly; picky, pious women with overly dependent sons day-dreamed of her as a daughter-in-law. I wasn't sure why: she was not prim and not mouldable, either.

The nearest beach was long and open, covered in small rocks. There was a line of cafés, some of which would turn into nightclubs after dark. I took one look left and one look right and said, No shade. We paid to rent an umbrella and since the beach wasn't yet full, we took a spot near the water. That was where Amela, the caretaker's daughter, found us. She was the same age as us and Eva had become friendly with her the previous summer; she slipped with ease into our talks, our manwatching and our fears of time. Her hair was long, wavy, dyed blonde; her mother wore a head covering, but she did not. She had a physical energy about her that startled me. Talking to us that first day on the beach, she suddenly stood up, whipped a nectarine core toward the sea, and fell back onto the towel, all midsentence. She tackled her little sister in the yard and jumped out of chairs unpredictably. Most of her belongings bore evidence of this violence — her tubes of sunscreen were mangled and her sunglasses twisted. We played beach volleyball with her once and she was a better hitter than either of us; but Eva got an elbow to her cheekbone, and we didn't play again.

The beach was one place Amela's parents never went — they did not go swimming or sun bathing and never sat in cafés. At the beach Amela smoked cigarettes in secret and generally carried on a kind of life — for an hour or two at a time, anyway. Then she would have to get back, for the widow housed a dozen tourists at any one time, and Amela and her mother were in charge of cleaning, linens, miscellaneous chores. She was also that summer receiving letters from a Bosnian man who was the nephew of a friend of her father's. Her parents hoped to convince her to become engaged to him. He was a little bit older, had a military honour for having been wounded, and though he did not get that much of a pension nor yet the property he was promised, he was handsome and had not lost his mind in the war.

Amela's other admirer was Donatello. Eva, who knew him from last summer, described him to me as "an Adonis, only little," and from then we all called him *mali Adonis*. He was shorter than Amela by an inch or so, with a small, sculpted head, straight nose and black eyes, and a classically proportioned body. He was from Palermo and his infatuation with Amela began the summer before when he first vacationed here with friends. He had taken Amela out to dinner once, in a restaurant in town, but her father had somehow found out and a brief madness ensued — her mother cried and entreated, her father reasoned then threatened, her little sister wailed because everyone else was yelling or crying. Dinner with a man, alone, in a restaurant, could mean courtship — they feared she was planning to marry a man who wasn't Moslem.

"First they said I was too young, did I want to leave them already? Then, that if I want a man there are many good men and they will send me to Bosnia and I can have my pick. When I said there was no talk of marriage, they were relieved but a little offended — did I have dinners with men for fun?"

It ended with a promise from Amela that she wouldn't see her Italian again, in return for their promise that they wouldn't send her anywhere or stop her from going to the beach. I don't know if her father knew Donatello was around the year we were there; I'm not sure how much he followed what she did or extorted information. I wondered what he himself had been like as a young man, when he first married Amela's mother — what he looked like I could imagine, because he was boyish even now, but I wanted to know if he'd ever been awkward, insecure, lustful, and how that boy of twenty-something had become the family patriarch.

How much Amela loved Donatello or didn't I couldn't decide. When he met with us on the beach, Eva and I would sometimes go for a walk or for another macchiato to leave them alone. Or Amela and he would walk away toward the cliffs where we went to practise diving. When we were all together he found things to talk about with Eva and me; he joked with us, would get our coffee bill, make the walk to the water pump to fill up all our empty bottles. But these things seemed to us in no way personal — they were part of the cordiality owed us as Amela's friends. This, I think, was something we disliked about him — what we perceived as his perfect and uptight manners that seemed to mirror his perfect physical appearance.

Amela was terrified of being spotted with him; but she was also familiar with living life with a degree of risk. It brought tension to everything, an anxiety we came to share and sometimes resent, and it may have accounted for her unpredictable energy, the nearly manic movements. They could not meet at night; occasionally they could see each other in the evening, and then he had to hurry away from dinner with his friends to meet her early, so that she could still make it home by nine.

Many evenings the three of us played blackjack at the kitchen table in our room and drank flavoured vodkas mixed with soda or juice in great quantities. The soda and juice bottles we kept on the table, but the vodka we poured and then capped and placed in the nearest cupboard. Women our age were not begrudged wine or a spritzer, but the bottles of vodka could have put our integrity into question if Amela's parents or our landlady were to drop in. During these evenings we often fantasized about making some radical move: we discussed leaving our families and living together in some unlikely, humble but charming place, just three friends, not bothering to get married. One plan involved Eva's great aunt's house, in Seget, a village further south on the coast: it necessitated the aunt dying, which was inevitable, and also Eva somehow inheriting the house, which was not. But if fate granted us that, we could work out the rest; we might plant a large garden, learn to cook, even learn some basic plumbing and such, since the house would need the work.

It was in our rooms that we spent our time; we never went to the downstairs apartment in which Amela's family lived. They had an arrangement with the widow in which they worked for her and she let them stay indefinitely. We knew that, but we never did see where exactly Amela went when we parted in the hallway, where she slept, how her clothes were folded, or what she kept at her bedside.

One thing that bound the three of us that summer was that Amela had moved here in the same month (July) of the same year (seven years ago) that I had moved away from Eva. The war ending brought us not a return but a chasm between past and future that for all of us was fixed in that distant July. Another thing we had in common was that we all suffered from a distrust of our own free will.

"The most important events of my life, whether gifts or curses, have come from an unknown source," Eva said. That's rather how she talked back then.

And we recalled then that even Eva moving to my street when we were six was a bit of chance — had her grandfather not died unexpectedly, her family wouldn't have been forced out of the house and into an apartment on my block. He could have lived another twenty years and we wouldn't have met. We hadn't quit trying to make things happen, but we saw clearly that there was a disconnect between what we strived for and what came for us; efforts failed, but also, as Eva would say, gifts also fell like rain out of a seemingly clear sky and demanded genuflection and gratitude. Amela agreed with free will in principle, but saw little evidence of it in ordinary living. Like Eva, she had a great appetite for sugar — just one instance of something out of their control — and at the grocery store they bought jars of Nutella that would disappear in one sitting, not spread on bread but eaten with a coffee spoon (Eva's sugar habit may have been inherited — I recalled our mothers in their offices eating chunks of white bread dipped in white sugar).

Amela wasn't with us the day we met Emir and Slavko, two film students from Sarajevo, in a line up at the bakery. Like Amela, Emir and Slavko slipped into our days as if they'd been with us from the start. They were staying in a house that was being built by Slavko's uncle, who mostly left them to themselves. They couldn't cook many things, but they knew how to barbecue, were generous, and most days good humoured. We grilled bass and ate watermelon on their uncle's unfinished terrace and some nights collapsed there after dancing. I remember the patio chairs and our limbs dangling and draping over them, in repose or animation. Emir liked to sit on the floor and lean on my legs; Slavko usually ended up with his legs on the arm rest of Emir's or Eva's or my chair. Eva's long arms could reach the floor when she sat slouched. Inside the house, the brick and concrete were bare; three rooms were fitted with beds, and we spent late afternoons lying in their coolness.

I spent more time with Emir than with Slavko. Slavko and I liked each other, I think, but if we chanced to be left alone we were sheepish and struggled for conversation. I didn't know how to talk the way Eva did — she was good at small talk and also understood the slow uncovering that led to gems of intimacy or vulnerability.

Emir was of average height and well built, but you felt that he would get pudgy with time. He had this terrific thick brown hair that he pushed to the side across his forehead and which sometimes stuck out behind his ears. Slavko, though darker haired, darker skinned, looked like he might have been his brother — they both had a slightly protruding upper lip. Emir liked to read the daily news thoroughly and he liked also the tabloid-type weeklies, so in the mornings we stopped at the kiosk, bought one or two newspapers and one weekly, one pack of cigarettes and one pack of Pez candy, and under the umbrella on the sand we took turns reading — he got the newspaper first while I read the gossip, and then we switched. By the time of the switch, we'd already have told each other the main contents, and so the second reading was flightier. Eva and Slavko liked to swim — to "bathe" seems the more appropriate word, for they swam a while and then lolled about in the water, while in the shade of the umbrella Emir lay on his side, legs crossed at the ankles, eyes on the paper spread beside him, and I on my back, magazine held over my head, wondering if he looked at the shape of my arm, my rib perhaps, anything at all. But he merely read and saved contemplation of my physique for other times and shuttered rooms.

When Eva and Slavko came in from the water, they would sit next to us, half under the umbrella and half in the sun, and Eva would often lean on my knees and squeeze my ankles and call me the nicknames we'd collected for each other over the years. She and Slavko sometimes walked into the middle of an argument, because Emir and I did argue — over what made for responsible journalism, over the physical attributes of minor, but famous, television hosts, over me taking up more than my share of the umbrella's shade, over living abroad versus living at home. His family had lived in Berlin but returned to Sarajevo, and he believed diasporic life brought something like a gradual mummifying process, which ended of course with death. Because I spent those last sunny days mostly in the shade and Eva in the water, at the end of summer we looked as if we'd been on two different vacations — she dark and I touched by the sun about as much as if I'd been on a castle tour of Austria.

Amela appeared usually midafternoons and then we three would leave the guys, have a swim and a coffee at the bar. She and Donatello continued to see each other covertly, on the beach with us, or alone on some bench down an abandoned path. But Donatello too would have to leave. He seemed to me very serious and keen on Amela; as for her, we had to believe she was serious, given all the difficulties she went through to see him. He spoke English better than she did, but she also spoke some Italian: he described in detail his daily life in Palermo, she her family history. Or so she told us; I never saw much more than timid smiles between them. But Eva said she felt near them a vibe of inside knowledge that was sometimes emitted by long-time couples.

We were both strong believers in vibes and truths felt though unseen. And we both thought we should, as friends in a unique situation, provide a cover for Amela to have, at least once, some real privacy with Donatello.

Time was one obstacle — Amela always went for just a swim, a walk, an errand, and didn't stay out from noon until nightfall like us. There was no explicit rule in place against it, but to deviate from routine would be suspicious, might activate dormant prohibitions. Space was another — they could be alone in the forested areas past the beach, in a corner behind a cliff, but that was unsatisfactory. And the house of course was not an option — the widow and Amela's father and mother were permanent figures in it, one or another of them always disappearing into or appearing out of a hallway, washing a window, pouring water on the hot concrete and earth of the yard, or unseen, shouting out instructions about light switches or the tomato plants.

After our first time visiting Emir and Slavko's place, Eva said, "If it's going to happen anywhere, it'll be here."

Amela at first said she would be too embarrassed — of everyone. We worked on that. And we worked on the logistics: she would tell her parents a day in advance that she wanted to go with us up to the fortress that stood atop the town. This would clear, we figured, a long stretch of hours in which they would not expect her back.

On that planned day, our attention, I don't know why, centred on food. Donatello brought along mussels and there was much to do about how to eat them; Eva and I admired the abundance of the home-grown tomatoes, and we discussed at length whether figs should be eaten with or without their skins. We played rummy, and felt this was an ordinary day of afternoon lunching in the sun, and it nearly was. Then Eva and I said we were too hot, and offered to show Amela and Donatello the inside and the view from the second floor. In the upstairs room we chatted for a little while and then excused ourselves as if we were just going for water. It was all very scripted and once accomplished also very easy seeming. Everyone knew and pretended there was nothing to know.

So. This happened at that time in our summer, just past the halfway point, when we began to feel a creeping fear of the end. It was a paralysis, like turning twenty-five. Emir and Slavko had less than a week left.

"When we were younger," I said to Eva, the day of the mussels and the rest of it, sitting next to her on the rough white sheet of her bed in our room, "it was easier. We could put endings out of mind."

"Until they collapsed on us with terrible severity," she added, putting down the tweezers she was using to pluck tiny hairs around her knee.

Now we seemed to know the arc too well and could foresee the days rolling out. Time was not a straight line; it was a circle, a lap around the track, and the half-point of the circle meant we were on our way back to where we started.

The next day the three of us decided to look for another beach that was rumoured to exist on the other side of the "mountain" — so we called it, though it was in fact a not-very-tall hill. Eva and I wanted to hear what Amela would have to tell us. We told her parents we wanted to spend the day hiking and swimming and, somewhat to our surprise, they agreed easily, and Amela's mom even packed us a basket of spinach pies.

We climbed the hill, where the heat that was unbearable in town was tempered by the spruce trees. It was turning out to be a long walk, and we distracted ourselves by planning details of our house, the one we hoped Eva would inherit. While we were calculating the cost of repairs — insulation, mould — we suddenly saw a wall of cliff give way to a small sunny cove sheltered by forest. The water was a transparent green. There were ten, maybe twelve bathers, about half of them nude. We had been walking for more than an hour. We looked at each other, looked above at the sky, and laughed: discovering this hideout had to be a good sign for our future.

We climbed down and unpacked our basket. Settled on our towels, pies in hand, we encouraged Amela to tell us all about the afternoon with Donatello.

"It was strange — not really like anything I'd known before. But I'd never even come close before."

To the men she had known sex was a game of resistance — the man's part was to cajole and coerce and the woman's to deflect, and Amela played her part skillfully, for which she was given credit and respect. For the woman to give in without a fight made the game pointless; in that case she was the loser, but she also spoiled the man's victory. The ideal was a timing of advances and retreats that allowed for something to happen and for each player to show his or her skills. In concrete terms, it meant that only some small, tortured pleasures could be got from the whole thing, which Amela, as the woman, had to pretend were teased out against her will. Then the lines were drawn — the final no was said, and it was respected; the men did not rape, though the whole thing was a curious simulation. The trouble was of course how one could complete the act at all, given the rules.

We decided that afternoon that sex and its variations had not much to do with love, less with looks. Though Amela did think it had to do with love; after all, it had prompted Donatello to vow his love to her.

"He also said he's glad we waited, and did it the right way." We laughed at this — Eva and I — but not Amela. I knew what Eva would say next.

"Men think they have to act as if they don't want sex in order to get it. It's a reward for the wait. It's another kind of game."

Slavko and Emir were a relief in this regard — one could shut the blinds, take off one's clothes, and know it was neither a down payment nor a concession.

Eva insisted there was such a thing as technique, but I argued it could not be like learning an instrument. Back then we even thought it had little to do with the rest of a person's character; it was all curiosity with us, then, and we thought curiosity would die if faced every day with the same view. We looked around at the aging nude bodies surrounding us and we wondered about sex at forty and sixty and eighty; we wondered about everything at forty and sixty and eighty, because we could not understand time. We did agree that time was slowest when life was fullest; months of inertia and routine conflated time — a week ago was a month ago or three months ago. Both trauma and great pleasure stopped time, broke it into a before and after. Violence suffered, witnessed, a painful parting, all were permanent moments, repeated, alive.

"I think I have a chronic ache, here," Amela said, putting my palm on her left shoulder, "from the time my brother laid his hand there, the last time I saw him. His hand shook."

So, we concluded, time dies but small bits of it survive.

We stayed on that beach until our basket was empty, the sun set, and all the other bathers left. Then we again climbed up the hill and down the hill.

That evening, as we were clipping our towels to the clothesline on the balcony, Amela's dad, who was below us, sanding a bench, called out, "Well, are there enough Italians here for you yet?" It was the time of the Italians' *ferragosta*, and they seemed to overrun the town.

"It would be better if they were fewer," Eva yelled back, laughter in her voice.

"Well, you watch for them," he said. "Once you get one after you, they're hard to get rid of." We looked at each other — it must have been a warning, but it was the friendliest-sounding one we'd ever heard.

෨෨෨

After the afternoon at Slavko's, Donatello was a man with one priority. He was to leave soon and seemed frantic. On the beach he followed Amela into the water, out of the water, laid his head on her hip if she turned on her side to talk to us, pulled her away for another walk when she really had to get back.

"Do your friends miss you?" I said to him once, while he drummed his fingers on Amela's thigh.

"They are not my close friends. We've gone to school together, that's all."

It was a straight, uptight answer to a pointed question. Amela was becoming distraught trying to find enough excuses to stay out of the house. He talked of their future as a battle, something they had to be brave for, keep faith in. She seemed wild in those last days — at home she had a controlled surface of calm, jokes about the usual household stuff; with Donatello she was more anxious than ever about being seen; with us she was distracted to the point of being unable to talk, could hardly sit still long enough to finish a coffee. She was always rushing, and she turned over glasses, knocked down stools, and more than once slammed into people.

We continued our beach reading and our lounging with Slavko and Emir. Slavko and Eva had an easy understanding, while Emir and I still argued, and I privately accused him of spinelessness and a lack of passion. And at home sometimes, Eva, underslept, took his side, pointed out passion could not be demanded or expected, and maybe it was not him but me. She was right, but the way she said it hurt the most — as if she'd had quite enough of my complaining and of me in general. Furious, I made private resolutions never to return. Of course she knew my thoughts, but would not back down. We each counted up our small betrayals and sat with them in the trenches. And I would think that this friendship too would now die and that we'd kept it alive as long as we, or anyone, could.

Two days before Slavko and Emir would have to pack up their Opel and drive back to Sarajevo, they had the house to themselves for a whole night, and we made it our farewell. I remember the excessive quantities of mackerel on the barbecue and the light-coloured red wine that none of us could feel at all for some time.

"It is not the wine that is weak, but we who are too strong for it," Emir said, while turning over a hefty slab of a mackerel, with a head and eyes. We other three were half-curled in our chairs and Emir now and then cut off a piece of fish and fed it to one of us after bouncing it in his hand and blowing on it to cool it. We hardly moved, only extended our arms to accept Emir's bites and to pick at the fruit and bread and cheese on the table.

Slavko said we should come to the Sarajevo film festival; it was to start in seven days. Eva said we could — I didn't have to fly out for another fourteen days.

"Let's do it," I said, reaching out my palm to touch her hand. We could not really do it, but the invitation, our acceptance, made it seem like the vacation, this night, would never end — there would always be another thing to look forward to. Just as after the eating there would be dancing, a walk on the beach in the darkness, cool rooms, fine Turkish coffee in the morning.

Then we heard the gate opening and Amela, breathless, hair piled high on her head in a massive bun, beach towel slung over her shoulder, hurried toward us.

"I ran over here — I only have an hour." She fell into a chair, reached for a glass and poured wine.

"Donatello wants me to go with him to Palermo," she said. "He's crazy."

"What?" Eva said.

"But what would you do there?" I said.

"I would live with him. He's crazy."

"Your parents would go crazy," Emir said.

Amela broke into a high-pitched laugh here.

"He's really not normal. He wants me to come in September. He'll pay for my ticket on the ferry and the train."

"Palermo," Eva said, as if trying to make sense of things by remembering Palermo's position on the map or perhaps conjuring its landmarks, some square Amela would be walking through.

"Where would you live?" I asked.

"He's renting a room right now, while at university, but he said he would rent something bigger, something with a kitchenette and private shower."

"How long would you even be allowed to stay in Italy? You couldn't work, could you?"

She couldn't answer.

Eva said, "He's twenty-six." It was part of our mania that summer to know everyone's age, and she might have thought his age could give us a clue about what should be done.

"Do you know where I saw my mom today?" Amela said. "At the little ice cream stand where the beach begins, just past the docks. I don't think she has ever gone there, as long as we've lived here. She was buying my sister a cone. We only ever buy ice cream in tubs, from the supermarket. I was sitting on that low wall a ways down with Donatello."

Eva and I looked at each other.

"She could not have seen you — it's too far."

"I saw her."

"The trees near the wall would hide you."

"It doesn't matter," she said cleanly. We were quiet then, heard the sound of a spade hitting the ground in the garden one house over, the sound of a spraying water hose in another. Amela said, "You don't know the winters here. People think I'm lucky to live by the sea. The winter is a desert. There is no one on the streets. I go to sit in the library, which closes at four. The librarian sometimes wants to go home early and sends me off at three. Our electric stove at the house is only for the living room and we all sit there, watching game shows. I go to a friend's house and her family is doing the same thing."

"Here," Emir said, holding up a fish, "it's really cooked now."

The mackerel was plump and lovely, and he lowered one on each of our plates. But except for Amela we were all already full. Moving tiny bites from our plates to our mouths, we surveyed the big moon-slices of watermelon, the peaches, the salty sardines spread on the plate, the cheese floating in olive oil — it all seemed evidence of our overreaching.

"What possessed us," Slavko said, suppressing a cough, a piece of fish meat caught in his throat. Eva and I covered our mouths and tried not to laugh while chewing. Amela was eating very quickly. It all seemed, all of a sudden, terribly funny. I looked at Eva, and I thought of her as she had been once, coltish and skinny, with a bowl haircut, saw her as she had been moments ago when she reached out her lovely braceleted arm to pinch a grape, and saw her now laughing with her head thrown back; I saw Emir with that shag of hair, Slavko, Amela with her characteristic rushing, how she seemed to me to look like her father right then in the handsome structure of the cheekbones and the nose; and I looked at Eva again, and she was looking at me, and I saw that she knew what had passed through my head as I knew what had passed through hers. And though I had thought of the things to come, I thought also that this moment might be enough — like a smooth stone, it sank, settled, and remained.

☙ ☙ ☙

During our last few days at the house there was a turnover in guests, and Amela was busy mopping and scrubbing and ironing bed clothes. Donatello was about to leave, and she still had not given him her word. We were nearly out of money, and we ate only fruit and bread with canned pâté. On our last afternoon with Emir and Slavko, I stayed under the umbrella on my towel, while they three swam. Donatello found me where I was and crouched next to my head so that I could see his smooth toes, proportional and hairless. I lowered my sunglasses to look at his face.

"I must see her before I leave. She knows I leave tonight."

I found her in the darkness of the hallway, bending over a dust pan. I carried two ice cream cones I'd bought on the way, and she took one from me, called to her mother that she was going for a walk. We hurried along without saying anything and she stuck the cone face down on top of the first, overflowing, garbage can we passed.

Emir, Slavko, and Eva had returned from the swim and Eva was wringing out her hair. Amela and Donatello walked quickly away.

"Maybe there is something wrong with him," I said to Eva. "Are there not enough women in Italy? Why go through the trouble of importing one from here?"

Eva turned to look at the two figures getting smaller and smaller.

"I don't know," she turned back toward me, "but it's a catastrophic idea to marry the first man you sleep with."

"She doesn't have to marry him," Slavko said.

"What is she going to do, go to Palermo to become a hotel maid?"

"Probably can't even become that," I said.

"She should go," said Emir. "They could have beautiful children."

"She doesn't know him. Does she? Who knows what he'll be like when she's over there," Slavko said, frowning slightly.

All Amela could say when she returned from her walk was, "He's crazy." She was relieved to have him go, I think, and so were we. Her future was being decided, and it could not be done in the presence of the man who'd tried so suddenly to determine it himself.

We said goodbye to Slavko and Emir standing by their car, in which things were packed heedlessly, piled in the back seat.

"We will see each other again, somewhere," each of us said, in turn, formally. But nobody brought up our visiting them in Sarajevo for the film festival. They drove away with a honk and a wave through the rolled-down car window, and we stood for a few moments, dry mouthed, on the burning pavement.

That night Amela came up to our room. We were tidying — we had few clean clothes left, had stopped putting things in their drawers — and already the salt-smell in our bathing suits, the knick-knacks from our beach bags, the return train tickets we'd dug up and would use in two days, were tearing into us. Amela sat herself in a kitchen chair and began to organize the things on the table.

"I called Donatello yesterday — from the post office," she said, stuffing a card deck into its box. "He's left me money to call him."

"He's thorough," I said.

"My parents think I should go to Bosnia and visit, you know, the other guy." She took a worn picture from the back pocket of her jeans. "He's pretty nice," she said.

He did look pretty nice in the somewhat fuzzy photo.

"They know," she said. "They must have known since our story about the fortress and the rest of it. And then that entire day we were away."

"What did they say?"

"Nothing."

"Then how do you know?"

"They would have made a scene — wouldn't they have?" I said.

She bristled at that. "It's not as if they're hysterical. Oh, it doesn't matter."

"Maybe if you explained to them," I said.

"Donatello liked to recite a line from a poem for me, something about wanting to" — she giggled — "eat my skin like almonds. It seemed strange to me and I liked it. But maybe I didn't like Donatello that much. After we did it, he went to the bathroom for a long time. I started to think he went to cry. Then I thought it may have been a mistake, all of that."

We had poured vodka into glasses of pineapple juice, but it was too early — they didn't sit well. We were surprised at first and a little offended at such easy discarding of Donatello. We'd gone through the trouble to get them together, had spent hours trying to ignore the childish petting happening beside our beach towels, under the café table. It could have been time spent differently, at the beach over the mountain, for instance, talking each other through the paralyzing fear of the inevitable.

"So that's how it will be," Eva said. "A little bit of desire and a little bit of coercion. Like grey propaganda. Truth and lies mixed together, and we move right along." It was an unexpected thing to say, even for her, and uncharacteristically bitter. It froze us for a moment, glasses in hand, staring at her. We recovered enough to bring the glasses to our lips and laugh a little.

"We should exchange mementos," Amela said. "Keepsakes, you know."

We decided each would write something on a piece of paper, something that would remind us of the summer, and give it to the other two. Amela's paper had Donatello's line from a Neruda poem, about skin and almonds. In that regard, I thought, he was accurate: her skin was that pale colour of a raw almond, and her hair, had she not bleached it, would have been the brown of almond skin. I'm sorry to say I've lost Eva's paper, and can't remember what she'd written. A few letters went back and forth between the three of us for a while, communal letters, drawing on the energy of what we'd had while together, and hardly touching on our lives as they were lived day to day, as they surrounded us wherever we sat writing the letters, in our three separate places. Eva and I didn't return the next summer — Eva found a job and could not get vacation time, and I spent the summer working too, and camping in southern Alberta with some new friends. We don't know how Amela faced thirty, which we'd feared so much, nor forty, for that matter — like us, she must be well into her forties now. Once, not so long ago, I looked for the writing I did about the period, and then remembered that I had destroyed it, in the affect of some resentment — against Eva or Emir or just myself as I was then. But I wished more than anything that I hadn't, that something existed that would tell me it was real, the moment was permanent and we were once really together, on the verge of being no longer young.

# Everyone Has Come

THE MOUNTAINS ACROSS THE INLET are spotted with snow. A float plane comes in — tiny, soundless to me, a toy. Closer, through the window, I see the worn white siding of my neighbours' house, our own same old patchy lawn, the kids' bicycles and little shovels that I will have to put away later. No one is at home but me; they won't be back for a little while, and then I will think about what to prepare for the kids to tide them over until dinner time.

Years ago, in Bosnia, when the war was still going, I'd been separated from my family by the fighting. But we were going to be reunited: I was on a bus full of refugees that was going west, to where my family was waiting. With me was my friend Lela. Before we ended up on that bus Lela and I had lived under the siege as best we knew how, and before that we were philosophy students at the university. We had only just got through our first year when the war started up, which is too bad because we were having a really good time — girls at the philosophy faculty were the most popular, and all the guys wanted to date us. We were respected, I don't exactly know why; I do know we despised money — who cared if you studied economics, or tourism?

But what I'm thinking of has to do with when the bus finally got to where it was going, when I first saw my family again after all those months.

It was early evening when the bus arrived at the station in Split, the city my family had got away to. There was a big crowd of people there; they had been waiting since dawn, the bus was so delayed. When I spotted my mom and dad in the crowd, they were searching the bus windows with their eyes, but they couldn't see me yet. I saw my brother yell something to my father, saw my mother pull on my father's · sleeve. It was a bright day, the sun had just gone down. Lela and I got out together, into this crowd of anxious, terrifyingly hopeful people.

I waved and yelled across the noise, like everyone was doing, "Mom!" I yelled, "Dad!" The look on their faces when they saw me. They hugged me and hugged me and cried and cried. Mom looked a little wild, Dad looked old, my little brother was wearing his hair short, really short.

Then we waited with Lela for her aunt, who was supposed to get her, but didn't seem to be here. Not far from us was another family, a father and grown son smoking, pacing, a mother sitting on the bench, her arms twisted together. They were still looking, waiting for someone, though the bus had nearly emptied now. We smoked too, I think, as we waited. My mother had me by the forearm, my dad, tall, would let go of my shoulder only to squeeze it again and again.

After some time we heard a deep moan, "Sanja, my Sanja, where are you." It was from the woman on the bench. I saw the father and son look at each other then look off again at the crowd. I knew a Sanja, Lela did too. We had had some lectures together. But there are lots of Sanjas. This one was a tall girl, and pretty and, well, it probably doesn't matter too much now what she was.

Before all this at the station, during the bus journey, we had stopped, in the middle of the night, once it was safe, and we were told we could go outside and stretch our legs. That was good for Lela because she had had an asthma attack on the bus, and it was I who had to push at people to give her breathing room, but really there was little room for anyone to move anywhere, and there were curses, and the scene made the atmosphere hotter and ranker than it already was.

So thank God we could go outside, and God, it was a beautiful night. Warm, and a clear sky, with a bright moon, just short of full, its edges fuzzy. Lela said to me, "What will you do first?" That's something we'd talked about many times before—and often at our worst, when we'd come back from a run for water or bread particularly shaken up, or on the nights when the shelling went on so relentlessly long that it made us mad, desperate. We said we would take the longest shower in the world, drink a cup of real coffee, put on a lot of makeup and go out on the town. But at that moment I could only picture that all of us, my parents and my brother, would go home, and that there would be food, yes, and coffee — but I couldn't picture the next step, the falling asleep or the waking up.

Lela's aunt did finally show up at the station. And already Lela and I were in different worlds, that's how it goes. When Lela asked her to, her aunt hastily wrote down a phone number on a receipt from a coffee she must have had at the terminal earlier and pressed it into my hand. And then there was Lela, looking just like any other person walking away. Mom and my little brother and I stood waiting for Dad to bring back the car. Mom's hands were clasped around my wrist, forearm. The buses stood empty but that family was still in the same place. There was a yelling exchange between some other men, and then two of them, fat bus drivers, climbed into the buses and drove them into the garage.

The woman on the bench started weeping. Her moans echoed along the whole station. "Everyone has come, only my Sanja isn't here," she cried. She cried, "Only Sanja is missing, why is my Sanja missing." On and on.

It is difficult to listen to such cries. The woman gasped for breath violently like Lela had gasped earlier on the bus from her asthma. But here's the thing about it: for some reason I then pictured my own family in their place, and when I did that, when I imagined them still waiting for me as everyone around them picked out their loved ones and left, when I saw my mother moaning and my father and brother stone-faced, when I recalled the hope and fear on their faces as they looked for me, when I put them all in that place and took myself out of the picture, well — only then did I realize the thing for what it was.

Then what I remember is my brother hurrying towards me with a fresh hot *burek* he had just bought at the bakery, him putting it in my hands; it was heavy, and steaming when I unwrapped it, and then I started to cry.

She cried like she would never stop crying, that's what my mother would tell people for years.

As we were leaving the station, the sun was going down and a man in blue overalls was sweeping the platform. Another man, older, was standing near the entrance to the terminal, dressed in a fine old-fashioned suit and neatly shaved, his face calm, as if he were ready to wait the night through. And that family, the mother bent over at the waist and holding her gut as if it were in danger of spilling out, the father and son looking into the distance with lost eyes. I think now I should have turned back and said something to them, offered help, asked their name. The Sanja I knew was Sanja Brkić. Both names, first and last, are so common, and it couldn't have been the same girl, anyway. The traffic was bad through the city and Dad drove slowly. We were starting and stopping a lot. My dad said, "Now that we are all together, everything will be all right." The *burek* sat in my lap, still warm. At some point before we reached the house I must have started to eat it.

Now from Vancouver, I call my parents on the long-distance plan sometimes. If it happens to be an odd time of night for them in Split, they say, "Is everything all right?"

"It is," I say.

"The kids, your sweetheart, are they all right?"

"They're more than all right," I say.

It's better that way.

# His

THE YOUNG SOLDIER LAY NEAR the edge of the forest, in the brush behind a hillock. He'd lain there for several hours, propping himself on his one good shoulder and alternately watching and not watching his other shoulder bleed through the jacket he'd tightened around it. Morning fog was just lifting. Not far from the edge of the forest was a large meadow, with streams and bushes, and beyond it the start of a village, with narrow house fronts and orchards or vegetable gardens extending behind the houses.

Old Mr. Hrgović, better known as Hrga, scanned the grass and the brush and the line of trees, and spotted the soldier not far from where he stood. Hrga could even see the bloody shoulder and could read the awkward unselfconscious posture of a person in all-enveloping pain. The front line had been near Hrga's house for months now, and he had lived in his house, on this land, for some forty-five years before that. He remembered that other war, and had fought in it too; this war was still young, but already he was full up with what he'd seen and heard since the first blockades of the summer, the first mortar attacks, and the first news of burning houses and bodies at the sides of roads. The roads, the forest, the hillocks, and the grass, the orchards of this Slavonian village, could not be anyone's but his — he knew this without needing to articulate it, without complication. Those trying to occupy it were insane, that was clear to him. He felt both sides — the Serb side and his own Croat side — to be intrusions. And his side he had to tolerate. The soldiers, some of whom he knew from the village and most of whom were decent and ordinary, came by his house and he fed them when he could and shared his brandy with them.

Last night there had been heavy fire and by sunrise he suspected something had moved, the Serb forces had been pushed back. Through the night he'd smoked cigarettes in the dark under the walnut tree. It was his tree and his yard. He did not want to stay inside. Whose business was it whether he hid in the house or sat on the bench he'd built under his tree? Now the morning was dewy and cool with a smell of wet earth and wet leaves. He'd walked out to see how things looked. He kept walking, beyond where he should have, into a small wooded area that had recently become no man's land. He kept walking because he had felt some new anger during the night. His sons and daughters were in turn angry with him for living like this, alone, so near the front. For weapons he had a rifle he had hunted with for decades, a handgun, and a few hand grenades. His children all lived abroad and two of them had grandchildren of their own, and he kept all the photographs he was sent in a neat row lined up next to the bread box.

The soldier reclining against the hillock heard the steps coming toward him, the shifting swoosh of the grass. His head was too stiff to move and he angled his eyes as far as he could to see who was approaching.

To Hrga, the man's eyes seemed at first dead and then insanely focused. He took off his cap and leaned over the man, as much as his back would allow, not very low.

"Where are you wounded?" he said.

The soldier's right side was all blood, blood that had spread from the right shoulder, had soaked all of the jacket tied around it. The left hand was bloody. He wore faded fatigues and a black shirt with lettering — a sports shirt. His rifle, a Kalashnikov, was in the grass next to his good left arm. Near that arm was a wet pack of cigarettes — Hrga looked at the brand, but he had already understood whose side the soldier was from. The man let out a croak and Hrga knew immediately he was thirsty, dried out. He'd been that dried out once. He straightened himself and looked out toward the river, and then back in the direction he'd come from. He knew these fields but he could not stay here now.

"Nothing but for you to come with me," he said, more to himself than to the man.

Everything was quiet, at the moment, in all directions. Hrga was further from his house than usual, but not especially far — had he not used to set fox traps not far from here, in the years before the war? He thought he knew where the Croats were standing guard, and he knew the Serb side was even further in the other direction.

"I'm going to move you now," Hrga said.

"Where to?" the soldier croaked. In the hours he'd spent in this spot he'd dragged himself to, shapes like clouds of gas, in colours of black, and rust, and pale green, had inflated and deflated in slow succession in the darkness behind his closed eyelids. In the last hour they had been appearing in front of his open eyes too, obscuring the grass and the trunks of oak trees. Their inflation and deflation had a rhythm, and he thought that if he was forced to move and lost this rhythm he would not be able to control himself anymore.

"Don't worry," the old man said and crouched beside him. He felt he was with one of his children when they were very young and had been caught in a transgression and hurt. There was in the soldier's body and eyes the same terrified, hopeful, naked surrender. And in Hrga, the same parental anger toward the child who had caused the disaster, yet also pity at the child's pain.

"Your shoulder's gone," he said, "but did it get you anywhere else?"

The soldier wanted to speak but after those first words he could not activate the mechanism again. Instead he looked toward his twisted ankle, the left one.

"We'll start anyway, slowly," Hrga said. He moved the man to sitting. He picked up the pack of smokes, put it in his own pants pocket, and slung the Kalashnikov over his shoulder. He put the man's good arm around his neck and his hand around his torso. The man smelled metallic, and yeasty, like a drying mushroom, and sour. His pant leg was wet.

The two men stood up. The grass under their feet was still wet. The day was not sunny, but lit by brightness that comes from behind clouds and gives hyper-real sharpness to everything. In front of the soldier's eyes clouds and balls of light were exploding and threatening to topple him.

"Steady now," Hrga said. He didn't know if this was a dying man or not. When he'd lifted him he'd seen the blood that had soaked the ground under him.

When they'd reached the hillock before the road, the soldier said, "I can't." They stood for a moment, and then the old man began moving again, slowly, putting all his muscle into propping up the soldier. They crossed the road and made it to the house from behind, through Hrga's orchard.

Hrga had taken to sleeping in the room that was both kitchen and living room and kept the sofa bed pulled out all the time. On it he now laid the soldier. His own arms trembled with exertion. "All right," he said, mostly to himself. "It's good now."

He brought a glass of water to the man, which he filled from the pot of it he'd boiled last night. After the man drank it he brought him another. Then he brought out his brandy and poured two small glasses, which they drank at the same time.

The soldier winced in swallowing. "It's a good one," he said. His chest expanded after he'd drunk the water and his voice was clearer now.

"It burns, doesn't it." Hrga crouched by the sofa, feeling the crunch in his knees, and unlaced the man's boots, took them off with a grunt, and then found a clean bed sheet and gauze and a towel and scissors. He cut the man's shirt straight across the front and pulled it away from his body. He wet the towel with water from the pot and squeezed the water from it on the man's wound.

"It's gone to hell, hasn't it," the soldier said. The removal of his stinking, soggy, leaden boots was a great, if temporary, relief.

"You have your head and you have your legs," Hrga said. He stuffed gauze and bandaged, cut the sheet into squares and wrapped it around the shoulder, under the opposite armpit. The soldier passed into unconsciousness for minutes at a time and then returned into pain. He was young and scruffy, with a dirty beard and bad skin. Hrga brought aspirin, four in the palm of his hand, a pointless offering. The next thing would be food, he thought. He was hard up for bread. He opened a can of pork and heated it up.

"Listen," the soldier said, "I should go to the bathroom." His eyes were glassy and bloodshot, and his face shone with fever.

Hrga nodded and stood up.

"No, I'll do it myself," the man said — but he found he could not prop himself up with his good arm alone.

So they went together down the long hallway to the bathroom. The old man helped him sit on the toilet, and then he turned away, started scraping at the grime of the sink. Then it occurred to him to give the soldier a new pair of underwear and pants. "Wait here," he said.

He found clean things he hadn't worn in a long time — he'd been wearing his overalls for months now. When he returned to the bathroom the man was crying silently and there was a new line of sweat around his hairline. The old man asked him if he could stand. He kept crying. Hrga waited. He held the folded wool pants, underwear, and socks in both hands, and he waited, and the man kept crying.

He looked out the small, high window at the bit of sky and a branch of his walnut tree.

"All right," he said, "all right." He got down to his knees, with difficulty, and pulled off the man's pants, then his underwear.

"Some things just have to get done," he said, with more shrillness than he'd intended. His knees hurt a great deal, as always when he tried to kneel or crouch. This pain, and the soldier's unrelenting soft crying, made him irritated, so he shook out the clean underwear, shook out the folded pants, and worked as quickly as he could to pull them both halfway up the man's thighs.

Then he could not bear it anymore and creakily lowered himself to sit on the floor and lean against the tub.

The man stopped crying. To avoid looking at Hrga, he looked up, and he noticed the small window high in the wall, and he saw the sky and the tree branch. He imagined standing on top of the toilet bowl and opening the window to look outside: there'd be new air, and the sight of a familiar yard — a shed, a water pump, defunct chicken coop, grass between concrete. And so he managed to use his right arm to hold on to the edge of the bathtub and raise himself to standing, and Hrga, seeing this, stood up too, with difficulty, and pulled up the underwear and the pants quickly over the man's hips. As Hrga tugged up the zipper, the soldier said thank you, which sounded odd to both of them, a politeness suited to cafés and grocery shops, to favours done between friends. Hrga said nothing in return and they silently made the long walk down the hall together.

Throughout the day and evening Hrga puttered about, and the man stayed on the sofa, finding the rhythm of his pain, and sometimes blacking out or dreaming. His face in repose was blank, his mouth slightly open — fleshy lips, straight nose, and straight, thick eyebrows on a wide face, pockmarked from acne. A handsome man, the old man thought, despite the bad skin and dirty beard and too-long hair.

Late in the evening the man was most present, and they ate and drank and smoked cigarettes.

"Do you have children?" Hrga asked.

"No. Wife can't have any."

The television was turned on, with the sound low, and the living room smelled of warm food and cigarette smoke.

"I have five. Not one of them lives here. My wife died two years ago. It was hard for me when she died, but I see now that it was for the better."

"I think my wife could do without me. Only my mother will miss me. Where are all your children?"

"Is your mother old?"

"Seventy-one. She was old when she had me. She has a bad heart." The man's voice was strained. Hrga brought him more water, then refilled his brandy glass.

"Whatever made you leave her and come down here to take what's not yours?" Hrga said.

The man looked straight ahead.

Hrga then walked out into his yard and sat on the bench and looked into the darkness over the low wall surrounding his yard and orchard.

In the night that followed the man slept on the pulled-out sofa and Hrga on a small bed that had stayed in the corner since the children used to take their naps on it. The soldier did not move much in the night, but he often exhaled heavily. The room was blankly dark, with only the broadest outlines, and it smelled of blood and stale bedding. Hrga focused his eyes into the darkness and imagined the outlines of the furniture. In the night the reality of what he could and could not do became stark. Officially, he should have turned the soldier over to the Croat side so they could exchange him for one of their own. But underneath the rules, underneath the neat lineup of men simply changing sides on some crossroad, some former school house, lay a dark corridor of unofficial space and time, ruled by those with the guns, and what could Hrga control about what they did with those guns? All their violent longings, all the beautiful certainty of self-validating power — you have it, and therefore you must be entitled to have it — what could Hrga do with those? And were they right?

And Hrga could not return him to the man's own side either. Odd, then, how the soldier's existence seemed now like a kind of nonexistence — he was not any place, not any place where he could be found by those caring to find him, not anywhere he could stay. Hrga thought of the soldier's men, why they didn't return for him — maybe Hrga had beat them to it.

He knew later that he'd fallen asleep because he dreamt — himself, in the shade of his tree, and outside the gate, crunchy noises, like wheels on gravel, and light gun fire, and distant rumbling, and he knew that he should be threatened and also that the noise was irrelevant.

*His*

He woke up when the soldier's phlegmy snoring broke through to his consciousness. He rose out of bed and walked over to him — his eyes were glazed again and he was sweaty. The old man thought, he will die here, and what will I have had to do with it?

"What can I bring you?" he whispered. He found more aspirin and made the man swallow it, and went back to his bed.

In the early morning they shared bread with big spoons of rubbery cherry jam. The soldier could not eat much. The day outside was bright and the window let in cool air. After the bread and jam breakfast, Hrga sat in a kitchen chair next to the sofa smoking the man's cigarettes. Hrga was thinking of his children, and then of this man and his mother. There were things he wanted to understand.

"When my youngest son came to say goodbye," Hrga said, "before he was to fly on a plane to Toronto, I wouldn't walk him out to the gate. I just sat on that bench and watched him and his mother at the gate, she holding his face and crying. He probably thought I would get up and follow. But I didn't. Instead I raised my hand to say goodbye. They both stood facing me, like they didn't understand. Finally my son nodded and left."

"I know," the man managed to say. Every time he closed his eyes the familiar clouds of gas inflated in great rapidity and in acutely bright ugly colours, and with increasing intensity he felt the insistent yellows and oranges pressing on his retinas, his eye sockets, his brain.

He wanted to say more, but when he began to speak again his words devolved into gurgles.

Hrga thought he could still be rallied. He thought there were things they might still tell each other. So he made some cold compresses out of old towels, and once he applied them the man started to breathe evenly and to fall into a kind of sleep.

Not long after, a group of undertrained, malnourished soldiers came through Hrga's gate and walked into the house without knocking, not expecting anything but breakfast and drink and a table to sit at. They saw the man and they took him away — this after eating and drinking and washing up and cursing and re-lacing their boots. Hrga said they should take him to hospital. They said they might though he didn't deserve it. The young soldier seemed not quite conscious as they moved him out to their car. They were, variously, shifty-eyed and boisterous and decent and tired and out of their depth and in a perfect depth. Hrga watched them pull the man along, forces within them aligning or conflicting.

Hrga followed them outside the gate, and after watching them drive away, the back of the man's black-haired head visible through the back window, he stood looking, across the road, beyond the houses and their fields and orchards, in the direction of the forest, which was just visible from where he stood. The old man saw now that the fields and the forests were not really his, after all, no more than anything was anyone's, no more than his children, whom he'd also tended and lived alongside of, were his, not in the way that word, possessive pronoun, could be used to mean freedom to control. He loved them—or were they just a part of him, intensely familiar? — but that did not entitle him to anything. He went inside, to the kitchen, and took a side of bacon out of the cupboard. No one is entitled to anything or anyone, he said to himself, slicing his bacon into small squares. He placed the pieces one by one into an uneven-bottomed pan in which he always fried bacon and eggs. He lit a match to turn on the burner. A quiet hiss, before the restrained sizzle of the fat. No one, nothing, he said, as he moved to the fridge and carefully took out the three remaining eggs with his calloused, stiff hands. He lined them up next to the pan, the fat really lively now, shooting up, and cracked them one by one. Before the whites were cooked, he took the pan off the burner. The bread in the bread box was hard and he patted it down with water. He sat at the table and cut up the eggs into bite-sized pieces so that the yolks spilled over and mixed with the whites and with the bacon fat. He tore off chunks of bread and threw them into the pan, then used his fork to pick up egg and fat and bacon on each piece of bread.

This was the way he'd eaten eggs for many years. Only this time his hand trembled slightly and occasionally he lost a piece from his fork. He stopped saying things out loud. He ate this way until he had sopped up everything, until he moved the last piece of hard bread in a circle around the little black pan, leaving nothing behind. Then he washed up — the table, the pan, his hands and face. He walked out to his shed, where the soldier's Kalashnikov was still propped up. He picked it up. He closed his eyes, pictured the faces of each of his children, from oldest to youngest. With a tired, stiff heart, he lifted his arm, managed to put the barrel to his temple, and pressed his finger to the trigger.

Three days later, three soldiers found him. The oldest among them had known Hrga since the start of the war, and although he was full up with all of it too, and they were all tired and stiff, still he insisted that they carry the old man's body to the sofa in the living room, and there they laid him out, straightened the limbs, wrapped a shirt around what was left of his head. In the shed they cleaned up as best they could the human tissue clinging to the wood, the shovels, the old flower pots still filled with soil. They poured buckets of water on the blood stains. Only then did the two younger soldiers look through the old man's cupboards, and find the side of smoked bacon wrapped in brown paper, and the bottles of brandy underneath the sink, all of which they took with them.

# Ninety-Nine Percent of It

JONATHAN WAS IN THE PASSENGER seat as his girlfriend Tatiana attempted to park his Dodge Avenger into a narrow corner spot. Tatiana had passed her driving exam on the first try — this was last year — but Jonathan had always figured it was only because her examiner was a fellow Romanian. Now he heard the sound of a tire — it was the back right tire — grazing the curb; the front of the car was nosing to the left, and Tatiana suddenly erupted into laughter. She pushed the transmission into park and covered her cheeks with her hands while she laughed.

"Oh my goodness," she said, "my goodness, Jonathan, my driving is desperate."

She spread her hands to indicate the position of the car as proof. She said the *good* in *goodness* as if she were saying the German *gut*, with the same kind of flat "U". Jonathan noticed this flatness. He observed her small fleshy lips, the way her hands moved to her face, as they often did when she laughed — such things had endeared him once.

"You can park it Tet, just calm down."

"Thank God," she said, between hiccupping laughs, "that you are so serious, my love," and she petted his cheek, "so collected."

What became clear to Jonathan during this small incident was that he couldn't be with a woman like this. That what he wanted was a sensible woman. A woman who could park a car and shut up about it. He wanted this the way he wanted a cold drink after a long day in his humid, un-air-conditioned cubicle. In this moment everything about Tatiana — her translucent pale skin, her round head on that unusually thin neck, her dangling earrings, her long fingernails, indeed her very existence in the world — seemed to him impractical. He wanted a sturdy woman, head firmly in place, hair cut straight, comfortable shoes.

He knew that his model for this kind of woman was Shannon from his office. And it was Shannon he was thinking about as he walked hand in hand with Tatiana — having himself re-parked the car — towards their apartment. He thought of Shannon while listening to Tatiana's footsteps clucking along in the gravel, and to the *flop* sound as her foot, with each step, separated from the sole of her sandal.

It was Sunday, and she had picked him up from a day with his son Jack, almost seven years old.

"You know what he wants to start training in? Judo. And he's so smart, Tet; he loves math. He could beat his mother in math any day."

When they got upstairs Jonathan reheated a pork stew that Tatiana had cooked the day before. They ate and then watched television in bed, and Jonathan continued to eat crackers. Tatiana, facing half away from Jonathan toward the TV, threw back the cover at one point to reveal a pale thigh. Jonathan had to admit it was a lovely thigh, long and smooth, and he followed its outline all the way up to the ratty boy shorts she wore to bed, with their thinned out bottom. How is it that she was dressed so *intentionally* when going out, but would wear any old garbage to bed? Nonetheless, here was the thigh, a princely treasure gleaming white amid the rubble of vari-coloured cotton and fleece bedding. Some crumbs from the cracker he was eating fell on the thigh, but that didn't tarnish it. Thigh with cracker. He licked his finger to scoop them up.

Tatiana turned and tapped his hand, "Baby, I have an interview tomorrow. You know I'm nervous." He said, "It might be just the thing," though he didn't quite want sex either. She smiled, grabbed the duvet by its edge, in a sweep of her arm made the thigh disappear.

అఅఅ

Jonathan met Tatiana at a Romanian-organized dance party held at a Latino night club. She arrived like a picture out of a winter-wear catalogue — in a soft white coat, red-cheeked, with a glimmering silver scarf thrown heedlessly around the neck, dark curls spilling over everything. Only later he would see that it had taken her years of practice to look effortlessly put together. She was twenty-two, engaged, and had driven two-and-a-half hours, with friends, to come to this club. He was thirty and just divorced. He had a brief feeling of regret when he recognized that he was going to be in love again — so soon, when he wasn't even missing it yet.

They now lived on the edge of a freeway. The condominium development where they lived, paying off Jonathan's mortgage on a one-bedroom suite, was a block down from the five-lane throughway that became the main highway out of the city. Surrounding the road were large commercial parks — with boxy restaurants, gas stations, motels, a huge supermarket, a huge home-and-hardware store. Jonathan claimed it was a good location. But to get from one of those places to another meant walking across huge parking lots and, where there were no sidewalks, on the side of the road. So Tatiana didn't often walk to work, one of those boxy restaurants called Burt's Grill: there was the oddness of being the only pedestrian in sight, and a feeling approaching humiliation when she had to wait long minutes for the light to turn green as streams of cars drove on.

Burt's Grill, like many others, had a patio that filled up in the spring and summer with people in slacks, jeans, sports jerseys, all of them indulging in extravagantly described meals, sensitive to subtle shades of slights from their servers — a plate overlooked, a slightly sour tone. For view they had the slow movements of the parking lot, the pushing of carts, men fitting large boxes into backs of vans, trucks unloading at the warehouse entrance of the hardware store, the flow and stop, stop and flow of highway traffic. When she first moved, she had wanted them to live closer to the river, in the old part of the city. But he intuited that she was glad he owned something; at least he was not a divorced thirty year old with a kid and no property.

❧ ❧ ❧

158

"I don't know if I have the job. I think maybe I don't have it. I think the guy maybe didn't like me. Though he said I have everything they're looking for. At the end he said that. Jonathan?"

He was eating tomatoes on toast and reading the editorial columns of the paper.

"If he didn't like you, that's not good," he said. "Liking is ninety-nine percent of it. Ninety-nine point nine. But I'm sure he did like you."

"No, he didn't."

He felt a pang of regret for her insecurities, as if they were his own. Simultaneous with it was the yearning to be rid of this emotional participation in her small daily miseries.

When she did go to get dressed for her night shift, he could see her, from his vantage point of the kitchen counter, flitting between the bathroom and the bedroom. In the large hallway mirror she arranged her hair and put on lipstick. She wore all black — iridescent leggings, a narrow skirt, tight button-down shirt, long silver earrings. She was leaning into the mirror and patting the blush up toward her cheekbones, the heel of her one foot raised, as if she were about to take a step forward. From the bedroom window, the late afternoon light gave her figure a luminous outline, and he considered the fact that this is what he would be leaving — this lovely balancing woman, this vulnerable bird. He did it as a mental exercise, to see what he felt about that, to experience right now and thus expel any possible future regret.

That night he drove by Burt's Grill on his way out for drinks. Around the same time, after the dinner rush, Tatiana was standing next to the salad bar, in front of Charlie, the head cook. Charlie was saying, "I'm going to ask each of you individually: six side orders of garlic bread came through to the kitchen, and nine are gone from the stock. I counted them before the rush. So where did those three go?"

She didn't know.

"Food goes disappearing here," he said, "food goes disappearing at such an . . . an . . . " he searched for a word here, "a fucking *unprecedented* rate, that it has to boggle your brain; it has to make you go wonky, you know? No one has any respect." He said "respect" with a tone of bitter disappointment.

"Charlie's going to lose it one of these days," said Fran, another server, when they were doing their cash outs later that night. Tatiana didn't care at the moment that Charlie had been losing it for a long time, she simply wanted freckled, gap-toothed Charlie not to exist. Pleasant Fran was separating her coins into stacks. Tatiana was smoking and wishing to have Dara here instead of Fran — Dara was her best friend who now lived in Fredericton and was taking a master's degree in German literature. Dara moved east soon after Tatiana had moved west to live with Jonathan, and now a vast country lay between them. Jonathan didn't like to bring up the topic of Dara with Tatiana, since it always ended with her becoming moody, or angry at not having Dara nearby, and somehow, irrationally, her moodiness made him feel guilty.

Fran was now saying, "Do you know who came by here the other night? Remember Brian who used to work here? I love that guy."

Tatiana remembered him; they had once drunkenly run their tongues over each other's faces and hands under each other's clothes, by the bread shelves in the back of the kitchen, but it was nothing she ever thought about afterwards. She didn't know what else to say or to talk about with Fran, and they finished up and walked, separately, out into the breezy night.

Tatiana dreamed of work. The dreams were similar to one other, nightmares of impotency — for one reason or another she couldn't get to her tables or to the food orders that were getting crusty under heat lamps, and she always woke up without succeeding. As for Jonathan, if he had any problems with his work at a program for adults with mental disabilities, they had to do with relative boredom. His colleagues he mostly liked, but all the interactions with them had already plateaued at a kind of casual, impersonal, uninteresting friendship. There was only Tom, with whom he had worked for years and known since they were roommates — he and Tatiana now regularly got together with Tom and his wife Leanna.

But with his sudden awareness of Shannon — sudden, though they had worked together for months — workdays became a happy tally of his encounters with her. He had figured out long ago, through a particular half-moment's glance she once directed his way, that she was not indifferent to him. Her parents were part Dutch, part German, and part Scottish. She told him this among other things, and her face was inexpressive, her skin smooth, plump, and practically blank. He had never seen her frown and wondered if she even could. There was a neat, unimaginative elegance about her body and the way she dressed it. He wanted to see that body unclothed, if only to confirm that it was a perfectly straight-forward body, real and unpretentious.

He wanted to tell someone about her, and he'd been considering telling Tom. He also wanted to ask Tom about him and Leanna, how they tolerated each other, their sex and their guilt. They were drinking pints of beer that night with another friend, a client they had befriended long ago, Alejandro, who had lately been diagnosed with Aspergers syndrome. Jonathan and Tom liked him immensely. His condition gave a name to his lack of social graces: if they told him they liked his scarf, he might say, "It's ninety-two percent mohair and eight percent acrylic." Dark-haired, olive-skinned, Alejandro was not actually Spanish, but the son of a Bosnian mother with a Spanish obsession and an entirely absent father — Irish, going by the name on the records.

"Tom, you still like talking to your wife in bed? Or what?"

Tom just said, "Fuck off," but Alejandro stood up, rattling the table, and glared at Jonathan.

"I have to get out of here," he said. He waved his arms for Jonathan to get out of his way so he could leave the booth. Jonathan did. Alejandro was tall and scowling as they saw him walk out.

They drank more. After a fourth or so pint, Tom said, "The problem with love is that everything is a betrayal. Last week I was telling someone what I think about this deregulation at work, and Leanna was there, and at home she said, 'I never knew you thought about that, why don't you ever talk about things like that with me.' So we had a fight. You have a single independent thought and don't share it, it's a betrayal. It's like religion. You can't even covet."

They looked around the bar for women they might covet, but found none, at the moment.

Later that week, it was Tatiana's night off, and the two couples went out for dinner. While shuffling a crab leg on his plate, Jonathan thought about the ride home from work with Shannon, a few nights before: she had lingered while saying good night, and the lingering seemed to be about the need for a handshake, or hug, and in the indecision of the moment he had put his hand on her shoulder. He moved it and said, "Sorry. I guess I just wanted to touch you." It was an awkward thing to say; his guard had abandoned him.

"And your family, how are they?" Tom was saying to Tatiana. Jonathan didn't listen for the answer, for Tatiana's way of talking was familiar and uninteresting. He especially didn't want to hear more of her insights on cultural relativism: if he called their apartment small, she would say, "It's small, yes, but in Europe a middle-class family of five would live in it comfortably."

He winked at her, entirely from habit. He remembered the way the word "love" used to fill up his mouth and spill out; he could remember telling her that his mouth was full of the word, and the two of them marvelling at it together.

But the shells of the giant Alaskan crab legs strewn all over their table mocked him. "You sit here and indulge and reminisce when you should really be taking charge of your life," they said. He moved his beer glass and sent a shell of tail tumbling, grazing Tatiana's skirt, then falling to the floor. She gave him a familiar look, a combination of the quizzical "what was that about" look, and the "you're a clown" one. He bore her looks with practiced nonchalance. The butter from the shell had left a mark on her skirt, and he dabbed at it with a napkin and ice water from his glass, while she continued some story, and Tom and Leanna laughed at him.

∂∂∂

Shannon's body was just as he had imagined it, sturdy and somewhat athletic, but with a layer of womanly fat on all parts. The sex was not long, or spectacular, but the sound of her coming filled him with great, mysterious satisfaction. Shannon lived alone in a house, and she had a dog named Bessie and a cat named Stu; when she went to walk the dog, she wore sweatpants and an old dirty windbreaker. Jonathan still considered telling Tom about her, but was that a sensible or an insane idea?

That was mid-July; at month's end, when it was hotter than it had been the entire summer, Dara came for a visit. He was uncomfortable around this pale, dark-eyed woman and the way of talking and hand holding she and Tatiana shared. But he was relieved — Tatiana was preoccupied and that left him free, unseen, released from his guilt. A few times he even called Shannon from home. Jonathan Stewart, she said on the phone once, you're going to get yourself in trouble sneaking off to call me like this. There was that hint of complaint in her voice again, which troubled him. That night he repeated his mental exercise with Tatiana as he watched her, from the kitchen, sitting and reading on the edge of the bathroom sink. They were alone, briefly. He thought she was sad and waiting for him to notice. It didn't occur to him that she might not want to talk to him either.

A wall had stacked itself up brick by brick and Tatiana had no desire to climb to the top and see whether he was lurking on the other side. Through the bathroom door she could see him bent over the kitchen table. She wanted to remember him as he once was to her, when he was seemingly beyond her reach, older and assured, physically larger somehow, comforting, but provocative and fresh too — untainted, unlike now. Before him she had been with men whose mentalities were as familiar, as accessible, as any room in her own house. But mousy-haired Jonathan, slightly freckled, Protestant, seemingly plain in his tartan V-neck sweater, was outlandish. Had they pledged, formally, never to let each other become miserable, or was she projecting a thought and building it into a scene? There he was, flipping through a magazine, his expression different from the one she saw on his face last night: out front of the building, while he was having a cigarette and talking on his cell phone, turned just enough for her to see his face and its sheepish smile; then his hand running through his hair, his foot kicking at something on the ground, laughter. She kept reading now. He got up from the kitchen table, walked by the bathroom, threw her in passing a warm smile, and continued to the living room.

The morning Dara left, the two women woke up on the sofa, chilled, parts of their faces and shoulders creased with the pattern of the cushions they slept on. They had talked long enough into the night to hear the patterns of waking in the apartment below and the garbage trucks in the back alley.

They woke up sluggish, heavy, and afraid of their imminent parting. At the airport their embrace was compromised by Jonathan's impatience and the deafening urgency everywhere around them. Later, when Tatiana recalled the day, the catastrophe of it would seem to have begun with the heaviness of the morning and the spoiled goodbye, all part of what came later: that same afternoon Jonathan would leave the apartment and go to another one-bedroom suite on the other side of city, in a quite similar short and brown walk-up.

When he and Tatiana got home from the airport, she made them two cups of tea and said, maybe now we can talk. It was not exactly intuition that made her do it, but an idea that it was good to fight against inertia and try to communicate; she would rather have left it alone and spent the day and night looking for tiny reassurances in the way he made lunch, looked at her, lay next to her. Instead she was met with Jonathan's frighteningly serious face.

"God, Tatiana, I'm sorry. I'm just not happy anymore."

"Maybe you're not the only one." Not till an hour later did she bring herself to ask if he had someone. Their tea mugs were half full when he got up to go. He took his old school backpack and she watched him start to fill it with razors, shaving cream — but then he seemed to give up and simply pulled taut the string on it, and stood in front of her.

When she was alone in the apartment, the place became eerie because it had stayed the same. Hours of solitary thinking while sitting at the kitchen table produced this: she was not sure that she still wanted him, but she wanted to have the chance to decide for herself. She took a walk, first along their street, then across the freeway, past all the large stores, and stopped near an elementary school. She sat on the ground beside the fence. A few years earlier she had disappointed *everyone* by breaking off her engagement, but she had not been afraid — not of loneliness, joblessness, boredom. All her life she had felt mysteriously inferior to everyone else; but when she fell in love with Jonathan and applied herself to making that love possible, she felt suddenly lifted to the level of other, worthy human beings. Now her own optimistic younger self seemed a fool.

When she returned home, her heart was beating fast because walking alone she had become afraid — of nothing in particular, only perhaps a hollering that came from nowhere, figures far away on the other side of the street. The living room gaped at her, the windows looked out to indifferent trees, the human sounds in the building were of people she didn't know. The apartment was cool and she found there was no heat coming out of the vents. He had driven off in the car, but had left behind so much — his laptop, stereo, a CD collection that took up half a wall. Golf clubs passed down from his stepdad, an Irishman whom he revered. It was silly that she was here with all this stuff; she would call him, tell him that they should talk like two sensible people, objectively. She dialed his cell phone but he didn't answer, and she eventually fell asleep waiting for the call back.

When she woke up, something was different. She began going through his things. In the jacket of an old psychology textbook she found a small photograph, taken in a photobooth, of Jonathan and an orange-haired, big-eyed woman. Was it Jonathan in younger days? The poor quality of the picture made it hard to tell. She put the picture aside. It was almost four in the morning. She took the golf clubs down to the garbage, wrapped in a quilt. She shoved them as far as she could beyond reach.

෯෯෯

Only weeks later, Jonathan was surprised at how much claim Shannon had already made on him. Much more than Tatiana had at that stage. When he showed up at her door, Shannon jumped up and down in delight. The moment brought to his mind the fortuitousness of the coincidence — that she wanted him, too. He told Tom, sitting on the corner of his desk. After work that day he talked to Bessie the dog: "you still like me, right, you big mutt," he said while shaking Bessie's big ears. He was happy to walk the dog, and to talk to her.

With time people from work began to invite him and Shannon to potlucks, to hockey games watched in pubs, barbecues. He knew that Tatiana had been the barrier; at most get togethers she asked the wrong questions, laughed when others nodded solemnly. At the last barbecue they went to she had made a minor production of eating her steak off a paper plate, so that finally the hostess apologized and brought her a kitchen plate; and later, sitting next to the campfire in the backyard, curled tightly into herself, she had looked so caught and bewildered, so oppressed by smoke and mosquitoes from which she occasionally tried to escape with swats and turns, that he did the obvious thing and invented an excuse for them to leave.

On a day in late November as he was leaving work, Margaret, one of the older clients, said to him, "I know how you look at me." And she smiled in a derisive, crooked sort of way. He had often been a little unfriendly with Margaret, for she could give him a hooded sidelong glance so full of animosity that he felt he could not, within the scope of his own sanity, respond to it with a smile. "I know what you think of me," she repeated, and he said, "Sure, Margaret, I know you do." And he made a face at himself in the glass of the doors as he turned, adjusting his collar, to walk out. He didn't think there was much room for self-awareness in people like Margaret, but while steering the old Dodge, he started thinking about his coldness and whether it had actually affected her.

When he got home, Shannon was re-reading Jean Vanier's *Becoming Human*. She was splayed on the couch in a childish sort of way, and she sat up and stretched when he came into the living room.

"I'm really enthusiastic about this book," she said, and then, "Jonathan, I'm so happy when you come home." And she took him into a kind of tight, almost wrestling embrace. Her optimism was, to him, something harmless, if inexplicable, like his mother's collecting of decorative plates.

"Well, you don't say, Shanny," he said while he pinched her and rubbed her head with a knuckle.

"Sometimes," she said, "sometimes it's like you think I'm just saying cute things. Like, 'look at little Shannon reading a book, isn't that cute?'"

"Oh, Shanny," he said, "I just love you."

Months after he left Tatiana, there was still the matter of the apartment to be settled. He had told her to stay until she found something, and she had said she would leave as soon as. But fall became winter and even with the sporadic heat she had in the flat, she didn't move. Jonathan ran into her one afternoon, close to Christmas, at the new Italian supermarket that had opened nearby. For weeks he had made a habit of going there after work and sitting at the little café in the corner. He saw her in the bakery aisle gazing at the cakes under the glass; her hair had grown out, but otherwise she looked just the same. She agreed to sit down for a coffee. In the mostly empty café, he was suddenly self-conscious, afraid of being overheard while sounding banal. She was polite. She asked him how work was.

"There was re-organization. They cut some branches, and we're unloading clients. Unloading employees, for that matter. It has to do with cost-effectiveness." Cost-effectiveness was an inside joke between them. They applied it indiscriminately and inaccurately to refer to arrogance, hypocrisy, hot air.

"Yeah, Leanna mentioned something."

"Oh. Well there is a man I believe responsible, Tom does too. But the man is a nice man, and so Shannon disagrees with me. She — she believes in goodness, and she believes in belief. You know?"

He thought that yes, she knew, she just wasn't biting. She looked away when he said Shannon's name. But he had been seriously disturbed and he wanted Tatiana to see that. He was disturbed because he could no longer keep work at work; it crept into his life and his pleasures; his dreams filled up with Margaret's cold stares, with himself looking like Alejandro and then convincing himself he was still dreaming and waking again and again, until he woke into reality in which he was finally himself. Tom was acting a little distant, too busy, passive-aggressive perhaps, and that offended Jonathan. Alejandro wasn't answering his phone calls, and Jonathan thought obsessively about the arc of that friendship, the slow and hopeful beginning, how he and Tom had prized all the gestures of communication and intimacy, and now, how cruel the shutting out seemed.

He was disturbed because he was lonely next to Shannon's sunniness, depressed by her relentless optimism. He had tried; he had sat, open palmed, patient, keeping his tone of voice even, reminding himself that he loved her, and he tried to tell her things as he saw them, supported by obvious facts and logical connections. But she had refuted him, told him not to patronize her, and finally that they would have to agree to disagree, which he couldn't do. "Look," she had said, "I refuse to see the world this way. Don't you see how poisonous it is to be cynical?" He had seen, to his dismay, how proud she was of her stance; her refusal to see what he knew to be the dark truth was to her a mark of integrity.

The person who would understand his dismay was, of course, Tatiana.

"I'm thinking of quitting," he said. "I might be managed out anyway. And you, how are you?"

"I might move. We have to figure out the apartment before I go, I mean, you have to pay me out."

"You already have a number, am I right?"

"And you should know there is a problem with the pipes. The heat comes and goes."

"Since when?"

"Since you left, actually. Do you know who came by? Your friend Alejandro. Didn't you tell him you moved?"

"We don't talk much about personal things. When did he come by?"

"Last month sometime. He brought over some CD for you. I tried to invite him in."

"You probably shouldn't have bothered," he said.

Tatiana looked around; she had to get back, for she had promised someone to be home when they called. She was giving English instructions to a graduate student from Finland, the recipient of a number of scholarships in the area of plant biology. She had let him into her bed once, and unleashed, she now feared, a growing affection on his part that she didn't know what to do with. He was a tall bulk of a man, with sharp, angled features, not the chubby, doughy look she expected of Nordic peoples. His English was really very good. The familiarity of Jonathan suddenly made her embarrassed about the Nordic giant. She put her few things together and got up.

"So I'll call you with the number. No, I'll email you. The sum shouldn't be a problem, right?"

"But where are you moving to?"

"It won't be just yet," she said. She sat back down. "Maybe back home to Constanta. But there are other options." She was faced with the difficulty of finding the right, or an easy, manner of speaking with Jonathan. The difficulty of fending off dread.

"Wow," he said, "wow. I can't imagine you being gone."

"What's wrong with you?" she said. She got up again and in a moment he saw her through the store windows taking a minute to adjust her scarf, carefully, to pull on gloves, before setting off in a brisk, characteristic trot.

❧❧❧

"Well you won't really pay her whatever she asks for?" Shannon said. "No, no, no, Jonathan, that doesn't make sense."

"I'm just going to pay her out. She'll only ask for what she put into the mortgage."

"Well I think we should come up with our own number, that's all. Is that okay?"

"Do you want to come up with a number? In fact, why not ballpark it. Throw out a number — how much do you want to give her?"

"Fuck you Jonathan," she said, and began to laugh. "We could have been living there for the past, two, no, three, months."

They were walking Bessie in the park that stretched on the edge of the little complex of walk-ups, a park similar to tens — hundreds? Jonathan ventured — of others around the city. Shannon carried her usual paraphernalia — little shovel, plastic glove and plastic bag. She bent over and did the work, without a shadow of a grudge, and as she did it she looked inelegant, like an oversized child collecting rocks.

When Jonathan walked Bessie by himself, he took along the tools but never actually picked anything up. He pictured Tatiana in his apartment, alone, overcoming despair to make some move in life — he saw it clearly, and with certainty, and felt acute pity. My pre-emptive exercises have failed, he thought. Here I am, prey to regret. That mock-theatrical talk was his and Tatiana's too. He wanted to tell her, right now, about seeing her in the mirror and exorcising her out of himself.

The truth was that Tatiana had no immediate plans to move anywhere. Only, she had applied for jobs in Ottawa, Winnipeg, Montreal. Her Finnish giant said he would be sad to lose his talented instructor. Aside from his physical beauty, he was sharp and thoughtful. He answered questions with consideration, and he had good manners — he knew how to absolve people in awkward situations. Tatiana saw this fine skill wasted on people who didn't notice they were being done a favour, who mistook grace for naïveté or even weakness. He was forgiving of stupidity, rudeness, of getting overlooked in a restaurant. He lived in a bright lovely flat near the university, which he filled with plants, including a ceiling-high rubber tree, and striking colour studies on the walls. She wondered where the money came from. He liked to drink sweet wines and ports.

They laughed a lot; she would miss having people to laugh with. He said, "People are nice here, but friends is different. They are not your friends very fast. But you, you're different." For a while before she was introduced to him, she had kept the phone ringer off and detested the blink of the answering machine. Though Dara considered Jonathan a jerk for the way he'd left, Tatiana didn't really, not any more. The fact was that Jonathan no longer wanted her, and everything else — the shocking speed of the thing, the mid-afternoon exit — was aesthetics.

∽∽∽

In January Jonathan brought over an electric heater, and an envelope. Inside the envelope was a paper with a number written on it.

"I'd like us to be, if possible, on good terms," he said. In answer she said, smiling, "Impotent overpowering rage." It was easier to talk now. The expectations they had built up of each other and tried to play along with were laughable, she saw. They'd built a beast that was now deflated, a clown with his face off.

She was plugging in the heater, on her knees, her back long.

"Oh, Tet, what a waste."

The imbalance she was seeing in him she'd never seen before. They sat on the bed, their movements suggesting sex, yet she, at least, didn't really intend it. Regardless, her shirt was up around her armpits and his leg between her legs.

He said, "I quit, did you know that? I wasn't just saying it that time. I'm free." She asked why, while running a knuckle over the bumps of his spine.

"She couldn't understand, you know? We had a big row. Her cheerful blindness is impenetrable. You know Alejandro, right? He tried to kill himself again. And so finally I thought, there's nothing you can do for people like that. I said that to Shannon, there's nothing you can do, or if there is, at least you cannot love them, you can't become invested in them. She said that's an awful thing to say. She took it very seriously, but so did I. You can never get back what you put in."

"I said that," Tatiana said, "It was me who said that to you." He had her calf in his hand. He said, "You shouldn't move. Please." His eyes were closed and she didn't know if he meant move her leg from his grasp, or move away from the apartment and the city. She was holding on to his shoulder blade, as he pressed his forehead to her neck. The phone rang, and in a moment the voice of Olli, the Finn, filled the room. She was supposed to be at his place right now and he was inquiring what had happened. He sounded serious and even pedantic; they laughed.

"Where the fuck did you find *him?*" Jonathan said.

But when their laughter quieted, she wanted to defend him, say Olli Jokinen had a better sense of humour than Jonathan himself.

"Others?" he said.

"Never," she lied.

"There were for me," he said, and she answered that she knew.

That night Tatiana lay on him so lightly, slightly sweaty, her hair matted to his arm. He thought of Shannon, the sex they had the night before, her white straight-forward body, her breathiness, soft moaning. He didn't like breathiness, didn't like to see people with their eyes closed and mouth open, getting lost in ecstasy, like evangelists, born-again Christians, madmen.

Light from a streetlamp outside the window fell on Tatiana's midsection. He thought of her saying, "All my life I've felt inferior to everyone." They'd been in this same room when she said it, just days after he'd moved to Shannon's apartment and come back here to talk. He had thought, why say that? It invites cruelty; it will grind the last bit of love right into this fake hardwood. He had miscalculated. He had once thought that he could, he would, stay with his wife, no matter what, forever if necessary, just never to be separated from his boy. He had believed Tatiana without a second's doubt when she said she didn't care how her family would react when she dropped her almost fiancée and moved. He'd been wrong so many times. Tatiana didn't stir, began to snore lightly, with mouth half open. The light on her stomach wavered and went out.

He'd lived in this place for some five years, but the lives of the neighbours were a blank. Maybe some of them lay awake right now too; some must be suffering. He tried to estimate the size of the mountain he would have to climb to be with Tatiana; no, he tried to convince himself, for the sake of being sensible, that there *was* a mountain to climb — in the moment it seemed to him that the path to her was an open plain.

The light came on again, tittered, and stayed. Answer me, he projected silently to her body, tell me what's better. His boy was apparently happy, very amiable, with good grades. He practised judo, and like so many other Canadian boys, rich or poor, he collected hockey cards. Jonathan could not be certain of anything.

The light went off again, then on; perhaps it was what woke Tatiana. She opened her eyes, and closed them. It was what he liked about her: she could let things be, did not demand. She suppressed, that was a joke between them. She didn't think she was owed anything, and she didn't think she was God's special creature. He'd derided Shannon, once, when they fought, for saying that. What was Shannon doing now? He thought of the irrepressible want that had led him to her: it troubled him that the symptoms are always the same. It meant he was vulnerable to sensations that he could not control; it meant that danger of being swept up again lurked everywhere.

He put his hand on Tatiana's cheek; when he moved it, she opened her eyes again, and he sat up a little.

"Can I come back in the morning?" he asked.

"Do," she said.

So he faced Shannon that very night: what surprised him, at first, about Shannon's reaction, was the shock. Why would you find it so unlikely, he asked her, finding his own anger, doesn't it happen all the time? She sent him out, he could barely put his shoes on, she was calling him names even as he walked down the stairs. He went back to Tatiana, and it was weeks before Shannon even let him back in for his clothes.

෨෨෨

Weeks later Tatiana would still be having dreams of him and other women, of the sort she'd had before. Talking should have helped, but the dreams were a barrier between them, a taboo. In the mornings he asked, with trepidation and anxiety, in a humble and casual voice, how she slept. Sometimes she admitted the dreams, and if she didn't, that left him interpreting her face and discovering with dread that she was lying. Other times he didn't ask but noted the unfocused look in her eyes, her heavy movements. He could be relieved only when she was visibly happy, when she woke with bright eyes, silliness, playful kisses. Her happiness wielded a power over him against which he seemed to have no defences. He was still not working, and they were always waking together, eating cereal and bagels, reading, migrating around the apartment. When the heat was out they would spend the day cooking, going out for walks, or sitting in diners. She worked only three shifts a week. Something would have to be done eventually, something concrete that made money. Sometimes they drove somewhere to go walking: the arts district, campus, or neighbourhoods in which they could admire unusual houses and old trees.

Olli dropped out of Tatiana's life, without her registering his disappointment. For weeks she kept meaning to call him again, in the same way that she kept meaning to steam-clean the carpet or look up people with whom she used to ride in a car for hours just to get to a party. When they were out walking on campus once, they saw Olli with a small Japanese girl. He looked at Tatiana and looked away.

"Hey, guess who that is," she said to Jonathan; it was better like that, to make light of it.

The winter was long and snow was abundant; the side streets and alleys did not get cleared, and everywhere were small hills of hard-packed snow, and deep grooves that hopelessly trapped cars. In February the Dodge broke down. They talked to hardly anyone but each other. Tatiana called Dara on the phone; she hung out with Fran after work only rarely; she remembered Olli's airy apartment, the fine ports, the light curvy glasses, his solid tall body. Looking around for a job was difficult; it meant packaging all of her self into a foreign object, using the right "key" words. In February she worked for an upscale women's clothing store and was fired within the month; she could not make a sale, was told she lacked the right spirit. She was fairly used to this kind of failure; she was glad that she wasn't going home to an empty apartment — it was a cold apartment, but at least occupied by someone other than herself.

The end of March was still bitterly cold. Jonathan got off the bus after a twelve-hour shift at his new, temporary job in a group home. There was a person inside the bus shelter, cowering under blankets. Cutting across the parking lot of the supermarket, he watched a woman try to shove a boy into his parka, bending his arm so forcefully that the boy started to lose his balance, and she shook him straight. Stupid bitch, Jonathan thought.

"Hey," he yelled, "keep your abuse at home." But he was far enough from her that she turned only in a cursory way toward the voice.

"Yeah, you," he yelled again, but it already felt like he was yelling into his own private tunnel. The boy got shoved inside the car to be taken to some miserable home, which he would learn to love and hate and would handicap him for the rest of his life. Jonathan heard the slam of the car door as a lid closing on a fate.

The sidewalk was freshly snowed in and a man was pushing a shopping cart with his belongings right on the road, causing a backup in the lane. The man was walking with long strides and an indifferent expression. The cars drove slowly along until the man turned away into a motel's driveway; no one honked. Assholes, Jonathan thought anyway. He was fed up with being cold. When he got home he found Tatiana boiling water on the stove, the oven turned on with its door open, and the portable heater in the living room on high. Once again he undressed in a freezing bedroom, and layered on two sweaters.

"So that asshole still hasn't fixed things," he said, coming out of the bedroom.

"Nope," she said, looking up from the chest of drawers she seemed to have just finished assembling, a screwdriver still in her hand. "He was here, though, doing more fiddling. Said they're waiting for the other plumber."

"He came to stare at you some more. The guy's a creep." She didn't respond. She stood the drawers up and began to push them toward a wall space next to the couch.

"Just let me do it," Jonathan said as he reached for them.

"Don't touch me. I mean don't touch them." She looked straight ahead and he backed off; he watched her strain, lift a little, then push, her fingers white from the effort. Skinny, dangly, emotional, she had put together a whole chest of drawers, had used all sources of heat, had probably even gotten up the nerve to talk to the creepy condo board president about their new condo fees; he saw she had done all this, and tidied up the house, and put out snacks and tea, and proofread an essay about German Romanticism that Dara had emailed her. She had done all this, his poor Tatiana, and he never gave her any credit for things. He knew it was a battle for her and she was battling uphill. She was suffering for each small thing, while he, he only cared for his dark moods. He trampled everything with his callous remarks, gave her nightmares and insomnia. Even with these perceptions he could only stand there feeling his heart melt in this cold room. His Tet, his dear Tet, if only he could make it up to her. The chest of drawers now in its place against the wall, she sat down on the floor and bit into a pastry. Her frown was gone, and she looked at him with a blank expression.

"I got a job," she said, "if — if I'm willing to move to Montreal by May first. I'd applied a long time ago. Assistant manager of a new magazine. I want to do it."

He sat in the lounging chair opposite her.

"I'm gonna do it," she said, "you can come with me or not come with me."

"I'll come," he said. She was afraid of this, him saying yes immediately. In his head he began to think about flights from here to there, how often he would be able to afford to visit his son or to bring him out there.

"Why did you put together the chest if we're going to be leaving?"

She snorted. "It helped me to think."

Her pastry was excessively, deliciously sweet, and Jonathan was watching her chew it. She thought, they would have to work on it, after all.

"Are you glad, Tet? I just want you to be happy. Of course I'll go with you." He didn't know if she could see the anxiety in his face, but he felt it keenly.

"I am — " she shrugged, "I am resigned to my fate."

"You poor sad maiden."

Despite these phrases that were familiar to both of them, he wondered — maybe she had thoughts he wouldn't even imagine. He remembered what she'd told him, about that waiter at Burt's Grill, how easily she let it happen. How eagerly perhaps.

"I want us to make each other happy," he said. There was the sound of water running through pipes. In his mind, he prayed, to no particular deity, that it would all come out all right.

# Peanuts

THIS MORNING THE SATELLITE GUY is at our house. He is young, tall, modestly good looking. After I lead him into the living room, my daughter Amanda brings him in a Coke. I see him do a double take at her, and then steal another glance as she walks away. This isn't out of the ordinary, of course — my daughter is an unusual beauty. I kind of wished she would give him a second glance or sit in the living room and chat with him. I could picture her rather well with a guy like this. But she's not terribly talkative with strangers.

Now, people say Amanda looks like me. And she does — but there is a difference between nice looking and gorgeous, although it's hard to say where precisely that difference lies. Amanda looks a little bit like me and a little bit like my sister Grace, and yet Grace is quite plain, I'm pretty, and Amanda is stunning. If you catch sight of her in half profile, there is something extraordinary about the angle of her jaw and the elongated cheek. Her grey eyes aren't big, but they're wide, and above them sit two perfectly straight, long eyebrows. If you looked at it simply mathematically, you might say her face is too long, but I think most real beauties have something appealingly incongruous about their face. The resemblance between us reminds me of a picture I saw once, of a supermodel and her three sisters, just an impromptu photo, and in it all the women looked quite a bit alike, had the same straight noses and the same wide eyes, and yet only one was beautiful.

Just as the satellite guy is packing up in the living room, Amanda does in fact walk in and give him a big, wide smile. It is this spontaneous, genuine smile that she's had since childhood, which often, like today, makes me well up with affection for her. And just as the guy leaves, Dan arrives from work. He's carrying files under his arm, and his step is light but a little tired. My husband still looks youthful, but sometimes I think he's getting some old-man habits. Every day when he gets home from work, he goes upstairs briefly, washes up but doesn't change, just takes off his watch, his tie, changes his socks, and comes back down and pours a little glass full of whisky. Then he sits in the middle of the sofa with his feet up on the stool, sighs a little bit, and this serene half-smile hangs about his lips.

Dan has also started cooking and collecting recipes from the *Canadian Living* magazine. He watches — well, we watch — travel shows and cooking shows, and we make note of not only recipes but drink mixes and all-natural skin treatments and detoxifying vegetable juices. Today Dan kisses me fully on the lips and smells my hair, and I pat his hip. Once he's settled in on the sofa, I bring my coffee with me, curl up next to him, and he calls me love and asks what I did today. He calls Amanda over too, and she sits on the other side of him, and they proceed to talk sweet nonsense to each other, rub noses, squeeze each other's kneecaps. He then turns to me with a look that seems not only serene but wistful. In a few minutes Amanda is up, off to begin the elaborate process of getting ready for a night out, which will leave the bathroom moist and fragrant and the doorknobs greasy with lotion. And Amanda too will become moist and fragrant, and flushed and sparkling. It can be my favourite part of the night, to see her bounce down the stairs, all made up like that, and then bounce back up because she's forgotten something, and then down again, and so on. Regularly Dan and I forget whatever it is we're watching on television and just marvel at our own daughter.

I have to say, however, that the guys she goes out with are hardly as interesting as you might imagine for a girl like her. And she seems to date casually, a few months with this boy, a few weeks with another. Without fail they are polite little men, and very stylish either in a teenage kind of way, or in an imitation of the young professionals. Most of them have highlights in their hair, blond or honey-brown, and they wear well-tailored suit jackets and square-toed shoes. Inevitably, as I open the door, there is the young man saying, "Good evening, Mrs. Reikson," and leaning in to shake my hand. They are all like that, eager to make a good impression. Often they bring a bottle of wine, and try to make amusing comments about the traffic or the weather or the design of our house, which, to be fair, is indeed a marvel, architecturally speaking, even among the other well-built houses on our block. Tonight, though, it's Amanda's girlfriend Talia ringing the doorbell. Amanda emerges from the kitchen, a big yellow pear stuck in her mouth as she's using both hands to button up her jacket. She waves goodbye, they leave, and

Dan and I go upstairs before coming back down to watch television.

I read somewhere that people don't age gradually, but in spans: every seven years or so all our cells replace themselves. Apart from that, it's amazing to me that a person goes from infancy to old age, yet every day wakes up looking the same — each morning the same person in the mirror, yet suddenly that person is middle-aged, then old. No wonder it takes us by surprise. But I also think there must be a point in everyone's life when they first realize they are aging. When I was about twenty-two or -three, Grace and I were on vacation on the West Coast. We were trying on bathing suits, and I remember looking at her body — a body I knew well — and seeing that it would pass into a different stage. She was a splendidly built girl, tall and long-legged, with these small, fragile shoulders, little breasts, a long neck, and thin arms. She was all like that, slim and long, but not sharp or muscular anywhere, just round and elongated. But that time I could see how her tummy would eventually round out, her breasts come to look even smaller, how her thighs would get heavy, and she would become something else. And as I saw her body pass into another stage, so I saw, of course, my own body as one in transition.

Dan cuddles with me until about midnight. I stay up watching a travel show on the Outdoor Network. I'm wearing my embroidered silk robe, my favourite, and thick thermal socks, and I'm as comfortable as one can be. I've finished a glass of steamed milk, and I feel myself finally drifting toward sleep. The clock is showing ten after two in the morning. The narrating traveller on the TV is now in

Nepal, attending a wedding of one bride to four brothers. Does this really happen, I wonder, and then I don't care anymore. I turn off the television. Just then I hear a car out front, and I peek through the half-open curtain to see it stop on the sidewalk and Amanda get out of the passenger seat. As I'm walking to the kitchen it occurs to me that Talia's car is a different model. When Amanda walks in, she is surprised to see me — I'm hardly ever up when she gets home. I ask drowsily how her night was. She looks rather drowsy herself. Her eyes have lost all their makeup, her lids are sitting low, and her cheeks look puffy, like after a nap. On a second look I realize she is missing an earring. For a moment I'm struck by the splendidness of this sight, my daughter tired, disheveled and caught off guard. In fact, I feel like hugging her. But I don't want to ambush her; instead, on an impulse, I ask, "Who was that who dropped you off?" But I instantly regret prolonging her discomfort. It's clear she just wants to go upstairs.

"Huh? We ran into some people from school, that's all."

Amanda isn't prone to lying by any stretch, and when she does it she looks positively embarrassed. She gets a little frown between her eyebrows. I wish her goodnight and walk up the stairs without looking back down.

The next Friday Dan comes home from work late.

"There's just a bit of trouble at work," he says. He beats the armrest with an open palm while mouthing the words: "trouble." He is an executive assistant at a public relations firm — a small company, as far as their type goes, but quite successful. Dan's been with them for fourteen years. Every so often he comes home with "a bit of trouble." He tells me, rather disconnectedly, about a questionable contract, a minor one, and a client concerned over conflict of interest — "So?" I ask.

"So nothing," he says.

I make him take off his tie, and fix him a drink, since he refuses to eat. We watch television.

"Millie," he says after a while, "this place needs dusting." He swipes a finger alongside the leg of the coffee table. Little things irritate him when he's got a bigger problem on his mind.

By the end of next week, Dan tells me they've ordered an independent investigation into the bungled account. This hasn't happened to him before, as far as I know. When Amanda comes home from her dance lesson — her dark hair all windblown, her cheeks pink, stunning even in her white windbreaker — we sit in the living room, the three of us, the TV on but the sound low, and actually we all drink, even Amanda, and we talk sporadically, cautiously about Dan's situation. Dan drinks bourbon, and Amanda and I gin with cranberry juice. The small assortment of bottles sits on the table and we keep refilling as we please. We don't have supper, except for the mixed nuts that always sit on the table and some crackers with cream cheese that Amanda brings in at one point. Finally, around ten o'clock — I don't even know where the time's gone — we all get thirsty, and after going to the kitchen for water Dan decides he'll go up to bed. He pulls on my earlobes, kisses me. I say I'll be right up.

The next day the article comes out in the local *Announcer*, a long column on the second-last page of the business section: "Shock, controversy at Beiland Inc." And underneath it,

"Several middle level executives may face suspension or charges". Dan's name is not on that list, but it is mentioned below, followed by "implicated."

"It was bound to be written about," I say as we're sitting across from each other that afternoon. He's rather intently staring into space.

"Of course," he says, with a little frown, as if annoyed that I've interrupted a reverie. "But I wouldn't have thought it." He looks up at me — is it wistfulness, this expression? — then looks around the kitchen, pausing at each corner, as if it weren't in fact his own kitchen.

"If I could go back in time," he says, and laughs, the laughter issuing from behind his hands as they cover his face. I get him to put his head in my lap. He pretends to resist, and we have a mock tug-of-war. I call him my boy, my skinny boy, too skinny to marry, like my mother used to say. I call him my love and my life sentence. Amanda comes home from school and she looks to be in a dark mood too. But I let it go.

The weekend passes slowly. We don't do anything. The tickets we had for the ballet on Saturday we give away at the last minute. Dan says he has no patience for sitting still for two-and-a-half hours. The phone seems to be ringing constantly, until we just shut off the ringer. There are messages that I don't care to listen to. One is from Grace: "Millie — and Dan, I was hoping to," she begins, but I cut it off without listening to the rest. On Sunday, neither of us leaves the house. We don't get dressed, and we listen to old records. We dance a little bit around the coffee table, getting tangled in our housecoats. We drink. By the time night falls we are drunk and impenetrable.

On Monday, Amanda is home early from school. I'm cooking some frittatas and thinking about the ballet on Saturday. I can't believe we gave the tickets away to the Van Tiers from across the street. The same people who call us only immediately before and after asking for a favour. The same Beatrice Van Tier who called me this morning — two days later — to say they loved it, what a stunning performance, and then cut me off with, "Sorry I can't chat, dear, I got some people on the way." I wish now that I had ripped the tickets into little pieces and swallowed them, rather than given them to that smug bitch. But I hadn't, so here we are now. Amanda sits down on the stool at the breakfast nook and picks at the corners of my frittatas. She thinks we should go do something, she and I, get out of the house for a bit, do some shopping. My car is at the dealer's, I tell her, but she says we can take the bus. I look outside through the window.

"It's warm out," Amanda says. "Just a little muggy."

But it's not the weather I'm evaluating, not quite. I would prefer to be home when Dan gets back from work. Instead we leave him a message on his voice mail. "Amanda and I are jumping ship. Remember us with love. Or call my cell if you need us."

We walk a block to the bus stop — Amanda wants to go to the thrift store.

"Are you actually going to buy anything here?" I ask her as the bus lurches to a stop.

"I always do," she says, though that's news to me. Inside, the store is bustling, which is explained by the big cardboard signs that say fifty percent off. We move in the narrow space between the overstuffed rows of clothing. I think about last night; Dan wanted to talk in bed for a long time. We ate a huge supper of veal, late, and I think it kept us up. What Dan wanted to talk about, mostly, was stuff from the past. About the time when I worked as a waitress in a little diner, how he would sit around until closing time, and then count my cash while I cleaned the kitchen.

The whole time as Amanda and I move from section to section, women's clothing, men's clothing, housewares, there is a very fat young woman in front of us, with small feet in thin cotton runners, wearing tights, and wheeling a big cart. She coos to her little child, whose little socked feet are hanging from the seat in the cart. After we have been here almost an hour, I can't stand to look at her anymore, nor at the rows of old shoes — they are too pathetic. But then I see the toy section and think that perhaps the saddest things are the little bags of goodies: old cloth dolls, and Barbies, and colouring books, maybe a Rubik's cube, stuffed inside clear plastic bags stapled shut.

"We should go," I say to Amanda, "it's going to rain."

Through the store windows I can see the overcast sky. We get into one of the lineups — they're both easily twenty people long. Finally, at the till, the man wearing the orange store vest smiles widely at Amanda.

"Hello, stranger," he nearly sings. She turns to me.

"Oh, Mom, this is Earl," and to him, "this is my mom."

I shake Earl's extended hand. He says, "Good to meet you." He greets me as if it's the commonest thing for him to be introduced to customers while working his cash in the middle of a sale rush.

"Found some nice things, did you," he says as he folds Amanda's shirts into a plastic bag. He smiles at me as I hand him money.

"I'll see you," Amanda says to him, as we're leaving the store. I can't help but throw a second glance at Earl, which only confirms what I already caught of him — a shortish figure in his late twenties, a round face framed by short black hair and a cropped beard. Outside it's steadily drizzling.

"A friend of yours?" I say.

"Yeah," she says.

It's only when we get off the bus and are walking toward the house in darkness, that Amanda stops. We're both wet by now; I can see our house a little further down, and the lights are on inside it. Amanda has put her hood on, she is sniffling, and there are smudges around her eyes.

"The thing is. The thing is, Mom, I think I'm in love." She rubs her nose a little.

"With Earl," she then says, and with her thumb points to the direction we've just come from. I half expect this Earl to materialize in the light of the streetlamp and stand waiting for my response. Instead there's just the sound of rain, a car driving down the next block, and my fallen-in-love daughter standing at the edge of a puddle. Of course, I think. It seems perfectly clear, and yet I don't understand it.

"Mom?"

"Who *is* Earl?" I say. She looks confused. Confused and somehow annoyingly apprehensive.

"I mean, who is he? Is he your boyfriend? Where did you find him?"

Her face changes, closes up. "I met him at a friend's house. He's thirty-two. Years old. But I love him."

Well then. "And for how long have you loved this Earl?"

"Kind of a long time now. Almost five months."

I don't know what else to say. I take her hand and lead her, in a sense, toward the house. She's silent. I want to say something else, perhaps something nice, but I don't have it in me.

Inside, I leave her in the hallway unzipping her jacket, and call out to Dan. The lights are on in the kitchen and living room, but he's not in either. I go upstairs. In the bedroom, he is on his knees in front of the walk-in closet. All around him there are boxes, and papers — stacks of them — and unopened photo albums, and sweaters, and computer disks. I spot the familiar glint of the purple-glass key chain attached to the safe key, though the room divider in front of the actual safe seems untouched. To my left, on the thick, ecru-coloured, imported rug, is a large stain, its edges peeking out from underneath more sheets of paper. The duvet is crumpled on the floor beside the bed.

"What are you doing?" I say when he looks up at me.

"What? I'm looking for something. The miracle that will prove me innocent. And the thing — don't step in that, babe, I spilled some whisky." All the while he is eyeing the things around him and moving them slightly.

"You know what really chokes me, Millie, in the end? That it's just peanuts, you know, I mean, all this, for what? Peanuts."

"All which?" I say. When he was much younger, Dan used to sit like he's doing now, kneeling with his legs spread open.

He leans forward then, so far that he digs his forehead into the carpet. His hands are still at his side.

"And how was your day, dear?" he asks then, from his hole in the sand.

"It was fine," I say, and I bring myself down to sit on my haunches too.

"A strange night, maybe. Dan — " I extend my hand and lean in his direction.

"Where's Amanda?"

Amanda is in a world in which five months is a long time, I want to say. Amanda is in love. But I don't say either just then.

"She's here," I say instead, just as I start to crawl toward him. And indeed, we both look up then to see her standing in the doorway.

# Barcelona

OVER THE LAST TWO WEEKS, Amanda has been moving her things into a spare guest room down the hall from her and Earl's bedroom. She now spends more time there than anywhere else in the house. So far she's moved only a few books, her laptop, some underwear and pyjamas, but the change has put the entire household on edge: her aunt Grace, her mother Millie, who walks around looking perplexed and afraid, and of course Earl, who has so far been quiet about this problem. Earl strokes his beard a lot and occasionally smokes a cigarette somewhere in the yard, out of view.

When Amanda started being down, crying in the evenings in secret, dressing badly, Earl decided optimism was the best attitude to adopt. Better encourage her than dwell on the sadness. He is nearly thirty eight and has suffered from depression before; Amanda is twenty four and until recently has seemed to everyone confident and happy. Now, no one is sure what Amanda does in her room, alone there for hours. Sometimes they'll find her with one of those thick women's fashion magazines spread out in front of her; Earl understands the magazine is probably a cover, but a cover for what? Nothing, it seems. She can get a little angry when they disturb her, and if Earl asks whether she'll have supper with the others, she might impatiently tell him she'll eat later. But following that, she might also take his hand, smile, apologize — give him temporary relief.

It is the end of July, and two months since the four of them have returned from a vacation in Barcelona. Millie pleaded and persuaded the reluctant Amanda into the trip, because she wanted, in part at least, to mark their togetherness, to affirm how pleasantly Grace, Millie, Amanda and Earl have lived together. Millie's sister Grace is getting remarried in three weeks and they won't be under the same roof, most likely, ever again. Grace has lived here for nearly a year, ever since Dan, Millie's husband, left for the States on business. Grace and Larry's ceremony and reception will be right here at the house: the property is large and slopes onto a ravine; you can stand at the far end of the yard and see the shimmering surface of the river. There is lots of room for a small, outdoor wedding.

One part of Millie hopes Dan will come back for Grace's wedding as he's said he would. He's also promised he'd be flying back regularly and hasn't been back once in more than a year. But another part of her would prefer not to have the interruption of him at the wedding: let him come when there are no guests, when the house is empty, formidable, silent except for the rustle of the poplar leaves outside, and Millie is ready and waiting with two glasses of scotch on the coffee table under the sixteen-foot ceiling. Or let him not come at all. Sometimes she feels as if he has never lived here, has never slumped his slim frame onto the sofa and put his feet up after work, has never greeted the neighbours with friendly obscenities, as if it was always she and Amanda or she and Amanda and Earl here in the house. Many times already she has bartered Dan away for the return of the Amanda she used to know.

Today they are having dinner together, but Amanda has not shown up. Everyone worries about her since she's changed the location of her pyjamas, and especially since she's told them that she wants to go back to Barcelona in the fall, for an eight-week course in Spanish language and culture. Millie has acquired the habit of writing her worries in letters to Grace; these letters often contain things she most wants to say but doesn't, and she slips them to Grace in passing, on her way out to work, or even while they're sitting in the living room. In the last one she wrote about a dream she had in which Amanda, looking not quite like herself, told her that there was no heart left in it, and Millie, panicked and heavy with foreboding, tried to understand what *it* meant, what the *it* was. She wanted to ask but for some reason could only touch Amanda's hair, which in the dream was inexplicably blonde. She gave the letter to Grace while Grace was having her one nightly cigarette out on the front lawn; so far, she has not brought it up.

"We have to fix up the yard," says Grace as she spoons mashed potatoes now onto Millie's plate. She is just the kind of person to fill your plate when you'd like it to be filled. Millie watches with admiration her sister's tall figure, with a straight posture, thick around the waist and hips.

"Is Amanda upstairs?" Millie asks Earl.

"I knocked earlier but got no answer." He's flattening his potatoes with a fork, and his shrug, as he answers, is almost a twitch.

"I'll go look."

"Oh, she'll come on her own, let her be," says Grace. "Though I do need to ask her about the tablecloths."

They've put Amanda in charge of certain things to do with the wedding, the chair and linen rental, because it seemed a good idea to keep her involved and give her a preoccupation that could not, as far as they could see, have anything painful about it.

"Good luck getting her up in the morning if you don't," says Earl. They're in the habit of talking about Amanda as if she were quite inaccessible, though she goes hardly anywhere and spends most of her time upstairs.

"I'm sure she's not forgotten. She wouldn't forget. She's efficient with these things," says Millie, and everyone knows that in saying it she's only remembering a time gone by.

When they start stacking the dishes, Amanda comes in from outside. Her brown hair is limp and her jacket undone. She's gained weight in this last year and it shows most clearly in a layer of pudge around her jaw. She was once known for her beauty, and that she is indifferent to it now, is killing it with her indifference, makes the change in her seem, to Millie, an even greater loss.

"We all thought you were in your room and didn't want to bother you," says Millie. The look on Amanda's face is part of the inaccessibility: a closed face, eyes averted to just below eye level. No one is sure if it's a good idea to ask what she's been up to.

"You out for a stroll, Mandy?" Earl smiles, lifts his eyebrows, but the feebleness of his voice is disagreeable even to him.

Amanda doesn't meet his eyes, but makes a sorrowful little grimace as if the question hurts her, physically, and says, "What?"

Watching her now Millie could weep. Her splendid, beautiful daughter, the kindest person one could imagine. Earl tries to take her hand, lightly, when she passes him to get to the stove and fill her plate.

"Oh, what," she says, sighing.

"Well, Groucho Marx." He's trying to tease. A friend of Millie's, a therapist, told them that they should try to coax her out of herself, not let her retreat. Still, this is painful to watch. Millie feels actual tears somewhere behind her eyes.

"We have to clean up the yard," repeats Grace.

"Easiest thing," says Earl. He is a professional landscaper. "I'll do up whatever you like. Take just a few afternoons."

"We are so lucky with you two," says Millie. Beyond the kitchen the sun is setting and they all have a golden glow.

Earlier, Amanda was walking through the ravine on the other side of the river; it was warm and there were joggers and cyclists and other strollers out. She could not stand to meet anyone's eyes, including the few side glances of men; she carried a notebook and waited for the urge to write to build in her. She quickened her pace and at the next empty bench sat down and poised her pen over an already half-filled page. Some time later she was startled by voices.

"Does she not hear? Miss, do you mind?"

"She's pretending. Unbelievable. Hello, Miss, hello there?"

They were two joggers, hardly older than her, and the man had one bloody knee and a scraped chin; they wanted to sit down, and Amanda was sitting in the very centre of the bench. Horrified, feeling her face flush, she closed her notebook and barely muttered, "I'm so sorry," before walking quickly away. She kept going until she was out of sight for them and found another bench. Now she sat on its edge, and opened her notebook again, keeping her pen ready while steadying herself. She could write only a sentence: *That was a nasty tone.*

Still thinking now of the streaks of blood running down the man's shin and of the woman's angry face, she is glad to be home and walking upstairs, to the guest room. She lies down on the bed. This is the only place she gets some relief. They demand things of her each day, all day; things she can no longer give. She cannot eat dinner with Earl in a restaurant, can't talk about films or about some friends' break up or drink wine at one of his friends' house parties, or answer sincerely when he asks what she's been thinking about. She cannot make love. She doesn't know why, but she just can't. She hasn't been able to since before Barcelona, before spring. The winter, when she was let go from her job at the photo shop, was bad. Neither can she sit with Millie on the sofa, watching some travel show and holding hands, like they used to do for hours in the year and a half after Dan was sent to prison. She can't spend the afternoon book shopping with Millie, nor work through an elaborate recipe with her, nor listen to a story from her and Dan's past, some blurry and dreamy time.

She can hardly bear the familiar old feeling she still sometimes gets around Millie: love that is a pulsating tenderness for her mother's small frame and brown curling hair.

Oh, she knows they think that she gets all the time she wants to herself. She knows they talk of her as if it is they who bend to her demands. She's accepted that as just one unremarkable injustice that cannot be fixed. She is sorry for all the things she cannot provide. And she wants to express, somehow, that she is sorry: when the pulsating tenderness appears, it shames her. The shame needs either a dark room, or an action, a gesture. This morning she shocked Earl by making him breakfast — of waffles, bacon, poached eggs, sliced nectarines, and croissants with cheese — because she remembered that they used to, when he worked early mornings and she had early classes, cherish a chance to eat together and linger over coffee.

She doesn't begrudge Grace her happiness, but regrets that Grace and Larry will not move in here. Out of the house, Grace cannot be counted on for her calm presence, her company for Millie, her evening drink with Earl, her general lack of demands, explicit or implicit. Amanda sits up on the bed, adjusts some pillows to prop her up. The time of Dan's trials — the one that was declared a mistrial, then the second, then an appeal — was a line that split her and Millie's life into two. They found consolation in long talks over coffee and waffles, or wine and sandwiches, in the nook near the kitchen window. It seemed as if they were engaged in one permanent conversation, and coming home from work or school they could continue it without warm up, as if it were the real stuff of their lives and the other things only the technical requirements.

She remembers telling Millie about Earl: there is her mother's face in the rain, the curling wet strands of hair at her temples, her own thumping heartbeat. Millie had hardly ever been angry at her, but Amanda feared she would be angry now. Neither of them knew then that Dan would be arrested for fraud in a few weeks' time. Who is Earl? Millie demanded, and indeed Amanda didn't know how to explain him. He was fourteen years older than her. He painted houses for a living, worked cash in a thrift store, and did whatever else he could to help his mother pay off the farm he'd grown up on, the one his stepfather nearly gambled away. What could she say about him? I know the kinds of men my mother pictured. And she pictured a procession of them, one after another trying to impress her daughter. But I only wanted my stocky cashier.

To think of them all as they were then pains her. She will walk down the hall, down the stairs to her mother's room and stroke her hair. She will find Earl and tell him she loves him and that everything, after all, will work out. But she can't. It is enough that she is supposed to call someone about renting chairs. She dreads this. Dreads the sound of her own voice hesitating and uncertain. She used to be able to do things. When Millie and she were left alone, she was efficient at calling the plumber, cancelling insurance, firing the accountant, talking to men who called, even after Millie changed and unlisted the house phone number. She was good at talking with her mother, too, at getting her to like Earl.

After her dad was released, came home to a house that seemed emptied of his presence, Amanda moved out with Earl. Oh, those days — they lived in a small flat; there was a wallpaper photo on the living room wall; Earl's friends were always dropping in. She liked Earl's friends. She tries to count back the years to when precisely that was. That tires her. She moves the pillows propping her up and stretches out on the bed again. Last spring her dad went to Phoenix on a business venture. He's supposed to come back, but she no longer waits for it. It seems to her that around the time he left, Millie began to shrink. Her posture changed and she lost about an inch of height. She began to speak in a murmur, knock plaintively on doors, eat her meals out of small side dishes. She had survived the investigation and Dan being in prison, had accepted Amanda's imperfect lover, but there's a limit to what one can take.

So Earl and Amanda moved into Millie's house. None of them wanted to sell it. Amanda would again do — she thought she would, everyone did — what she used to be good at: taking care of things and cheering up her mother. She moved into the house so that she might one day find Millie baking a German chocolate torte, with one of those upbeat chirpy waltzes playing in the background, smoothing the icing patiently and almost hypnotically, winking at Amanda when she caught Amanda watching. I used to endlessly come across one or both of my parents in some unaware moment, always the observer on the edge of the picture, surprising them — happily, it seemed — with my presence. Every now and then, they do try to bake together, but Amanda has so little to say. The fake cheer exhausts them both and each needs a lie down afterwards.

Amanda wants to return to Barcelona. It was with apprehension that she broke this news to everyone, at once, and explained taking the course. She should have told Earl first; she would have if it weren't so hard to talk to him. Sometimes if she looks him straight in the eye she feels that collapse is imminent. What form the collapse would take — that's still vague for her. The only secret is that there is no Spanish language and culture course as she has told them; or rather, there is one, she's looked it up, she knows how much it costs and what it involves, but she won't be attending it. How she'll explain it later, she can't quite think about; she hopes it will not matter once she gets away.

What Amanda remembers about the city is the smell of men: during mass at the Basilica, she noticed the discreet colognes emanating from the fresh, upright collars of the men in the row in front of her. There were other smells: the colognes were beneath the fragrance of wood and old prayer books. She loved the cafés too, with the breeze carrying the scent of coffee, and the pairs and groups of men and women, packaged, perfumed, sometimes perfect and sometimes too worn; it all made her heady.

The rooms of the two bedroom apartment they rented in Barcelona smelled of new furniture (the furniture was sparse) and of linden trees. They had to clean up after themselves, but a woman came with washed and folded linens and towels every other day. Her name was Lula and she was thin and stunningly pretty and looked perpetually fatigued. Whenever Amanda saw her, she either held her young boy at her hip, or her posture alone suggested a great weight; her lids hung low and she gave the impression of a person continuously exhaling. She wore dresses in bold colours — fuchsias and blood reds and aquas, which hugged her waist, hung below her knees, and showed plump cleavage. Her dark hair was thick and wavy and pushed back from her face. The combination of this mane, the bright colours, and the perpetual weariness was both beautiful and slightly disconcerting.

On the second day there, they passed by while she was talking to an old man in the hallway. He was Arthur, the owner of the apartment; Lula was his daughter-in-law, the wife of his son Jude — they all lived in apartments in the same building. On the stairs Arthur invited them all for lunch and they obliged. Amanda liked old people and Arthur was just the kind of old man she liked — good humoured and slightly satirical, as if one could not be otherwise having sampled the ways of the world. He treated all of them with interest and politeness, and her, in particular, as someone who knew less than he did of how the world breathes, but also like one who will eventually figure things out. His courteousness approached flirtation — or did it do so only in the mind of the generation that did not expect to have chairs pulled out nor coats taken care of? Arthur had come to Barcelona from London some thirty years ago, and stayed. He liked talking to Amanda about the nineteenth-century British novel, which happened to be one of the last courses she had taken in her degree, and so the titles and gentlemen and the madwomen were still fresh. Based on two or three informed responses he had assumed, probably, a much wider breadth of familiarity than actually existed, but having a commonality made them free to talk of other things.

Jude was not intended to have a part at all; he was merely the son, beleaguered by a beleaguered wife, who was waiting for him to become a lawyer so she might hire a sitter or housekeeper and get some sleep. He was a man who needed not diversion or stimulation, but a bigger apartment. He was young — as young as Amanda — but with a child, a toddler, and this small, striking wife. His hair was the slippery blond hair of an infant and his face the kind that passed for good looking in television dramas about small towns — an earnest, manly, serious face. His mother had been Catalan but his appearance showed nothing but Arthur's deep Anglo-Saxon roots. He was not supposed to be in the picture but there he was, the poorly defined figure somewhere near the edge of it. He smelled like cedar, like woody cologne with a whiff of something orange; on the two hottest days, she could smell his skin, coppery and yeasty. There were Arthur and Lula's scents too: Arthur's like just-ironed clothes, and sometimes like caramels that he often chewed. Passing Lula in the hallway, Amanda smelled hair oil and lilac, and there was a hint of orange around her too.

∂∂∂

She was supposed to meet Arthur for an afternoon drink, but she was late. He had waited for her at a corner table of the café down the street from his house, his regular place, where he took his coffee every other morning. He liked putting on his suit pants and a dress shirt to walk over and be served.

The wind blew wisps of his white hair as he thought about the girl: she was a bit of an unexpected pleasure, a breeze when you thought all the windows were closed. He was not sure that she was as young as a girl; the precise age of the young eluded him. Regardless, here was a person he could get used to talking to. She had a lovely manner, a nervousness that showed in the movements of the hands, and a habit of staring at a person for moments after he or she has stopped speaking. But that entourage of hers — why did they all travel together like that? Though the mother was lovely. Attuned to the daughter — when the girl saw a fly in her lemonade, the mother's eyes immediately searched out the waiter. Did the girl notice that? The mother seemed nervous. The aunt and the boyfriend were not nervous. When the mother looked for the waiter to inform him of the fly, the boyfriend leaned toward her until she noticed him and stopped. Then he went inside the café and returned a minute later with a fresh drink.

The three women resembled each other and he covertly spent much of their lunch trying to pinpoint the similarities and differences. Around them the girl did not talk very much; that's why he had enjoyed their brief stroll alone, yesterday, more than the time with the entire package. He thought he was starting to understand about this family and the girl. And so he came on the idea of making her an offer: he could spare an apartment in the off-season, and he liked talking to her. He realized he liked her a lot more than he cared for his daughter-in-law.

But now the girl was late. He had nearly finished his coffee and was starting to feel nauseous, a symptom, he suspected, of a new blood pressure medication. The day was hot, too, and he was uncomfortable. When he saw Jude walk by, as he often did, on his way home for lunch, he waved him down and asked him to wait for her and tell her that Arthur had to return home. He put a bill into Jude's hand and walked away.

Amanda was hurrying along because she had misjudged the time again. Often half an afternoon passed before she realized it was no longer morning. When she saw Jude sitting at the café table, she thought that she must have got more badly mixed up, until he explained. Jude's smell was a thin edge of cologne mixed with clean coppery sweat; she could see the sweat at his hairline and on his neck.

"Will you have lunch with us? Lula has made some kind of tuna pasta salad, I think."

Because she said nothing, he added, hesitatingly, "Do you like tuna?"

"Sure, yes, thank you."

If Lula was made uncomfortable by the unexpected company, Amanda could not discern it. She smiled through her sleepy lids and pointed Amanda to a chair. She wore a turquoise dress, and held the boy in one arm as she set the table with the other. As they ate, the boy turned his eyes to Amanda repeatedly, prompting Lula to say, "He likes you," the first thing she'd said since the initial hello. Jude was the one keeping up a conversation by asking Amanda what she and the others had visited.

Amanda had no memory for names and dates of art works, or names of streets, and found it impossible to keep talking about places and things she'd seen.

"He seems very bright," she said of the boy. Shortly after, Lula rose from her seat, put her plate in the sink, and said, to the child rather than either Amanda or Jude, "We're going for our little walk, aren't we." She stopped near Amanda's chair and said to the boy, "Wave bye-bye to the lady." With that Jude and Amanda were left at the table with their plates still half full. He moved his plate to the side and she felt it meant that the visit was something of a chore for him, one that could now be concluded without loss of politeness.

She walked out of the apartment minutes later, turned the corner and followed a route she remembered. She was heading toward a vendor's stand where she had seen, the day before, a print she liked: of a field, an open road, and an old-looking horse, in repose; it was a generic print, but she liked the horse, which looked pathetic and unfriendly. There was the stand, with a small crowd near it, browsing or waiting to pay, several Spaniards involved in a conversation with the seller. On the last occasion she saw Arthur he'd told her that if she ever wanted to return to Barcelona, he'd be happy to let her stay in the flat. At the end of summer for instance — she could return at the end of summer and stay as long as she liked. As a young man he had found that it benefited him greatly to experience new surroundings; he'd spent a transformative three months on Greece's Saronic islands. She pictured herself walking down this street alone, past the fountain and up the stairs, into a quiet apartment, empty, entirely hers.

She found and took hold of the print, but the seller was still in conversation and she turned toward the street. A pair of young men was passing by, one of them twirling something like a short, thick cable. She would have turned away to try to get the seller's attention, but in that moment the man suddenly ran up, very quickly, and loudly smacked the cable — it was hard to tell what exactly it was — across the bare thighs of a woman standing near Amanda, just looking at some postcards. Up close Amanda saw that he was not a man but a teenager. He ran back swiftly to his friend, and they continued walking at a lively pace, jostling each other, turning back to laugh. The look on the woman's face was one of white shock and shame and pain. The man who was with her stared after the laughing boys with bafflement and concern, an expression he might have worn while watching news of violence in distant parts of the world. The woman wanted to rub the place she had been hit, but her hand merely hovered near it as it was becoming a blotchy red welt. Amanda looked away, to overcome the shame she shared with her. No one else seemed to have seen, or comprehended, what had happened. Amanda said, "They are awful," though she did not know what language the couple spoke; nor were they looking at her.

She put the print back, realizing she could not, anyway, bear to draw attention to herself and ask the vendor if he spoke English. Nasty, she thought, and stopped on her walk home to take the notebook out of her purse and write it down. At the flat she complained to Earl of a stomach ache, and wrapped herself in the quilt on the bed. He brought her tea, a book, and she let him move the strand of hair falling across her eye, she let him lie next to her, and she did not go out for the rest of the day.

ॐ ॐ ॐ

But why did Amanda want to go back to Barcelona? When Millie asked her why not, for example, learn French instead of Spanish, Amanda said she had just liked Barcelona so much. This was not one of the things Millie remembered about Barcelona, Amanda liking it so much. To Millie Barcelona was all lush foliage, hot sticky air, and those corrugated metal shop doors, always pulled down at closing time. But what she remembers most clearly, somehow, is the baggy dress and funny little slippers Amanda wore day after day. It was a short, wide dress, with a deep front, and when they sat down in cafés the waiters — men, almost all — could see much of her bra.

"It's summer," Amanda would say, inexplicably, when Millie said the dress didn't fit well. It was warm, yes; in fact it was hot and oppressive and full of people. In the mornings, they took their coffee on the little canopied balcony; sometimes Amanda slept in and Earl and Millie and Grace had breakfast without her. "Let's leave her for the day," Earl would joke to lighten things. Then as Millie rinsed plates she would hear a plaintive voice behind not-quite closed doors, Earl's voice, gently coaxing Amanda out.

Millie sits at her vanity, a common spot for her, easy to write letters at, and with a good window for surveying the yard. She can see Earl making little snips at one of the dogwoods, building up a messy pile of the small white flowers by his feet. He's not protesting Amanda going to Barcelona, as far as Millie can tell. Would she know if he did protest? She doesn't know if she would know. Before he appeared, she had imagined Amanda with many types of men — tall and gallant and intellectual, kind and self-effacing and brilliant. What she got was Earl, his friendly-neighbour manner, a provincial familiarity, advanced age, and few credentials. But she certainly doesn't want to picture anyone else in his place. She has tried to help them where she could. She gave up the house to him and Amanda — she really only needed one room, two at the most — and a few years ago cashed in some bonds to pay for Earl's two-year diploma. But how are things between them now, she would give up many things to know. Amanda doesn't talk to her anymore, and Earl, of course, won't suddenly start. This tells Millie what she dreads, that things are getting worse. She remembers the old man in Barcelona, and his son and the housekeeper. It was months before the trip that Amanda's oddness began, and when they were in Barcelona, Grace said it was great to see Amanda engaging with people. She was right — the thing Millie had feared about the trip was that she would have to implore Amanda to leave her room at all.

One afternoon, standing by a fountain on the corner of their street, she'd seen Amanda leaving a café with Jude, not Arthur, walking with her hands in the pockets of her funny dress. Amanda came home within the hour, and Millie would surely have cut off her own ear to have Amanda lean into her on the terrace and tell her what she and Jude talked about. Why does a depressed girl have enough energy to talk to strangers and not to her own family? She was encouraged by seeing Amanda choose restaurants and discuss literature, but why should it have been others who got the pleasure of the real Amanda, the one Millie has been waiting to wake up to one day? Millie wanted to help Earl, if only she could. In their bedroom are pictures of Amanda and of the two of them together — Amanda with her mouth full of Timbits and her eyes open wide, or dressed as a 1920s flapper, with a long cigarette in her gloved fingers. Or Amanda and Earl hugging each other tightly on a bridge in Banff, nighttime and the reflection of lamps in the river behind them.

Earl has paused his work, stands stroking his beard and looking down on the lonely spiraea not far from the dogwood. Millie drops her hair brush, walks out of the room, through the kitchen, out the front door, and into the yard towards him. He turns toward her and smiles. She walks right up, holding up her hand as a shield from the sun, and asks him if he needs a drink — "nope."

"It's starting to look good."

"Be ready in a few more days."

"It'll be strange without Grace around, won't it?"

"I'll miss that old broad."

"Oh, Earl. It *will* be strange without her. Empty."

"She'll be over lots, I'm sure. If Larry goes away on some contract, she might come and stay here, hang out with you and Amanda."

Millie brightens a little.

"She's always welcome, of course. What's Mandy doing?" Millie was in the habit of asking Earl about Amanda as if they didn't all live in the same house.

"Oh, chatting on the phone or something."

But Amanda never talks on the phone.

"Oh. Do you think she's serious about this Barcelona thing? The language course thing?"

"Seems like it. Might be good for her. You know there's work in languages — translating, interpreting."

It irritates Millie when Earl says far-fetched things that sidetrack her from what she is obliquely trying to say. As if Amanda is going to go to Barcelona to begin a career in interpreting for the United Nations.

"Right. I was thinking I'd feel better about the whole thing if you were going with her."

"Really."

"It's only that she doesn't know anyone there. She hasn't asked you to go with her?"

He pauses, making Millie fear that she's been far too direct. Earl is capable, she knows, of shutting down conversation, her conversation about Amanda specifically, quite politely and unmistakably.

He says, "No, she's not asked me to come along. I probably could have. Work drops off in the fall."

Millie titters with something like fear.

"Well, I think she ought to have. You deserve some travelling as much as she."

He squints at her. "I guess she just wants to do something for herself." He keeps his eyes on Millie as he says it. She can hardly believe she is getting all this from him. What passes through her head is, What *doesn't* Amanda do for herself these days?

She says, "Oh, I don't know. Has she said that?"

"That's what I think, anyway. I don't actually know. She doesn't explain much."

214

"She doesn't?" Millie's heart rate quickens.

"You know how she is."

"So secretive. Oh, I can't tell you how it worries me. Just tell her you want to go with her."

Earl smiles. "She's free to do what she wants." Millie thinks of what to say next, but it doesn't matter — it's too late, the moment has passed and Earl is readjusting his garden gloves, and she knows of course what that means.

                            *ৡৡৡ*

"You could come with me to the concert on Friday."

The tone of Jude's statement had so faintly resembled an invitation that Amanda hardly knew how to answer. She, Arthur and Jude had been sitting on the patio of the corner café; Amanda had her hands on the table and on hearing the invitation interlocked her fingers. The suggestion seemed hypothetical, indifferent; only Arthur's just perceptible encouragement suggested it might be something else. She was afraid to accept what had not necessarily been offered.

Jude said, "I like to walk over from the park; you could meet me there."

"Yes," she said, "I will." She thought, I'll tell the others Arthur and Lula will be going too. But ought I not to invite Earl, if not Millie and Grace? Well, she had said yes. She would find a way.

He had not mentioned dinner, but after the performance he walked casually toward a restaurant not far from the park where they'd met earlier, and she found she didn't mind. When the first tapa arrived, a trio of slick sardines on pink-paste-covered bread, he seemed to relax, which revealed a brighter, more childlike face.

"So you are a graduate of literature."

"No, of media arts."

"Ah," he said. "I don't believe we have an equivalent of that here. Do you have siblings?"

"No."

"Ah. I have six, but they are all half siblings. So in a way I am an only child too. In a way I grew up alone. Did you grow up alone?"

"I grew up in a huge house, and all the friends I had in school always ended up playing at my house. My parents let us go into almost any room. They were what I think people call modern parents. They were very happy, that's what I remember about them and my childhood. I would exist all day in some imagined world, a fortress of couch cushions, and emerge suddenly into their presence, a shock of happiness."

She worried, for the first time, if he'd understood everything — the result of realizing that he was not English, after all. There was the Catalan mother, long dead from what Amanda had gathered, and a whole Catalan life. She noticed all the hesitations in his English, and his earnest listening.

"My parents seemed to me like very public people — you know? I think I was shy of them in my childhood. If I caught them intimate, I mean, like, my dad in his shorts, I was embarrassed." He paused. "You're here with your family."

She didn't say anything at first. She was watching the smoothness of his forearms and his neat, slightly plump hands, as he lifted a stray bit of sardine into his mouth.

"Yes, they like it." That was not what she had wanted to say. "We live together."

"In the huge house?"

"My aunt, my mom's sister, came to live with us — we could not keep up the house, my mom alone couldn't, not without others. She is reluctant to sell it." He nodded vigorously, as if to show he understood all about the weight of houses.

The waiter switched their empty plates for full ones, and there was some brief joke between him and Jude, a friendly pat on the back from the waiter. The humour, the ease, were new. Near Arthur he was pleasant but aloof, almost unreadable.

"Lula wants a house — though my father has several flats we can choose from. She would like to put all we have into a house. I like to keep something for the side — like travel, pleasures."

"A house is a lot of work," Amanda said, thinking of Lula's droopy eyelids. "I would not put all I have into a house."

"And yet to live in my father's apartment is not very good, you understand."

"I like your father," she said, and regretted it.

"And your mother seemed nice. You and I are the same age, I think, but your boyfriend is older, no?"

"Yes. I was young when we started dating. I mean, compared to him; I was seventeen. He was thirty-one. My mother, at first, ignored the whole thing so that it might go away."

"Of course," he said, "but you didn't care? I mean it didn't stop you."

"Oh, it could have. But I guess the happiness was already cracked by then and I didn't have a complete terror of spoiling it."

"Right."

"Only ordinary fear."

He laughed, lightly, and so did she. The waiter came again and this time the camaraderie included Jude holding on to his elbow and the waiter patting his cheek.

"Should we order dessert?"

They did. In Jude's flushed face she read a slight drunkenness. He leaned in.

"You return on the Sunday, you've said?"

For the first time in the conversation she didn't know what his words were intended for. The guilt had not started for her yet. The lights of all the restaurants, the glassware on the tables, shimmered. She was a woman talking earnestly over dinner with a man. It was what a person wanted from travel, memorable connections: light reflecting off wine glasses and a stranger's life unpeeling in front of you. No pulsating tenderness, no shame, no love, no remorse. Only civility, freshness. Possibility.

"Do you remember when the happiness had started to crack, as you said?"

"Oh, I don't know. Well, I do."

"Let's hear it."

౷ ౷ ౷

The room is shuttered and lines of light coming through the slats stripe the furniture. Amanda keeps it this way most of the time. Her long hair hangs down the sides of her face and part of it touches Earl's shoulder — that's how close they are, sitting propped up on the bed. He touches a strand of it gently. She used to put a lot of work into her hair. As for him, he hasn't physically changed since they've met: his fingers are the same, as is his beard, and the skin on his face is still perfect. He observes the room like a visitor. There's a magazine on the table near the window and a plain glass vase, empty. The room reveals nothing. He puts his arm behind her and around her shoulder, though he knows she might squirm away. This time she doesn't. This isn't right, he'd like to say. One ought to be able to hug one's girlfriend without fearing that she'll pull away as if she's been poked with something sharp.

"It doesn't have to be like this," he says. She closes her eyes. He wishes he didn't have to feel as if he were torturing her.

"I got a contract for October."

"Oh good." She opens her eyes. She sits there in fear of what he will ask of her that she won't be able to give.

"Spain will be warmer than here this time of year," he says.

"I suppose. I might even come back tanned."

"What day do you return?"

"The 16th, I think. I have to check the ticket. It's in the drawer there, you can look."

But he won't. Something about that feels false, her telling him to look at the ticket. He doesn't want to look at it. He moves his hand from behind her back.

Maybe he can take her out of this room, out from whatever fortress she has built for herself. He smells her hair, covertly.

She leans into him; she leans into him. He won't move, won't ask for more, won't say something to spoil it. He can get her out of it. It doesn't matter what will happen later, but he sees now he can get her out of it.

"What is it?" he says. "Because we can change things."

"Don't. I don't know. It — when we were in Barcelona, that woman who got hit."

"Which?"

"At the stand. I was going to buy a print — it doesn't matter what — they just walked by and hit her, with — a cord or something. I don't know. It's just that nastiness."

"Who were — did they hurt her?"

"No — you mean was she bleeding or something? No."

"You're scared that it could happen to you?"

"It doesn't have to happen to me. It's only that it's out there, always."

There is a timid knock at the door. They don't move to answer it; they know it's Millie. Then Amanda sighs and straightens.

Earl grabs her hand, says just what he means: "I can get you out of this." If not now, he will lose her. She is looking at him. He could cry but doesn't. Millie calls apprehensively, "Hello?"

At supper the previous night Amanda mentioned the good deal she got on her flight. The definitiveness of a plane ticket put Millie in a panic. Until Amanda brought it up, the supper was festive: Millie had cooked, Grace brought out a fine champagne left in the pantry since the days of Dan. It all threatened to destroy Amanda's resolve. Just yesterday morning all she could think was away, away — that, while listening to Earl's humming as he brushed his teeth and Millie starting the juicer. Then in the evening, while Grace was setting the table, Millie knocked on her door, opened it, and said simply, "Amanda, my love, darling." That "darling" cut like a polished, well-prepped blade. Later, sitting at the table, Amanda thought, this is all my mom needs, her family about her, an occasion to justify putting out the good china. Me, looking content. And who else but Earl would live in this house and grow to love this family of hers? Barcelona was a risk: it was one thing to be alone in a house full of people, and another to be alone in a stranger's apartment beyond which strangers waited for their bus.

So when Earl came to her room this morning, she was already worn down with a sleepless night and the dread of indecision and the struggle to hold on to the certainty that had been wavering consistently. It would have been a super-human effort to change tracks and reach out, hold on to him so he might help her. And when Millie knocked on the door, the easiest thing was to open it.

By the time she does, though, Millie is gone.

Millie has hurried down to Grace, who will not look at what she wrote for Earl.

"Earl's devastated," says Millie, refolding the letter, "he doesn't have to say it — I can see it."

"Jesus Christ," Grace says, "it's only a goddamn course." She thinks, enough of you and your letters.

"Do you really think Amanda would have anything to do with that bland quasi-Englishman? She'll be back before you notice she's gone."

The latter platitude is of course impossible, since Millie notices everything to do with Amanda, but Grace is exhausted. Since Dan left it's been too much of this. God bless Larry.

"You're always welcome here, Grace."

"I know," Grace says, "I read your last letter."

Millie again starts to unfold the one intended for Earl, but Grace turns away from the lined notebook paper. She has an idea of what Amanda wants in Barcelona; it's not Jude. Earl could have seen that, if not Millie. But Grace is not about to tell them. She has her own life to consider, thank God, and she will not get caught again; no, she will not read any more letters. Instead she will visit with baking for an evening or an afternoon, and her presence in the house will be only the breeziest, lightest caress of a kind hand.

ৡৡৡ

Jude is waiting outside the baggage hall doors. Amanda is sick — nauseous from the turbulent flight and sick with fear. She packed for the trip as if moving through a dreamscape, as a soldier who doubts her mission, has a bad gut feeling about it, but must put her hope in the wisdom of those who planned it. In this state, she was taken to the airport, Earl driving, Millie in the backseat. And with that gut panic, she had hugged her mom and kissed Earl, holding him tightly for a moment at the security checkpoint.

Landing in Barcelona, she wished only to take a taxi, give the name of a hotel where no one could know her, and, after putting a few drops of sleeping aid into a cup of hot water, escape into sleep. Instead, here is Jude—courteous, opening the passenger door for her, swinging her suitcase into the trunk. During the ride he keeps his eyes on the road and doesn't try to force talk, so that for some time the only sound is the smooth hum of the car's machine and the murmur of a voice on the radio.

After a while, worried her silence might be rude, she says, "It was good of your father to let me stay at the apartment." Jude turns only briefly, smiles quickly.

"He likes you. Anyway, he has other apartments." What she wonders is, what does he think she's doing here?

When they arrive he carries her suitcase up the stairs and says, "My father hoped you'd call him when you recover from the difference in time zones." On a pad of paper that sits on top of the shoe rack in the hallway, he writes down two phone numbers, Arthur's and his own.

She thought all she wanted was to sleep, but after he leaves, after she takes off her shoes and her watch and splashes her face with water at the kitchen sink, she opens the balcony door and steps out onto the tiles, which are warm — it is after ten in the evening, a hot night, though it looks as though it has rained earlier. She sees people walking on the street two storeys below, entering buildings, parking their cars and exiting them, talking and laughing and jingling their keys. She can hear their voices. She can hear a distant thump of bass from somewhere in the small building, and a thin sound like an amateur oboe. On the balcony below and to the left of her a man with a fleshy back and light brown hair is lifting undershirts from a clothesline, speaking to someone inside. She cannot understand most of the Spanish, but she picks out the words *mujer* and *dulce*. She can smell warm wet air and hackberry trees. Her heart begins to beat fast. It is not only fear. It is that she has not slept much in twenty-four hours and has not eaten on the plane. It is that she knows she will have to call home now, and either talk about the Spanish language course or say something true. It is also that she feels the difference between being dead and being alive. The ugliness deadens one, and then also a hollowness that is hard to ascribe to something specific. Arthur and Jude made her alive, briefly, and now the smells and the people. And her heart also beats fast because she sees that whatever she has begun by coming here, and whether it ends with life or death, this is only the beginning of it, and it will get much worse, before it ends, one way or the other.

꙳ ꙳ ꙳

Millie finds Earl in front of his laptop, his head down on the table on his hands, headphones on his head. She knows he dozed off waiting for a call from Amanda's computer. In the nine days since she's left, Amanda's made some vague but disconcerting statements. Millie still has the letter she never gave Earl tucked into the cover of some books that sit on her bedside table. She doesn't like to think of it now.

She touches his shoulder lightly and he wakes with a shudder. He was not exactly asleep; he may have sunk one layer below wakefulness, while thinking of the same things he's thought about on the other days since she's been gone — of the fact that it's been eight years. That he's not young, and that there is no consolation for him. All he wants, all he's wanted all along, is Amanda. For her he had

224

let himself get absorbed into her family's palace, for her he used to, years ago, leave parties early and drive across the city in blizzards, tipsy, so she might take a last cup of tea before bed with Millie and Dan. He wanted to love what she loved. Or he feared that unless he did, he would not last, like her friends never lasted. So he'd learned to understand Millie, had accepted the house, the daily precariousness of moods.

"It's nearly six now," Millie says, "and Amanda must be asleep over there." She says it gently. He takes off the headphones, rubbing the ache they've left around his ears.

"I wanted to tell you I talked to Dan. He wants to come home now. What with Amanda and everything."

"I heard there's a heat wave in all of southern California."

"Oh yes, he's hating it. Here it's twenty-two degrees, perfect. Will you come outside and eat? The air is so lovely. I baked rolls earlier."

"I could smell them."

"We still have to eat," she said, "don't we."

# The Time of the Apricots

ALEK'S GIRLFRIEND JULIET WAS GETTING dressed for a premiere at the Toronto International Film Festival — a premiere of a film based on her own novel, *Little Gods*. She wore a green dress, with a one-shoulder neckline, cut out into a sort of stair pattern descending from the shoulder to the bust and then continuing down in a curve around her back so that Alek felt he could not figure out how and where parts connected; the lowest stair on the front came close to her left nipple, and instead of an ordinary bra, she had to wear a pair of round, pinkish, gelatinous, self-adhering objects called nipple covers. Women really own such things, Alek thought. The dress, by some Canadian designer Juliet knew, was the intense lawn green of children's crayons — Alek thought it suited his girlfriend: her body was archly upright and muscular, and she looked like some kind of alien soldier, and he knew that he loved this.

She had brought over to his place everything she needed for the event, and he watched her from his sickbed, wearing his last clean T-shirt and keeping himself close to the mop bucket at his bedside. When she was dressed, perfumed, rouged, and shimmering, she stood at the foot of the bed with her happiest cartoon grin, wide eyes and wide mouth, arms bent at the elbows and palms turned up.

"Can you believe it? I'm going to TIFF!"

"I really adore you more than anything right now. You're going to TIFF! Look at you!"

"And I can't even reach you to kiss you, poor sick sparrow!"

"No matter, I will merely touch my finger to the hem of your gown . . . wait, no, the waist of your gown, and . . . my soul will heal."

She stood in the same pose and watched him move his finger up the waist to the first stair over her breast. Then he fell backwards.

"I'm saved," he said.

She clasped his calf in her hands, leaned over, and kissed his knee.

"Call me if you get worse." She unclasped her purse and took out the piece of cardboard on which Alek had drawn the figure of a man, with a speech bubble that read: "I'm so broke I can't even pay attention." The figure was drawn in blue sharpie all in one line, without breaks, in Alek's elongated drawing style.

"And in the meantime, I've got this guy," she said.

He did the drawing yesterday, when it became clear he would be too sick to go with her tonight. The strange, prolonged stomach bug that he got two days before the premiere seemed to him an act of infuriating randomness. He wondered if she found this fact as sad and upsetting as he did. Instead of him she took her friend Trixie, a writer who had in fact read several drafts of Juliet's novel and deserved to be rewarded for that slogging work. The novel had been published by a decent small press, averagely well-reviewed, selling the usual modest number of copies, and Juliet had been nominally paid for it. In all ways, it was an ordinary, good Canadian first novel, by a relatively young author (which these days meant thirty-five — Juliet was thirty-four when it was published four years ago), and not at all the kind of novel that gets optioned for a movie.

Since then she had been writing but had not, as she liked to say, "actually written anything." She spent about three years on a novel she finally gave up. She wrote two or three stories; also a few reviews, and one long essay she was still trying to get published. But no new novel, which she wanted so much—he knew this—that she could hardly read or talk about others' novels for the envy and shame that arose in her.

*Little Gods* was about a derelict hospital in a small interior B.C. town, where a woman shows up, claiming that the doctor and founder of the hospital was a fraud who regularly misdiagnosed people, including her own, now dead, aunt. The woman, Annabelle, gets a young man, Donny, whose own father died at the hospital, on her side, and together they scour the archives, spend nights drinking in an abandoned barn, gather a lot of opposition against their mission, and stir up a lot of rumours about the sex they're supposedly having in various outdoor locations. But in researching the doctor story, they in fact uncover their own stories: it is Annabelle's past that becomes the main narrative. And yet that narrative is slippery and inconsistent, and the townspeople accuse her of being the actual con artist.

It was a predictable move, Alek thought, this almost-red herring of the doctor false-identity story being replaced by a less sensational one, the mystery novel giving way to a novel of personal histories. It was also the kind of novel he might have expected to come out of Juliet: she was always digging for stuff in people's personal histories — his own, for instance — and he thought that in the digging she was looking for some confirmation of a story she had already imagined; or maybe just *the* story, the one that would make sense of the whole person. She had dug up first his divorce, then his move to Canada, then his life in Croatia, the war, and further back still, his childhood, of course. He wasn't sure any of it satisfied her. Perhaps she could not get a satisfactory story for Annabelle's character either, and so she made her unreliable; it seemed to him this unreliability was some kind of trend too.

For whatever reason, and probably, in his opinion, through an act of outrageously benevolent randomness, the novel had got into the hands of a Belgian director who happened to be a fan of Canadian fiction, and who optioned it for a film. After Alek met Juliet, their first conversations were about the film, the director, the French-language script — she liked the script (though whether she did or not was of no consequence), but liked to point out problems with particular dialogue lines, and Alek, for whom English was a second language and who knew zero French, listened anyway; she loved the title, which was adopted from one of her own favourite lines of the novel, her rephrasing of an Arabic saying, *bukra fi al-mishmish*, "tomorrow you're in the apricots" — in other words, good fortune is on the way. That's how she chose to look at it, anyway — it was also used to mean, apparently, "when pigs fly." No matter. It was the title she had wanted for the novel — "the time of the apricots" — but the publishers wouldn't have it.

And Juliet soon learned that the famous French actress who shared Juliet's name would play Annabelle, and the Canadian star recently exported to Hollywood, Eric Pantinople, would play Donny, the aimless, gruff, handsome male lead.

Now, also, the novel was being reprinted and reviewed in the European press, the *Guardian*, the Belgian papers, and somehow, it seemed, more generously for having the bright light of the film shining on it. Before all this, she could not have hoped for even a reprint of the novel, never mind the fairly healthy sales.

"It's your time," Alek said to her, "your time of the apricots." He couldn't say the phrase without thinking also of peaches and plums, ripe plums fallen from their trees and carpeting the orchard floor. As a child he'd had to walk through such orchards picking those soft, sticky, mushy oblongs from the ground, trying not to step on them and create more mush he'd have to clean out of his shoes later.

And then they learned of her six-figure commission.

Who handed out these miraculous bonuses, these hares jumping out of hats to turn into doves? When the commission came in, Juliet's job was serving dinner and cocktails at the lounge of the Fairmont Hotel four nights a week. With the original publisher's advance for the novel she had been able to buy exactly a winter coat and twenty discounted copies of her own book. With the commission, she could buy about half a house in a decent, even desirable, Toronto neighbourhood.

She was still, remarkably, ignoring this sum, letting it sit in a high-interest bank account. Alek couldn't get her to talk about what she might do with it. He was glad for Juliet, yes, he was. But there was a thin line of trepidation underneath the gladness. Trepidation seemed like the right word — a restrained feeling, like breathing very quietly for fear of disturbing some important balance. Maybe it was his fear of sudden change; but then again, fear might have been, already, the lining of everything with Juliet. When she was near him, she was unmistakably concrete — someone to be watched, touched, inhaled. Away from him, she lost her solidity; her voice became distant and thin, her skin paled and lost its texture, he could not imagine her eyes focused on him. And when she dissolved into this pale, flimsy spectre, so did he. He'd phone her on a pretense, just to bring her partly back to life — otherwise he'd have to walk around the neighbourhood, aimless and embarrassed, to get the nervousness out of his body. He disliked this agitated insubstantial walking man and preferred Juliet to show herself, to enter his proximity, so they might both be flesh and presence.

One small thing — relatively small, depending on how you looked at it — that the commission made moot was Alek's plan to gift Juliet a sum of money she could live on for a year, without working, to concentrate on that second novel she so wanted. He had been putting aside money, for this purpose, for more than a year, about a quarter of his monthly salary.

If she'd been someone else, such a gesture might not have been necessary even before the commission; she would have moved in with him, quit her lounge gig, and stayed at home to write, supported quite comfortably — and happily, on his part — by him. As it was, she continued to live one block away, in a walk-up similar to his except that hers was a rental, not renovated and turned into condos and sold, as Alek's was, at an insultingly inflated price. One piddly block she insisted on keeping between them, one street she crossed again and again, happily hurrying to her own bed, her own cups and plates and ferociously abundant hanging plants and record player and unorganized books, her own sofa by the balcony where she sat with a laptop in her lap, writing and brooding and ruining her back. Even knowing she was merely going home, he felt like she'd vanished, as though the corner was a cut-off point beyond which she could be anywhere.

And despite his own apartment having clean surfaces and dust-free corners, he liked being in hers. He was usually fed, and warm, and at rest.

When he had divorced his wife he was happiest to leave her home décor: the kitchen she called rustic European, with prints of stone-cobbled streets and wrought-iron café chairs and waiters in long aprons that made him feel like he was eating in any one of Italian supermarkets or cafés lining Little Italy; the heavy, refurbished walnut dressers in their bedroom that reminded him, not pleasantly, of childhood. But he missed the protection sometimes. He thought that must be the reason people build all kinds of imperfect, wobbly, dull, unpromising, contentious, ludicrous even, homes and marriages — to move through the world inside the bubble of them. Nothing was required when he lived with his wife: if after work he did all the chores she expected of him, it seemed they got on well enough. There were groceries to be picked up, clogged sinks, new patio furniture, a bookshelf to be built from scrap as a side project. There were visits, in-laws and nephews and other couples, and sometimes a beer after work with people he still called friends. If he showed up for all of it, shaven and well dressed, his life went on, mostly unthreatened, unquestioned, unchallenged.

But in another way, a lot was required, and they didn't get on well at all. Just to sit through an hour of television together, without revealing some resentment or creating a new one, was tense and exhausting. Resisting the urge to surf for porn when in his study was exhausting — or, if he didn't resist, upsetting in another way. It seemed things would stay the same unto eternity: and yet all kinds of things changed moment to moment — a sudden tension, dissatisfaction, a sly, slowly produced accusation, or — worse — a kindness offered, taken, a day of hope, then a long stretch of withdrawal. That was required, living in that back-and-forth, all the while the surface hardly stirred, a picnic laid out on a blanket in the grass, the wobbliness invisible from a distance.

And of course the unthreatened part turned out to be plain wrong. It was all precarious indeed, and the threat had been there for a long time, at least the two years during which Amira had her affair. (He found that, after the initial rage, the words, "Amira's affair," came to him easily, and with a mocking superiority.)

So out of the bubble he found he could take care of himself well. He got rid of stuff — furniture, books, dishes, knick-knacks. He organized the rest meticulously; the dream of perfect order, in which all objects have their place and no object is superfluous, every old photo is dated, every necessary receipt filed, boxes labelled, filing cabinets up to date — this dream came true. No expired cookies in the cupboard or old mustard in the fridge. Absolutely everything in its place. Perfect peace.

But then he met Juliet at an otherwise entirely boring mixed bachelor party, and they started meeting for drinks in bistros, and tugging at each other's belts and buttons in the parking lots of those bistros, steaming up windows, earning treasured bruises in unlikely spots. Like so many others all over the place.

She'd spent her twenties and the first half of her thirties in longish relationships, and one of those men she came close to marrying — they were as good as married, she said; they had a small house and a cat, and he was a political activist of some kind, and she had stayed up late into the night, on a slow computer, helping him do research. Then he left with someone from his office. Confusing for her, she said, because only a few months before that they were talking about getting married — just in case one of them needed his or her life support removed, they joked. And then he left.

He liked when she told him things like that. So he couldn't explain it — couldn't explain what troubled him. She kept saying yes to things, even boring things like office Christmas parties, even long vacations, and still he felt like — what? Like she could take it or leave it? She'd mention an event of her own, some book launch in a far-flung bar, and he'd have to ask if she wanted him to come along. "Oh, you'd like to come? Sure, come!" And yet, she also regularly came over with groceries and they peeled and chopped and simmered, and made happy, prolonged love. But then.

Why did he give her all the power? Did he? After he met Juliet nothing was enough, nothing would do but to be holding Juliet's sturdy hand, smelling her nutty skin, having her nearby, lounging on the floor on her unwashed cushions while she did yoga on the carpet, eating and spilling popcorn, perfect order be damned.

తి తి తి

The next morning, after the premiere, at Alek's place, Juliet said, "Can you believe I met Juliette Gagnon? I mean she only said hello. But the director and Eric Pantinople stayed a while at the afterparty. Trixie kept feeling up the director's camel-hair blazer, holding the cuff between her thumb and forefinger and saying, look how soft, Juliet, feel how soft. We drank these Chambord Royal slushies, slushies made in a real blender. Can you imagine the noise, again and again? And ridiculously tall waiters walking around with trays of tiny hamburgers, and small glasses of white chocolate mousse with jelly beans stuck in the middle."

She was drinking espresso with milk out of a gigantic round mug, a soup mug. Her muscular legs were stretched across a chair, his house robe that she always wore at his place falling around them to the floor.

It was the first morning in four days that he did not throw up, and he was cheered by that. He massaged her shin with an open palm.

"I really wore a ridiculous dress. Anyway. Everyone was so kind about the novel. Eric had read it too. Do you know what he sounds like, at first? A slightly prim high-school history teacher. Slightly stuffy and pedantic. Isn't that bizarre?"

"Is he short?"

"Short?"

"You know how you assume everyone in movies is tall, but in real life they're not. Like Tom Cruise is the famous example of that. He's really short, right?"

"No, he's tall. Eric Pantinople. Probably taller than you."

"Like over six feet?"

"He's not beautiful or anything. I mean maybe it's the posture. These people get so used being looked at that they start to carry themselves as if everyone does think they're beautiful."

"Wasn't he voted hottest dude of the year or something?"

"Anyway. What I was going to say was that he seems sort of stuffy — but then he has this laugh — you know this deep, back of the throat kind of laugh? And it comes out suddenly, as if he's surprised that anyone has said anything funny."

Alek could tell when Juliet liked someone because she got specific about them.

Now she nudged him with her toe. "Isn't that interesting?"

And that too — she found the person "interesting," saying the word with a voice full of wonderment. But in fact she was always saying, "Isn't that interesting?" — about the neighbour's cat, the mailman's socks, a random obituary in the *Globe and Mail*. He supposed that's what one needed to want to write novels, to find all kinds of things interesting.

"Isn't it a bit clichéd, the whole fame thing?" Eric Pantinople — posing on the cover of GQ with his abs polished, speaking with that fey jokey charm at inane interviews — didn't she despise such things?

"I told them all about the horse ranch idea for the novel. What am I doing telling strangers about doomed novel ideas? What have I been doing for the last four years?"

"Falling hopelessly in love, I think. I'm joking. It will come. Your time is coming."

"He said we should all come to Portland, where his friends have a horse ranch."

"Oh please. You can find a ranch anywhere."

"Indeed," she said, and made his hand massage her knee and then her thigh, and then they walked to the bedroom together, dropped their robes, and had some remarkably vigorous sex, given her hangover and his barely passed illness.

"Tell me something," she said afterward.

That's how she would begin.

"Tell me about the girl you were with during the war."

They'd gone through many war stories already — often he told the same ones a second, a third, a fifth time, repeating some parts verbatim and adding details to others. Sometimes her repeated interest made him wonder if he wasn't telling things right. Was there something about the experiences that he'd missed, though he'd been there? What was she looking for?

"I'd bike to her house every other day, unless there was really heavy fire. Sometimes I'd go in the day, sometimes at night. We could stay in her room unless the shelling seemed

237

really bad, and then we'd go to the cellar with her parents. There were air attacks, but more often shelling. You'd hear a long whistle before the shell hit.

"She was what you'd call a high school sweetheart. We thought we were more serious than all the other high school couples. We had this understanding early on that no one else was worth our time. She was intense and loyal. She had one best friend from grade school and then she had me. She still did stuff everyone did — which was to sit at cafés smoking cigarettes and to shoot hoops after school; but she never, for instance, played the phone call games, in which girls got together at one of their houses and phoned boys they liked and teased them to guess who was calling; she never spread rumours — she could not tell a lie. She was frighteningly principled. It didn't occur to me until later that she might have appeared humorless to people, no fun. I wanted to be near her so much that if someone had told me she was no fun I would have thought they were brain damaged. She was disliked, yes, but not so much: she was good at things, and good looking, in an athletic, healthy sort of way."

"Did you have sex?"

"Oh yes. In her room, a lot. Her parents knew. That was extremely rare, that they knew and didn't make a fuss about it. They were maybe the most sensible people I've ever known."

"And she made it through the war."

"Quite well. She's a doctor now. She studied in Sweden for a while, but she never moved away from our town for good. She's a doctor at the hospital where they took me after I was wounded. I know this because we email each other about once a year, and in between, my mother tells me what she hears."

"Oh. Did you never think of going back for her, after the war?"

"Once I left, I didn't ever think of going back. I mean I would have if things hadn't worked out, if I hadn't got permanent residency. But I didn't think of moving as a temporary thing. I didn't particularly want to leave home in the first place, but once I did, I wasn't going to think any more about going back."

"How could you leave her?"

"Yes. Well. After the hospital and the rest of it, it seemed as if she would have to be all of it or nothing. I thought, she'll go to medical school eventually, in the capital city, away from our town, and I won't be able to get into any university up there. I wasn't such a good student. But that wasn't really the whole thing. Once my parents put pressure on me about going, it was just one or the other. The moment of decision is actually blank for me. I remember us in the hospital, she sitting beside my bed — you couldn't do this often — talking about how we would adjust her room so that I could be comfortable with my leg, and also about how long before, and in what position, we would be able to have sex.

"I've no doubt she would have turned her room into a hospital rehabilitation room and waited for me as long as it took sooner than sleep with anyone else. But my next vivid memory is of us in my parents' living room, she helping me find, on the one bookshelf, the copy of *The Adventures of Sherlock Holmes*, which was the only book I wanted to take. I don't know if she was heartbroken. Somehow I don't remember talking about that. She did everything with me until the end, packed my toiletry bag. There was no talk of me returning. We were just seventeen, but in my mind we had the purposefulness and the realism of people between thirty and forty.

"Were *you* heartbroken?"

"How can I explain it? Maybe this is more than I should say. It's as if once I realized she wasn't going to be the foundation of my life, the load-bearing wall, I . . . well, I couldn't concentrate on her anymore."

"But she could have been — she could have been that."

"Yes, that's the mystery. And I can only safely remember the before and after."

"I don't know if I buy that."

"Well, I wish I did remember. Maybe it would be useful."

"But you had wanted to be near her so much."

"I know. I know. Is this poor material for you?"

"Very poor — it misses the most dramatic moment, the moment of decision."

"We didn't write letters. Phoning was still very expensive, and of course there was no email."

"Is she married?"

"Yes, recently. No children. I don't know if that's intentional."

"She works at the same hospital — it's been rebuilt?"

"Fixed up, expanded. There was donor money after the war, and though much of it was stolen, things did get fixed up. I've never set foot in there again, and I never will if I can help it."

They were quiet after this, and dozed, on and off, and talked between dozing, and the afternoon stretched away. And yet after all that, the soft intimate lull, Juliet started walking around the apartment, yawning, collecting all the things she'd spread around — her dress, her shoes, her earrings, the whole magical ensemble she had put on just last night when he had been so happy for her. She was always leaving.

"You need a rest," he said, and again he could not help watching her turn the corner.

Alek was not a writer, and not really an artist, despite his drawings of crabs and squids and robots with horse heads and people with long sad faces. He had once spent a lot of time drawing — in his old life, the before life. In this life, the after-war life, he was glad to find something he liked better: organizing, and managing. It seemed he could walk into almost any administrative nightmare and clean it up, with minimum hard feelings, sometimes in just weeks. It was a people skill, as well as a numbers skill, an intuition for balancing resources. Front in his mind he kept a goal, a vision of near perfection, and slowly, cautiously, decisively, sensitively, he made it real. People wanted to help him, to please him, to fit into the vision they didn't even know existed.

To do this, he understood, was indeed to create, as an artist does — to create order, to transform chaos into shape. Did not stories of creation open with, "In the beginning, there was chaos"? And then. Organization was a step away from invention. And invention itself a kind of reordering. All of life demanded this pruning away of the unnecessary, endless sorting, slotting, and naming. On a sticky note that she tacked to one of his kitchen cupboards, Juliet had written, with a blue sharpie and in his neat hand (she could imitate almost any handwriting, a skill as ambiguous as Alek's drawing), "Life is an endless organizational nightmare." He liked to sit down with a pile of mail Juliet had collected over months and to move through it until the junk was in the recycle bin, the bills separated, the miscellaneous stuff marked with sticky notes. Layers of mail and books and pages of notes and stray clothes accumulated around her with the cheerful persistence of weeds.

He was not a writer, but all that night he thought of images he associated with her leaving: closing door, blinds drawn. Cold wind. As he drifted to sleep, the images slipped up: Unfinished basement. Dried-out toast. Hard suitcase handle. He knew that if she had such thoughts she wrote them down. As he pictured her walking down the street, around the corner, into the vast unknown, again, he thought — how pathetic, that she would write such things down.

❧ ❧ ❧

Later that week Alek was going to tell her, finally, about the money he'd saved for her, because he decided she should have it regardless of the commission. He couldn't just keep it and pretend the whole thing had never happened; it seemed to him that to not even tell her about it was to lie, to leave some important part of himself hidden — and that was the thing that nagged him.

She was reading a review of the film in the *Guardian*, one leg bent under her on the kitchen chair. He put the pizza boxes he had walked in with on the counter. She was wearing new pants, beautiful dark-brown riding-style pants. He had to ask about them.

"Weren't these a good find? At the consignment store by the university, just yesterday."

He turned away to open the fridge.

"They look good on you," he said, opening the crisper drawer.

He was pretending to be looking for something in the fridge so that she wouldn't see his face, which he knew looked either angry or hurt. Because that was Juliet, that's what she was always doing: a quick outing to some thrift stores, quick jaunt for Mexican food, last-minute adventure to the opera, always alone, never inviting him. Juliet who acted put upon, claiming to never have enough time — enough time to write, enough time to cook dinner or watch a movie with him. Not even enough time to put away the piles of clothes that mushroomed in her living room.

He got a tomato from the fridge, and a beer. She started to browse for other reviews on his laptop.

"Come here and read these with me," she said, patting the empty chair next to her own.

And, as it often happened with him in these situations, he wanted more than anything to have sex with her.

On the carpet in the living room where they'd ended up he had his arm under her neck. The sun had gone down in the meantime; they could hear the evening birds. All the sounds carried with great clarity: you could hear the words of the man that a woman was talking to on a cell phone.

They had a throw from the couch over them. He put his nose in her hair.

"What does it smell like?"

"Earthy. Wet earth and rotting leaves. Like the under-brush in a forest."

"Rotting leaves. Mmm."

"And nutty. *Loamy.*"

Her leg was bent over his. Her legs reminded him of a horse's legs, with their assertive thighs and big knobby knees and visible tendons.

He told her all that, because it was true, and because she liked specificity, as writers would.

She pushed her body closer to his. She felt up his clavicle, shoulder, ribs, pressed fingers into them and paused on irregular parts. It was investigative, anatomical, not erotic. But, to him, more intimate. She had done this first with the back of his head, his neck, a long time ago, in the parking lot of a Loblaws.

"You smell papery. Slightly chemical. Like cosmetic cream residue."

To be felt, examined so closely, paid that kind of attention. He couldn't tell her about his gift, not right then — things were too good, right then, and he couldn't bring himself to change or add a single thing.

ॐ ॐ ॐ

But not too long afterward, just two weeks after the premiere, she took an early morning flight to Portland. He woke at the time he knew she would be up, getting dressed in her dark apartment, then cabbing it to the airport. They'd spent the past week in a series of dramatic, brinkmanship-style fights, and he could hardly believe she was really doing this, after all that. The morning had a preternatural stillness, a muffled quality, so unlike the sharpness of twilight. Such an atmosphere might have given him a feeling of heaviness, of moving not through air but something as thick and dragging as honey, but in fact he felt light — as if the scenes they had had over the last week had brought him to the edge and emptied him of something, cleaned him out.

He should have gone to work. Instead he found his keys for Juliet's apartment, and a roll of industrial heavy paper. He used the paper to wrap the portrait of her that he'd been working on for some months. The canvas was stretched on a rack that when stood up on the floor reached just above his waist.

This, too, was to be a surprise, like the money, neither of which he'd got around to telling her about because she'd shocked him with this announcement of a weekend trip to some ranch in Portland. It wasn't about Pantinople, she'd said. And you could come along, she'd said.

That was the part that offended him: You could come along.

More than wanting her to like the portrait itself, he'd wanted her to know that he had been drawing and painting again, because she was always telling him that he should. It was just the kind of advice he would usually find presumptuous and silly, but from Juliet he considered it, and maybe that fact, not the painting itself, was his gift to her.

Now that it had turned out to be a waste of time, he would have to waste more time deciding what to do with it.

He carried it, awkwardly, to her apartment. He imagined being Juliet, walking down the street lightly, turning the corner; he imagined himself watching, too; he was at once himself being Juliet and himself watching Juliet from his own window. Inside, he rested the painting gently against the hallway mirror. He breathed a little easier than he had for some time.

He found her granola and the cheap Ikea bowls and the organic milk and ate this breakfast standing up. On the fridge was the drawing he'd given her to take with her to the premiere, the long blue man, held up by a magnet in the shape of a lighthouse, and next to it a magnetized writing pad with distances and times, tightly scrawled in, keeping track of her runs.

Juliet ran the grid of Toronto neighbourhoods just about every day on what seemed to him a furious regime. He'd see her sometimes returning from a run, the sweat on the back of her T-shirt looking like ink from a Rorschach test. No exercise made her happy if sweat didn't begin to drip off the end of her ponytail. He'd done a shameful thing once, which was to leave a book called *Running Yourself Miserable: An Adult's Guide to Exercise Addiction* on her coffee table, planted casually among some magazines.

It seemed so obvious now. When he and his ex-wife separated, she started cycling compulsively and before the divorce was through she had become a lean, ropey, efficient body, a body he couldn't recognize. His much older brother's wife ran two ultra-marathons after their twenty-six-year marriage: the longer the pain, the more rage to expend. And it seemed to him now he could remember a plumper, less muscular, softer Juliet.

He walked into the bedroom, noted the roughly made bed. He looked through the drawers, surprisingly neat, except for one with apparently miscellaneous stuff, including old address books, and those gelatinous nipple covers. He looked through it, gently, opened the little notebooks — all before his time with her. An old receipt for a perfume, with numbers on the edge of it.

He had an idea for what he would do here, a vague idea that had appeared through his sleep, and might have been the thing that made him feel so light.

It was to organize: her books, certainly, which lay about and were crammed into their shelves, and also her CDs, her drawers, the miscellany of objects on her coffee table and various chairs — the sweaters and leggings and notebooks and lotions and USB sticks and cough drops; possibly all her clothes. Yes. She had once said that she loved recognizing him in the order of things — the neatness of her coffee table after he sat near it, the magazines stacked and perpendicular to the box of Kleenex; the towels folded and hung symmetrically after he'd had a shower.

He made a sandwich, chewed it while looking over the living room, thinking where he might start. But before he could get to anything, the buzzer sounded. There was an old-fashioned intercom here, one button downstairs for buzzing each apartment. Nine-thirty in the morning. He pushed the Talk button and said hello.

"Hi, Darryl here." Then a pause, as if that should be enough.

Alek shifted to Talk.

"What can I do for you?"

"Is Juliet there?"

Alek stared at the intercom.

"Juliet? No."

"Do you have her recycling?" When the man said this, Alek could hear a woman's voice behind him.

Alek, stunned yet compelled, said, "Yes. Yes, I have her recycling", and he pressed the button to unlock the lobby.

Was it a scam? They just wanted into the building? But after a minute there was some shuffling and whispering by the door — Juliet's door, the right door. Were they here to rob Juliet?

He looked through the peephole: yes, a man and woman. He took a long look. He didn't think they were here to rob. He thought he could tell those sorts of things. He opened the door.

Darryl was a middle-aged man, on the tall side, hefty around the shoulders and middle, in a denim jacket and jeans, the kind of sturdy denim thrift stores abound in. Hiking boots, worn out. There was a woman with him, a small, soft woman, wearing a nearly identical outfit. She hung back like she was not in favour of any of this.

"Hey man," Darryl said. He was leaning into the door frame with his shoulder and looking at Alek — it was not exactly a challenge, but an open measuring.

"Hi. So what did you say? That you want Juliet's recycling?"

Darryl looked at the woman as if he thought she should be the one to talk. When she didn't say anything, he turned back to Alek,

"We met her a while back, eh. She said we could have her bottles when we were around here."

"Juliet made me a sandwich last time," the woman said.

How on earth did Juliet meet these people?

"Come in," Alek said.

When they did, the woman seemed to brighten noticeably, and looked around with some eagerness.

Darryl made a *tsk*ing sound and pushed the woman's shoulder. "I told you it's all right," he said.

The push must have been a teasing one, a gesture of punctuation. But it also had a childish insistence and an intensity that reminded Alek of the angry physical negotiations between him and his sisters, the ways they snuck their hostility into offhand gestures, reaching for the eraser across a table and pushing the other's hand to spoil their homework.

"I didn't know!" The woman giggled, as if woken up, revitalized both by being inside the apartment and by Darryl's push, by having engaged his attention.

"So loosen up, jeez," Darryl said to her, shaking his head, though he was the one looking stiff and sour.

"This is my old lady, Mary, and I'm Darryl. Maybe Juliet didn't mention our names."

"Right. Do you want coffee?"

"I don't bother with coffee," Darryl said, as if bothering with coffee put you into a category of people he was not all that sure were people worth talking to — an idea nourished in his private, inviolable store of wisdom, which there was no point explaining to the listener.

"I go straight for the goods at post time. But Mary likes a cup at this time of morning."

Alek went into the kitchen and poured the one cup left from what he'd made an hour ago, and added milk and sugar.

"This all right?" He said to Mary when he brought it out. "Why don't you sit. Did you eat?"

"No way man, I don't eat until dinner," Darryl said.

Mary said, "Juliet made me a sandwich with some funny cheese last time. It was good." She sipped the coffee. "Hey, how'd you know how I like it?"

"I don't know if there is any cheese. I'll look. Why don't you sit on the couch."

Darryl wouldn't go in. He said he never took his boots off because if he did he wouldn't want to put them on again, and he wasn't gonna walk on the carpet in his boots. Mary did unlace, and padded over the carpet in thick white sport socks to sit on the couch. She looked sheepish, but also pleased, in a festive spirit even. She patted the cushions next to her, and crossed her legs.

"She's got so many books, doesn't she," Mary said, picking up one from the coffee table.

"Hey, don't touch everything, for chrissake."

"I told Juliet, this is such a pretty place. So homey. What'd you make this coffee with?"

Alek was in the kitchen, crouching in front of the open fridge. But he couldn't make sense of the contents — what should he get from the fridge?

"Are you looking for cheese in there, man?"

Darryl was right — he was looking for cheese. And bread perhaps, or something else sandwich-y — he'd just had a sandwich himself, hadn't he? But was that what he should do — start a whole sandwich operation?

"Say, would you mind," he heard Mary from the living room, "while you do that, last time I was here Juliet let me check my Facebook?"

He abandoned the fridge and walked out to the desktop in the living room, and turned on the screen.

"Buddy, I don't know if that's such a good idea," Darryl said. His tone was one of mock exasperation, as if Alek was going around doing baffling things, offering coffee, letting the fridge door hang open, allowing Facebook — but only Darryl could know, in his secret store of wisdom, why such things were out of order.

"I'm counting the minutes," Darryl said, a warning for Mary. "She's crazy for Facebook."

Alek was back in the kitchen. Forget the sandwich stuff, he thought. He found Juliet's stash of bottles and Tetra Paks under the sink, and began stuffing them into a large plastic bag.

"I got to keep tabs on my kid," Mary yelled from the desk. "That little weasel. You should see the things he's posting, sheesh! I'm gonna write him what I think of that."

"Mary! Get your butt out of that chair. We're going."

"All right, all right." They could hear quick staccato typing. "Juliet's my Facebook friend, you know."

Alek stopped what he was doing, which was arranging the containers so that they fit snugly against each other in the bag. When he looked up, it seemed to him Darryl, who was maybe watching him the whole time, was smiling in some way Alek could not interpret.

Alek handed him the plastic bag of empty mineral water bottles and beer bottles and milk containers. He saw on the counter by the toaster three granola bars — the wrappers looked soft and thinning at the edges, and the bars bent, as if they'd been squished at the bottom of a bag for too long.

He handed them to Darryl — or tried to: Darryl took only the bag of bottles and turned away.

"Thanks for these," he said to Alek, behind him. "Mary!"

Mary was already padding back, a dribble of coffee in the corner of her lip, which she dabbed away gently with her knuckle. She had a child's gait and she sat on the floor to tie up her shoes, like a child.

"Juliet's great," she said. "She gave me a pillow, did you know that? But I lost it. *Que serra.*"

"Adios," Darryl said, already walking through the door Alek held open, swinging the bag over his shoulder.

"See you later," said Mary, and Alek closed the door.

He thought, so she gives them her recycling. His hands weren't shaking when he sat down on the couch and picked up his own coffee mug, but they had that nervous energy that wants to squeeze something tight. He sat where Mary had first sat, and he felt a pressure, a weight that started in his gut below the ribs, continued through the lungs, then squeezed his esophagus and spread through his throat. "It's Darryl." "Juliet gave me a pillow." What the fuck? His face became flushed. It was outrageous. He looked for the word that described what he felt, and that was it: outrage. Shock and betrayal and anger all together. Shock that Juliet went around doing such careless, unnecessary things. He knew now why he'd let them in. To have evidence of what he must have already known: that she opened herself up and made herself vulnerable, all over the place — for what? So that these people, these strangers, thought they could come around, stretch out their feet, ask for sandwiches, and check their Facebook.

He looked over the place where the woman had sat at the desktop. The coffee mug was there, with one long drip down the side. It had left a faint ring on the mouse pad. He picked up the mug carefully, then adjusted the couch cushions and looked over the coffee table. In the hallway he noted the bits of dirt, twigs, fallen out from the ridges of their boots.

He swept those up, washed the coffee cup. He washed his hands thoroughly at the kitchen sink.

But the organizing will left him. He remembered neither what exactly he'd been doing before the buzzer sounded, nor with any vividness the details of the big ordering he had been planning. There was the blue man still magnatized to the fridge. The bag of granola, the milk still on the counter, cheap cutlery in the metal Ikea drying bin. African violets on the windowsill. The alley seen through the window, which he'd looked on many times before. Strange and ordinary alley. Books piled on the coffee table, without regard for size. All someone else's. What had they to do with him? What had he imagined he might do with them?

He sat on the couch. The shrapnel still embedded in his right thigh from nearly twenty years ago was itching furiously. He rubbed it through his pants with the flat of his palm. He thought, I'll have to carry that damn painting home, a four-foot burden of canvas and planks. Juliet's phone was on a side table next to the couch, within reach of his hand. The answering machine light was blinking, as it usually was, because she often left messages on there without listening to them. He pressed it — had he meant to do that, in his organizing rush, clean out her answering machine?

Now he merely played the messages randomly. He skipped to the beginning and listened, sometimes two in a row, sometimes skipping ten. The dentist, Trixie, the diabetes community association, a soft-spoken man named Rasheed. "Thank you for the tea, hope to see you again." Tea! A woman, Eileen, telling Juliet the office painting day had been moved to Saturday; another one from the same woman, saying she has to move Juliet's adjustment. Adjustment — that would be her chiropractor, whom Juliet saw every two weeks.

Nothing from Eric Pantinople. Did movie stars even call personal numbers and leave messages on answering machines?

She had helped her chiropractor move her office some months ago, and had gone grocery shopping for her once when the woman was in bed with a broken leg. The most blatantly unethical advantage-taking of clients without good insurance, Alek said. More than unethical — creepy. The woman's voice on the machine sounded meek and petulant and entitled. He never heard about the office painting, but was sure now Juliet had done it. He thought of playing the message again to note the time and date, but there was really no need to, he was certain enough.

Here was a story Juliet had told him: years ago, when she was about twenty and lived in BC, two of her boyfriends — men she was something with, in any case — got into a fist fight at her house, and the police called her at work — well, at the bookstore where she showed up once a week to work the till or do random tasks.

"We have two men here claiming they both belong in your house," the cop said, after her manager had passed her the phone — "which one is your real boyfriend?" One of them she had met while tree planting, a foreman named Samuel, who, post-season, got a job with a construction crew, and she moved to a cabin next to his work camp, a friend's cabin (her life was full of such coincidences), and hung about for the winter, without a real job or an indoor toilet. This dude Samuel was always randomly driving out to her cabin — no phone — to check up on her, and one time he found there a guy from the same crew, Ronaldo, or Roderigo, or something, sleeping it off, no sign of Juliet. She drove back to the cabin to find Samuel with a bloody chin and Roderigo being taken in.

"The funniest part," she'd said, "is that I wasn't even sleeping with that guy, Roderigo. He was just always after me, and that morning he had come to pester me, and I couldn't get him out, and finally I just went to work, leaving him there. The cabin door didn't even lock properly. Anyone could get in. I didn't even like the guy."

He was nostalgic, nostalgic for Juliet, for her anxious face as she ran up to an unlocked cabin, worried about bullish men she didn't even love.

He again looked gently through her drawers. There was no plan — he was an observer. He reached behind the books on the bookshelves. He read scraps of paper with short notes on them, notes to self about writing.

Rasheed was her pharmacist. In his looking around, Alek found a stash of business cards, one with the name Rasheed, Park Plaza Pharmacy, just a few blocks away.

He stayed in her apartment all that day and returned the next day, Saturday, after sleeping at home. And Saturday night he again went home to sleep and was back at her place Sunday morning.

She was supposed to be home late that night, he thought, but around 5:00 PM someone unlocked the door. He was ready for more weird intruders — why shouldn't Rasheed or Eileen or the bag boy at Loblaws have her keys?

But it was Juliet, with her hair in a bun nearly at the very top of her head. She looked maybe a little underslept, but ordinary, except that her left arm had a long, wide scrape, the kind you'd get from wiping out sideways. It was just freshly, lightly scabbed over.

She dropped her purse to the floor. She had no suitcase. She looked at him. He was holding a cucumber and ham sandwich — he'd been eating sandwiches for days.

She looked around. She seemed to look around quite thoroughly.

"What's going on? You've just been hanging out around here?"

"I hope that's okay."

She tilted her head sideways, and squinted, like you might look at a drawing you just did to see it from a different perspective.

In an impulsive desire to touch her, he put down his sandwich, onto the little ledge for holding keys. But then she brought her hand to her chest, making him notice again the fresh scrape on her arm.

"You've hurt your arm."

"Can you take my car and drive us somewhere?"

"What?"

"The car, can you just take it and drive? If I stay here, I'll scream."

"You don't have a car, Juliet, what car?"

"There is a car outside. It's a rental. I mean, never mind who it belongs to. You can drive standard, can't you?"

He walked over to the living room window and looked out — like in the movies, he pushed aside the curtain — and saw one car parked by the curb, a red Saab, an older, mid-nineties model. He liked Saabs, and the nineties' models were among his favourites.

"You rented a '95 or '96 Saab? Juliet? That's not possible."

"Of a sort, it's a rental of a sort. Is that relevant? Is that what we should talk about right now?"

And he thought suddenly — the restlessness, the shiftiness: drugs.

"Are you high?"

She picked up her purse, and walked the few steps into the kitchen; from her purse she grabbed fistfuls of things that she dropped on the kitchen table — ordinary things, pens and Kleenex and makeup compacts and loose receipts and two small glass marbles. She stopped when she'd hit on the car keys.

"I haven't been high since Y2K," she said, as she held them up to him. And though her movements a moment ago were impatient and rough, now the gesture, her damaged arm holding the slightly trembling keys for several long seconds, seemed like a plea.

So he took them. She hurried ahead of him on the stairs, didn't lock the apartment, didn't collect things back into her purse.

He approached the Saab as if it were a parcel wrapped in brown paper with no return address or name of sender.

No weird smell when he opened the door. Nice leather seats. Clean, with just a takeout container on the passenger seat. She pushed it to the floor and sat down and closed her eyes.

So he drove. He got out of the neighbourhood quickly, onto Bloor, heading west. She began to look out the window, intently, as if she'd not lived in Toronto for a decade. Rather with the same squinty, head-tilted look.

Near the end of Bloor, approaching Kipling, he lost his patience.

"Juliet? What is this for? What's the matter with you?"

"I'm fine while we're moving, I'm better now. I wish we could go somewhere far, be somewhere else. Where could we get to tonight and spend the night?"

"Spend the night somewhere together?"

Behind clouds both white and heavy with grey, stretches of blue showed — it was that kind of sky, jumbled and massive and tender. The greens of the trees had a stark, saturated quality; all the outlines and colours seemed freshly revealed. More than that: raw, lurid. For some masochistic reason, he drove north on Kipling, and after some time, Eglinton, Dixon, he was getting to the familiar landmarks he'd had no wish to visit in years — Rexdale, Albion, nearly Finch, where he spent his first, painful years in Canada. The childish, blunt, brutal, yet complicated hostility — not toward him, or not only toward him, but between everyone — ethnic groups, neighbourhood gangs, a hostility for which the war he had just gone through had not prepared him. Neither had the guide to Canadian culture he'd got at the embassy — published in 1977 — which said nothing about racism or segregation by high rise.

He pulled into the parking lot of Albion Mall, redone now, minus the K-Mart he remembered.

"Oh no," she said. "What is it? Do you have to use the bathroom?"

"No, Juliet, I'm just not going to keep driving without you telling me fuck all about what's going on." Fuck all. He found he could do English slang easily when he was upset.

"Do you want to get out and run?"

"Have you flipped?"

"Don't be so dramatic. I just noticed you're wearing running shoes. I just want to keep moving. I can run in these." She was wearing espadrilles, which he noticed everyone was wearing all of a sudden.

And it occurred to him that Juliet regularly made him say yes to strange, unexpected things.

"Fine. I can run. Fine. Then will you explain to me?" He could run decently, despite his bad leg.

They ran down Finch and into a park. He'd not spent any time in parks when he'd lived around here. The sky was getting pink and orange along with the white and the blue and the sodden grey. It's too much, he thought, you don't need all that in one sky. They weaved along quite energetically. Juliet seemed pleased. He felt about as perverse as he had when he'd asked Darryl and Mary to have a seat on the couch — but equally compelled to. After a while they could see the river, heavy and dull, and the rocks and sand and twigs on the bank as sharp and clear as in a close-up photograph. Then they descended slightly and cut in on a paved path.

It was a short stretch and at the end the path curved uphill and they trudged up it, Alek watching Juliet's straining legs. Soon they were in a residential neighbourhood he didn't recognize. They ran past high-rises, past people riding bicycles on the sidewalk, past families walking slowly, spread out like a moving wall of unhappy people with grocery bags. They got honked at when they ran diagonally across roads. Any red light and they changed direction. At one point Juliet cut through the yard of a house and they skipped softly over a hula hoop and then continued down the alley.

The sun was close to setting. Juliet had a ring of sweat around her hairline, sweat beading on the sides of her nose. He thought she had a slightly shifty, collapsible quality about her face. He reached for her at one point but retreated from touching her — you couldn't, not without breaking stride. It seemed that if they broke stride they'd be stranded, alone in the middle of nowhere, panicked. If they stopped Juliet's face surely would collapse into tears.

None of that if they kept going. You settle into it, and then you can go on, he thought.

But he couldn't, his lungs couldn't. They had expanded, but now they were pushed past their edge. Juliet too breathed in a heavy, though controlled way, her shoulders sagging, that vein on her forehead bulging.

She led them sharply downhill again — they were moving in a circle — down to the river, to a broad park with benches and barbecues and small foot paths curving up the hill into dense shrubs; it was chillier here, a cutting wind rose. They faced the straight long line of deep blood orange on the horizon. They were running toward it, and then the sun went under. He could see where the pavement they were on ended and another kind of trail wound up.

A group of boys and girls, with skateboards, startled them when they burst out of the bush and down this trail, with the loud roll of their wheels and their exclamations.

Juliet and Alek stopped, both panting, hands on their ribs.

The children stared at them.

"Are you dating?"

The question was not loud but reached them clearly. It was not a taunt from the boy who said it, but a slightly vexed inquiry, as if he genuinely needed clarification.

They couldn't get enough breath to speak. Alek's tongue was heavy from thirst and his eyes burned with the sweat that had run into them. They were a long way from the car. Juliet took off her left espadrille and he saw the side of her ankle rubbed raw. The wind blew harder, making her lose her balance as she put the shoe back on, wincing. It was clear they would not run farther, or back, to the car.

She sat down onto the grass with a small grimace and he sat next to her.

"I'm getting cramps," she said, between heavy breaths.

"We'll sit while it passes."

"It's my period."

She was holding on to her ankles. Her periods usually came at night: he'd find her in the bathroom, on the toilet, wearing a house robe, her head resting on a pile of folded towels stacked on her lap. She'd have the heater on in there, and if she lifted her head to look at him he'd see glaze over her eyes.

"Is it bad?"

"It'll get bad soon."

"Why did you want to run?" She was collecting her breath, and so was he.

"Darryl and Mary came by your place while you were gone."

"What?"

"I was — well, I was at your place."

"How do you know their names?"

"They came upstairs. I also learned you'd been helping your chiropractor paint her new office, and having tea with the pharmacist."

"Oh God."

She put her head on her knees. Without lifting it, she said, "The Saab is Eric's friend's car. I drove it from Montreal, where we ended up a day ago. It's been a terrible time. I got this scrape because I fell down the stairs, perfectly sober.

That's when I decided I'm going home. And Darryl and Mary just seemed nice. They started talking to me in the alley by the recycling bin, when I was coming home with groceries."

"Is that right? Juliet? Do you love Eric Pantinople? Or someone else? Please be honest."

She seemed to tremble, and when she lifted her head he saw that she was laughing, though with a grimace.

"I'm so sorry. No, I don't. It's just that he likes me so much. I don't know what to do when people like me. I'm sorry. Oh, it hurts now."

They were in a strange park and doing a stupid thing, and it did not feel like good things were on the way for them, but he thought maybe Juliet was giving him one true part of the story.

He looked at her curved back, her arms now around her middle. He'd witnessed several women in menstrual pain, but now he wondered what it was like inside — like indigestion, or a rotten appendix, or a bruised rib?

"This pain, what kind of pain is it? Do you know what I mean?"

She took a breath.

"It begins with heaviness, in the lower abdomen and lower back. In the ovaries, too. Deep, uncomfortable pressure. And soon everything inside feels inflamed and throbbing.

"When the pain gets going, there are these waves — sort of like something is churning your insides? Clenching and releasing, pushing against the heaviness. Maybe imagine swollen tissue and a hand kneading, pulling, tearing it up.

"Then you just want to huddle. Heat helps, and cold is terrible. The pain usually wakes me up, often after I've dreamt of it, and though it happens every month, I am always disoriented at first and never want to get out of bed. But I do, and follow my steps — robe for warmth, warm milk to digest the Advil, sitting on the toilet to give the illusion of relieving the pressure."

His heart rate had slowed by now and he was getting cold. "Can you walk? We'll hail a cab once we get out of the park."

"Yes. But do you know what I think of every time? I think, there are women in prisons and labour camps and sex trafficking houses all over the world having cramps at the same moment as me. Some are bending over rows of strawberries in some illegal farm worker operation in California, picking, picking, not allowed to stop, hours on end. Some are being beaten by twelve-year-old soldiers high on coke, in some other place. Some are being raped. And when I'm so overwhelmed with pain even though I'm sitting in my warm bathroom, fed with warm milk and an overdose of ibuprofen, it seems unbearable that women sleeping on cold concrete in a locked shack with no bathroom and certainly no Advil are also waiting out the pain. I think of waking up to the pain and that first dread, when you know something prolonged and painful is just beginning. I think of not being allowed to get up, even, just staying in that cold spot, not having a place to pee, starting to sweat, that hand inside you grabbing fistfuls of your uterine wall, squeezing your ovaries, raking blood and tissue with its insistent fingers, and you just staying put, for hours. Or, maybe you're forced to get up — someone is kicking you so that you get up and get to work. No one who loves you nearby."

She took several small breaths and exhaled with pursed lips, as if she were doing a breathing exercise.

"And then I think, how many women? How many right now and how many regularly? And you can't figure out the numbers. Say there are three-and-a-half billion women in the world right now. Say a third of them are menstruating women — a billion, say. Say out of that billion, one-hundredth is enslaved in some manner or another. I don't know. Say less than that. Say a tenth of a percent. That would be a million. A million women getting periods in some bad place they can't get out of. There are no such numbers, I know. The periods are not the worst of their problems, just one bad thing."

Yes, he thought, these are things one would probably rather not know about.

The kids who'd been hanging out on the trail above them now came down, jostling and energetic.

"Have a good night!" One boy yelled, and waved. Juliet and Alek both lifted a hand in return.

They limped to the road, hailed a cab, took it to Albion Mall where the Saab was still parked, bought ibuprofen at the drug store in the mall, and then he drove them home, to Juliet's apartment, where Juliet got herself settled to wait out her pain on the toilet.

He started the kettle. He looked through the cupboards for a good tea, something soothing but tasty and strong too. He found a lavender Earl Grey. All right. He shook out two tea bags, tapped the box playfully before tucking it back into the cupboard. He went into the living room and opened the blinds all the way and that still-jumbled sky gave the room a severe sort of light. The painting! There it was, leaning on the wall next to the window: he hadn't thrown it out. Then he looked at the couch, where Juliet might get comfortable in a little while, when she was ready to lie down: he unfolded the white wool-knit blanket and fluffed up the cushions. He remembered the tea and turned back to the kitchen. He skipped from one thing to another like a cat chasing a strip of light. He went downstairs and brought up Juliet's suitcase from the trunk of the Saab, and put the pile of stuff she'd dumped on the kitchen table earlier, before their drive, back into her purse.

He brought mugs of tea to the coffee table. He began to whistle, then caught himself, because — was it callous? He remembered his long-ago love, the last bike ride to her place, before he was hit. She had not saved him from that — that was why he could leave. He must tell Juliet this possible explanation. Sitting on the couch and looking at the wool blanket, he could imagine, momentarily, how it was for Juliet, how she could stay in one place and run through her mind impressions of the world and words she read, and how some impression would begin an invented world that she would scrape away at, and how much time that took and how she could not care, for the moment, that her mail was unopened and her answering machine blinking.

He jumped up again. "Juliet," he called softly, as he approached the slightly ajar door of the bathroom, carrying a cup of Earl Grey.

The thing was, his leg ached, her uterus contracted painfully, but here they were; he could make tea, there was heat and light in this apartment and a kitchen full of comforting things.

In the time he'd spent there on the weekend, he'd watched a few movies, including a rough cut of *The Time of the Apricots*, and had lain on the couch, browsing through Juliet's magazines, dozing, getting up for a snack and a beer now and then. The film resembled nothing of his own vision of it — a vision set in the landscape of his childhood, pale in colour, in washed out greens and blues, the novel's derelict hospital like the bombed out one of Alek's home town. A mish-mash of stuff, and an unnecessary, self-absorbed projection.

He pushed the door gently open. Juliet sat on the toilet, her shorts around her ankles, her head propped on a tall stack of towels on her knees, eyes closed, arms around her middle. When he entered, she opened her eyes and looked at him. He sat down on the edge of the tub and didn't touch her, just leaned in close.

"Terrible," she said. She was with him. They sat like that for a bit, not saying anything, feeling the heat of the tiny bathroom. Then he left her there to fix them something to eat, something they would eat later, when Juliet was better and had her appetite. He could count on that happening, and was glad for it, and he whistled in the kitchen, and didn't worry. He supposed that pain could be handled when it was known to be finite and in the confines of safety and certain not to lead to death or other damage.